KYD'$ WORLD

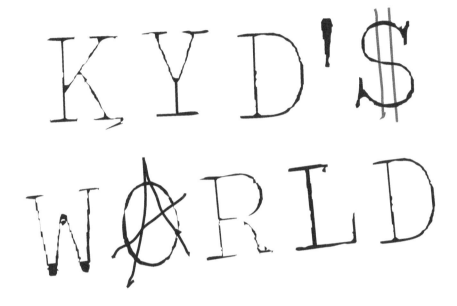

KYD'$ W⒜RLD

Ryder Stone

iUniverse, Inc.
Bloomington

KYD'$ WØRLD

iUniverse books may be ordered through booksellers or by contacting:

iUniverse
1663 Liberty Drive
Bloomington, IN 47403
www.iuniverse.com
1-800-Authors (1-800-288-4677)

ISBN: 978-1-4697-8208-9 (sc)
ISBN: 978-1-4697-8210-2 (e)
ISBN: 978-1-4697-8209-6 (dj)

Library of Congress Control Number: 2012903073

Printed in the United States of America

iUniverse rev. date: 4/16/2012

In Loving Memory

Simon

1

The cab driver pulled my bags out of the trunk and set them on the curb. I paid him, carried the bags over to the curbside check-in, and handed my ID and itinerary to the lanky guy standing behind the metal counter.

"All the way through to Portland, Oregon?" he asked.

"Yeah."

He typed something into the computer, printed out two labels, and wrapped them around each of the handles on my bags. His jacket was tight and the seams pulled at his shoulders as he worked to get things done. His entire uniform—a navy blue polyester—looked too small and constrictive. I hated polyester. It was hot, itchy, and felt suffocating, especially on these sweltering, muggy Florida days. I hated Florida.

As I watched him type into the computer again, I wondered about his life—if he liked standing in the heat outside the airport all day, dealing with rude, stressed-out people who were running late, checking bag after bag in that awful polyester suit. I wondered how much money he had in the bank, if he had a retirement plan or health insurance, where he lived, what he had in his refrigerator. I wondered if he was happy.

"You'd better hurry. That plane is scheduled to leave in half an hour." He smiled kind of condescendingly, like it was funny that I was running late or something.

I took my ID, itinerary, and boarding pass from him and walked into the terminal to check the status of my flight. He was right: only thirty minutes till departure. Fortunately, there wasn't much of a line at the security check. I placed my backpack and shoes into one of the rectangular plastic bins and watched it slide on the conveyor belt through the X-ray tunnel. I walked through the sensitized frame and stood on the other side, spread-eagle style, so the cranky-looking lady could run her wand over me. She nodded, and I headed to the conveyer belt to get my things.

"Excuse me? Sir?" the security guard called to me. I felt my breath shorten and pulse quicken as I glanced at the handcuffs hanging off the side of his belt. "Do you mind if I look in your backpack?" Without waiting for my answer, he unzipped it, dug around for a minute, and pulled out a set of keys. On the key ring hung a small photon light, a mini-Swiss army knife (missing tweezers and toothpick), and three keys: one to my old house in Boulder, one to my new Toyota 4-Runner (which had been confiscated), and one to my mom's house in Oregon, which was where I was headed.

The guard pointed to the knife. "I'm sorry, sir, but I can't allow you to carry this on the plane."

"That's cool." I slipped the knife off the key ring and gave it to him. "Sorry, man, I didn't even think about that."

"It's okay." He dropped the knife into a plastic bucket under the X-ray table, and I hurried to my gate.

I hadn't slept even an hour the night before, and now I was exhausted, anxious, and edgy. I'd packed quickly, just before dinner, because I'd wanted to get a good night's sleep. But, much to my frustration, I was wound up all night long. I lay in bed in the dark, and with every toss and turn grew more and more agitated and panicky. I didn't want to do it; I hesitated because it was always a little embarrassing and made me feel ashamed and weak, but around midnight, after three hours of agonizing insomnia, I broke down and called Sam.

It was only ten o'clock in Colorado, and I had hoped he wouldn't be in bed yet.

"Kyd?" He sounded concerned but not like I had awakened him or anything.

"Sorry to bother you so late," I said sheepishly.

"You're never a bother." Just hearing his voice made me feel better. "Is everything okay?"

After all my shit went down and I had spent all that time in jail, Sam was my first light. I was sober for the first extended period of time in years, which opened the door for me to really *feel* again. That, in turn, allowed the reality of it to sink in, and I was utterly consumed by agonizing depression, self-loathing, and hatred toward existence in general. Sam was a counselor at Willow Winds, the rehab center where I spent two months after jail. At age fifty-five, Sam was a recovering alcoholic, coke addict, sex addict, and compulsive gambler who was clean and sober for eight years. He had gone down about as far as anyone could go but somehow managed to pull himself up and learn to live again. I developed great respect and admiration for him; he became the first positive male role model I'd ever had. Sam had overcome his dark and shadowed past, and now he shined. His light roused my belief that I could do it too. I knew he could honestly understand and empathize with everything I was going through.

"I'm going home tomorrow ..." I hesitated. "To Mom's."

"How do you feel?"

"I don't know. Nervous, I guess." That wasn't totally true. I knew how I felt. I felt sick, like I wanted to throw up. Like I wanted to crawl in the closet, and shrink down, and disappear into one of the cracks in the back. "I don't know man. It's fucked up. It's just ..." I hesitated again, trying to remember why I had called him in the first place. "Over the past year I've been in jail and rehab and this fucking halfway house, and all I've wanted was to get out and somehow go on with my life. And now, it's finally happening, and I'm not excited about it at all.

It's the exact opposite; I feel all pissed off and tense and weird and ... depressed. I'm still fucking depressed. I should be happy, right?"

"There aren't any rules on how you should feel, Kyd," Sam advised. "Life can piss you off. It can be tense and weird and depressing. Why do you think you still feel this way, now that you're finally going home?" I knew he was prompting me to face the skeletons he and I had danced with so many times before.

I sat quietly, not wanting to believe that all this bullshit was my life. I wished I could wake in my warm, cozy bed to the sound of sizzling bacon and the comforting aroma of fresh pancakes, relieved to discover this had all been a terrible dream. But that wasn't going to happen "I'm having a hard time caring," I finally answered. "I just ... I just really don't think I give a shit anymore. I haven't in a while. There's a part of me that really wishes I could care ... but I don't. I'm done. Over it. What's the fucking point?"

"What are your alternatives?" he asked, though he already knew—we'd hashed through all this about a million times.

A part of me hated to go where I knew I was headed—even a split second was shameful. "I guess I can either have a bullet for breakfast ... or stick around and try to deal with my shit." I was sorry as soon as I'd said it and immediately forced a fake laugh, as if to indicate I was joking. But I didn't fool Sam.

"Your decisions affect the people around you too, people who love you. I understand your apathy, Kyd, but just try to take it one day at a time. After a while, something about it gets easier, and you just might learn to like life—parts of it anyway." Sam sighed wearily. "It's never *always easy* for anybody. But I believe we are here for a reason, and I don't think that reason is solely for some kind of mass experience that entails nothing but complete apathy and hedonism. That's a bad combination, Kyd. There's more to it than that."

"Yeah, I know." Sam and I had talked extensively about all

that "everything happens for a reason" crap back at Willow Winds when I'd felt on the verge of hanging myself in the closet. I hated hearing it—it was like holy water on the possessed—but deep down, it sort of resonated with me, and I felt like there probably was some truth to it.

"What's bothering you most?" Sam asked.

"I don't think I can do it. I don't think I can be normal. I'm not normal. I'm fucked up and sometimes I wonder why I'm even trying to ..." I felt my throat start to constrict and then a lump rose up to the middle.

"You can do it, Kyd." His voice was kind and compassionate. "You just have to reinvent parts of yourself; create new habits for yourself."

"I know," I whispered as a tear rolled down my cheek.

"Just take it one day at a time," he advised. "Do you have a counselor lined up in Portland?"

"Yeah, Mom found some guy."

"Good. Go to the meetings, Kyd, and be honest with your counselor. Let him help you. You're a sharp, charismatic, witty man. You'll be fine." I hated hearing him say all that, because I knew it wasn't true. "Remember," he went on, "breathe your way through it, and try to find happiness in the little things. It's there. You are completely capable of transitioning into your best self. I know you can do it."

The truth of it all—my "real truth" that I'm positive Sam could sense—was that I didn't *want* to do it. I didn't want to work to transition into a normal, boring, suppressed person with a normal, boring, suppressive job so I could slowly become just another hamster spinning The Machine's fucked up wheel. Sure I *could*. A person can do things all day long, but if he doesn't want to, then what's the point? The only other factor in my case—the thing that was really the bitch—was that I *needed* to. For me, it wasn't so much about "Can I?" or "Do I want to?" The in-my-face reality was that I needed to because I did not want to go to prison.

I replayed the conversation with Sam over in my head as I hurried through the airport, hoping that my wanting to stay out of prison was stronger than the don't-give-a-shit attitude that had been slowly seeping from me for years. I tried to switch my thinking back to the seemingly futile attempts to convince myself that I *did* care, that I *was* worthy, and that I really *did* want to be a good, normal, regular, menial, mundane person.

I ran toward my gate, and my heart skipped a couple of beats when I saw that the seating area was empty; I prayed I hadn't missed the flight. I looked with pleading eyes at the ticket agent as I pulled my boarding pass out of my backpack. She glared at me, picked up her little walkie-talkie-type device, and spoke into it. Then she turned to the other ticket agent, who was in the process of closing the large metal door that allowed access to the airplane. "Sarah," she said with a heavy sigh, "we have one more." As she took my boarding pass, I shifted my eyes downward but still felt her scowl. Sarah also sighed and reluctantly pulled the metal door back open. I scurried past, down the passageway, and boarded the flight to my next phase of hell.

I walked down the aisle, looking for 16A, which was next to the window, so both the slow-moving elderly woman and the short, pudgy man had to climb back out of their seats so I could get to mine. I quickly pulled my iPod and headphones out of my backpack, stuffed the backpack into the overhead bin, apologized to them and scooted past. The man quickly nodded; the woman compulsively twisted a tissue she held with both hands, refusing to look at me. As I sat down, a flight attendant gave the routine spiel about seatbelts, safety exits, oxygen masks, and electronic devices, while another attendant checked that our seats and tray tables were locked and in their upright positions.

I took a deep breath and tried to relax. The g-force generated by our takeoff anchored me to the seat. It wasn't so intense that I wanted to puke or thought my chest might blow up or anything like that; it was just enough to give me that good, tingly, butterflies-in-the-stomach kind of feeling, like a diluted Ecstasy high, extremely diluted like a million to one. I chuckled as I thought about how this takeoff, the plane racing down the runway like the endorphins of a dope fiend immediately after that fix, the one he's been jonesing for days after he's sobered up and gotten sick, was the closest thing I had experienced to a high in a while. I put my headphones on, sat back and closed my eyes feeling grateful for a little bit of time to check out.

When we landed in Miami, I just sat there while everyone else dodged the elbows around them, juggling their things out from under the seats and from the overhead bins. Once the plane cleared out, I got my backpack, exited the plane, and meandered toward the gate for my next flight, which was in a different terminal.

I walked through the airport feeling saturated with the electrifying buzz being generated through everything that was happening as people scurried past, scuffling around, each in their own frenzied attempt to juggle screaming children, pull over packed rollie luggage, answer cell phones, lug coats much too burly and burdensome for the balmy weather Miami was having, all as they crammed crappy airport food down their throats hurrying along to get wherever it was they were going. I stopped and stood there for a moment, watching, taking it all in, feeling a part of the dynamic vigor as it continued to unfold, the dialectic social process happening all around me, through me, to me. I was one of them—faceless, nameless—a legitimate thread woven tightly throughout this pure and just social fabric. These people were not interested in me. They didn't know or care a thing about me, my history, or the monsters that lurked behind and patiently waited ahead for me. In that moment I was just some Joe, fresh and wholesome, unpolluted by drugs and death, untainted from jail and rehabilitation. In that painfully fleeting moment that I wished could last a lifetime, I was just some kid, masquerading as a guiltless, blameless other in a crowded mass of seemingly sanctioned oblivion.

I arrived at my terminal. As I walked toward the departure gate I noticed the game on TV through a doorway. I had never really been into football but Tony, one of my roommates at Beacon, was a huge fan and watched it all the time. After a while, I found myself beginning to actually like it. You've gotta admire the athleticism of those guys. I soon learned the teams and players and by the Super Bowl, I was one of those guys who leaped from the couch, slinging potato chip crumbs across the room while shaking his fists and yelling at the TV like it made some kind of difference.

I walked through the door toward the TV and sat down at a booth. Dallas was playing Seattle. Seattle had just tied the game with forty-six seconds left in the fourth quarter. As I watched the play on TV, a girl approached me. She was dressed in a pair of nicely fitting black pants and a red polo-style shirt with the name "J. Chill's" stitched boldly on the left shoulder. She set a sweating glass of ice water down on the table. "Can I see your ID?" Her juicy red lips formed a sweet smile. She was cute and I felt my cheeks flush as I pulled my wallet out of my back pocket. She took my ID and glanced at it. "Thanks."

I hadn't immediately realized I'd walked into a bar, so I was a little caught off guard when she carded me. Now, I noticed the beer taps and bottles of booze behind the bar, as well as neon signs hanging on the walls—"Budweiser," "Corona," "Miller Light." And then, the Coors Light hottie, standing there, picture perfect, smiling out at me from a large cardboard stand-up, leaning in on and holding onto a larger-than-life Coors Light bottle, as her tight, little red Coors Light half-shirt clung to her big, beautiful titties, as I would, if given the chance. I hadn't walked into a bar in months—legally, I was prohibited. I looked around to see if anyone was watching. I immediately wanted a

Jack and Coke more than anything in the world. I could taste it.

"What can I get for you?" the waitress asked. Her smile was shy, and she quickly diverted her gaze from me to the small rectangular pad in her hand.

"Uh … I'm not sure." I knew I acted as awkward as I felt.

She pointed her pen toward the end of the table. "The menus are right there."

"Oh." I was a little embarrassed that I hadn't noticed them. I pulled one out from behind the neatly lined bottles of ketchup, mustard, salt, and pepper.

"I'll give you a few minutes." She looked at me and smiled again. I smiled back. I hadn't been with a woman in a while, and she was pretty hot.

Back in the day, I had more ladies than I knew what to do with. No shit—they all wanted me. I don't mean to sound conceited or anything, but it is the truth. I don't think their initial attraction to me was necessarily due to my being an intellectual heartthrob or "great guy" type. I guess I'm relatively good-looking and all—I mean, I'm not butt-fucking ugly or a complete social retard or anything like that—but I'm pretty sure the ladies I hung out with were more into the "incessant partying with a bunch of outlaws" thing. They probably were more attracted to my status in the drug culture than anything else—the perceived power, strength, and utter coolness that goes along with that whole thing, if you're into it.

I was a big baller, a high-roller, one of the kingpin drug dealers in Boulder, Colorado, and I made loads of cash. People treated me with respect because of it and feared me because of it. They had reason to. I've been in lots of fights over drugs and money, broken lots of bones—some of my own but mostly other people's. My crew—Jefe, Cloud, Tortoise, Nate, Cedar, Nico—all worked together, took care of each other, had each other's backs. Now that I look back on it, we were like a pack of rabid dogs. I was the alpha, because I supplied most of the work, but we were more of a working unit than anything. If somebody fucked with one of us, they fucked with all of us. We'd earned a reputation for being pretty agro and didn't mind using things to thump on people when they deserved it: crowbars, baseball bats, clubs, chains, skateboards—whatever we could get our hands on.

In the world of illegal drug dealing, most kids don't have the initial capital to invest in their business, so, a lot of the time, if I wanted to move my product, I had to front. Most of the time people paid me, but occasionally, when it came time for me to collect, somebody would wind up being short, or, not have the cash at all. Unfortunately, it did happen. But, in those cases, I tried to be cool and talk to the person—give him a chance to make it right. It was that easy. I had a kid work off a twenty-thousand-dollar debt once, no shit. It took him a while but he worked it off, paid me back, and it was all cool. On rare occasion, I'd front product to some nit-wit and he'd bail, trying to make-off with my drugs and having no intention of ever paying me—dumbass. Nobody likes a thief and our networking system in and around Boulder was pretty sick.

Tom found that out the hard way, stupid motherfucker. He owed me six thousand dollars and tried to skip town. Within two weeks my buddy Nico called and said he heard Tom was hiding out at some friend of his girlfriend's a little outside of Breckenridge. He told me where the house was and asked if I wanted him to come along. I knew Jefe and Tortoise would want to go so I told him thanks anyway but I thought the three of us could handle it.

Nico was very cool that way—a true friend, all heart, always had my back. I trusted him completely. He grew up in Denver and had been friends with Cloud for several years, which is how I got to know him. He was an incredibly nice guy and a killer fucking deejay who was totally passionate about spinning his vinyl. He had made quite a name for himself around the Denver music scene, and when he wasn't playing at parties or clubs, he spent the majority of his time at home behind his turntables and mixers, coming up with new and improved incredibly dope shit. Nico also sold a shitload of weed and he and I did a lot of work together. He had a good head for business, always had some cash to throw down, and wasn't too flashy or loud. I had a lot of respect for Nico and enjoyed working with him; he was a pro.

When I got off the phone with Nico, I told Jefe and Tortoise that we were going to Breckenridge to see Tom. At first they looked surprised but then Jefe asked, "How long do you think we'll be gone?"

"Pack for a few days. And bring your board. We might as well ride while were there."

We were on the road in thirty minutes.

Once we got there, it didn't take us long to find the house. It was just outside of town right where Nico said it was. We didn't see Tom's truck so we decided to hit the ski park and check again later. Sure enough, when we went back that night, Tom's truck was in the driveway. We had been hitting it pretty hard riding and drinking most of the day and were feeling a little haggard but amped right up as soon as we saw it.

"Fuck it, dude. We'll just knock on the door and push our way in as soon as it opens," Jefe said. He was one agro motherfucker. I loved the shit out of him—I'd known him since I was five—but he was fucking nuts, always had been. When we were in the fifth grade, this kid Justin, the class asshole, came up behind me at recess, knocked me down, and started kicking me. He had completely blindsided me, and by the time I figured out what was going on, he had stopped. I looked up and saw Jefe, with his hand gripping Justin's throat. His eyes had a wild look that I saw over and over again, years after. Within seconds, Justin was on the ground, crying and bloody, and Jefe was on top of him with fists flying. It took two teachers to pull Jefe off, and for the next couple of weeks, Jefe had to spend recess inside, cleaning the chalkboards and dusting erasers, but he didn't care. Jefe was my soul brother and deemed himself my protector at a young age. I did everything in my power to protect and take care of him too.

I could hear Jefe shuffling around in the backseat of the car. "Where's my fucking skate?"

I reached onto the floor of the backseat and grabbed my expandable police baton. I'd picked it up at an army/navy surplus store. It was only about eight inches long when it was closed but had three steel telescoping sections that friction-locked into place with a flick of the wrist. Its grenade-textured rubber grip on the handle ensured retention in any situation—the motherfucker never slipped. It was the shit!

Tortoise had this little wooden mini-club that he had jokingly named Thumper. He wrapped the handle with navy blue grip tape, and although it was small, it did the trick. We weren't really planning on all of us piling on this kid and beating him to death, but in a situation like this, you just never knew. You didn't know who was in the house, what they had or didn't have—dogs, knives, guns. Usually when we had to do shit like this, Jefe packed this 1911 Colt .45 that he traded off some kid, but not today, thank Christ. Packing always made me a little nervous. I understood the reasoning behind it and all—I mean, if they're packing and you aren't ... We never had to pull a gun, and I always figured we wouldn't, but it still made me uneasy. That was just somewhere I never really wanted to go. You pull a gun, you better be ready to use it.

We found a discreet spot a little ways from the house to park. We got out of the car, put our ski masks on, and sneaked toward the front door. It was quiet and still, but I could feel the energy of the woods, the night, and the adrenaline, and my heart began to beat faster. They had a wood fire going; I smelled it and could see smoke billowing from the chimney. The sun was starting to go down, the sky was clear, and the air was dry, frosty, and crisp; it was getting damn chilly fast. I didn't really feel like fighting. I was tired, cold, hungry, and didn't want to lose the nice buzz I had spent all afternoon working on. I really just wanted to go somewhere warm, get some more beers and a pizza or something, and kick it. But that wasn't going to happen; this was one of the most important parts of the job. We weren't going to get money out of this kid; I knew that. We were here to make a point. If you let people take advantage of you, then other people think it's okay. They lose respect for you, lose fear of you, and then you might as well close up shop because you're gonna get jacked every time. If people think they can fuck with you, they will.

I watched Jefe's clenched fist pounding on the door, as he held his skate by its trucks in the other. And then the door opened—just a little at first but enough for us to see it was Tom—and for him to know it was us. His eyes grew wide, and he put all his weight onto the door, trying unsuccessfully to shut it. Jefe threw his left shoulder and all of his weight against it, I threw my weight in behind him, and Tortoise followed us up. In two seconds, we were in.

Jefe always went wild with shit like this—eyes all bulged and glazed with delight. He was a big boy and when his adrenaline was pumping, he was nuts. I wouldn't want him coming through my door, all psycho and shit.

Once we got Tom down, I did most of the pounding because it was my debt. I didn't want to kill him or anything—that wasn't the point—so I kept my steel baton off of his head. Jefe and Tortoise just threw in a little kick or smack-down every now and then, more to serve as a little garnish o' fear to my main course of pain.

"Where's my fucking money, you piece of shit?" I said and pounded him in the face with my fist.

"I don't know ... I'm sorry ... I can get it," Tom said, his voice garbled.

A girl standing on the other side of the room was screaming

and holding her ears. "Stop it! Please!" Tears were streaming down her cheeks.

I looked up and saw this big dude come in from down the hall. He was older—late forties, maybe—and was wearing dirty coveralls. He had a bushy, strawberry-blond beard that covered most of the lower half of his pudgy pink face. "What the fuck is going on?" he demanded angrily, and I saw fear and confusion spread over him. His eyebrows furrowed as he took a step back, and I heard a baby crying in another room.

"Get the fuck out of here!" I yelled and lifted my baton.

Tortoise held up his club. "You don't want any of this shit, man. It has nothing to do with you."

The guy stared blankly at us. His mouth was hanging open, and he turned and went back down the hall.

I grabbed Jefe by the back of the shirt. "We gotta go. Come on, man. Let's get out of here."

Tom was lying there in kind of a fetal position, rolling to his right side, holding his ribs. He was pretty bloody but breathing and moving. We hadn't been on him too long.

The next thing I knew, Tortoise was driving toward the main highway, and Jefe was in the backseat, half shouting and half laughing. "That stupid motherfucker! Yeah, come on. Take our money, you sorry little fuck! Go and tell your friends who did this to you, you little piece of shit!"

The hot little J. Chill's waitress walked back to my table. "Do you know what you want?"

I glanced at the open menu on the table in front of me and thought of saying, "Yeah, how 'bout you?" Instead, out came "I'll have a cheeseburger."

"What kind of cheese?"

"Cheddar."

"Do you want fries with that?" she asked as she scribbled

something onto the pad in her hand. "They're ninety-five cents extra." She subtly shifted her gaze from the pad to me, and I saw the warmth in her cheeks that I was feeling in my own.

"Yeah, sure." I gave her the best cool "pimp daddy" look I could muster. It worked.

She looked back at the pad as she tried to fight back a big smile, but her face started to flush, and the smile broke through. She gently bit the inside of her lush bottom lip and looked back up at me. "Okay." I could feel her nervous energy. "My name is Carrie. Let me know if you need anything else." She turned around, and I watched her sweet little black pants scurry away.

I opened my backpack and pulled out *The Catcher in the Rye.* I had already read it twice, but it was an easy, somewhat mindless read that wasn't too chewy, and I liked how I could just relax and settle into it. I had started to feel like Holden Caulfield was a buddy or something, always around to keep me company when I was bored. I opened my book, leaned back in the booth, and looked out the window at the planes on the runway. I thought about freedom and money and all the places I could go if I had them. I looked at the planes and wondered how many of those people were going on a fabulous vacation somewhere tropical, where they would lie around, and their most pressing decisions would be where to eat and if they wanted another drink or not. Lucky fucks!

Then I wondered how many of them were traveling to a funeral of a best friend or a parent or to a hospice or hospital to visit someone they knew they might never see again after they got back on the plane to go home. I wondered if anyone came to see Tom after that beating we laid on him. I wondered if his mom ever knew about it or if she would even care. My mom would freak.

There definitely seems to be more desensitization of violence these days, though mostly for us younger kids. Violence is literally a joke; it's mindless entertainment with a twist for the masses. It's a fucking riot.

Like most kids in today's society, I was exposed to the whole violence thing at a relatively young age. One of my earlier memories is of Wile E. Coyote and Road Runner, who spent an entire hour at least five days a week entertaining children all across the nation by blowing the hell out of each other in all kinds of sadistic ways. I thought it was hysterical. Not too long after I became acquainted with Wile E. and Road Runner, I got a PlayStation, and Mortal Kombat instantly became my favorite game. It was the first game I played where I could do a roundhouse, kick a guy in the head, and have his brains oozing off my toes as he dropped to the ground, squirming like a half-stomped-on night crawler while I watched his life force drain from the bar at the top of the screen. It was exciting, almost euphoric, and it lit the fuse of my primal need for dominance. The hungry alpha male—savage and blood-thirsty—was unleashed.

I fell in love with the whole gangster/mafioso thing and when I wasn't watching *Scarface* or *The Godfather* or *Goodfellas* or *Casino,* I was listening to Snoop Dogg or Ice-T or Tupac. I wanted to be like all those hard-core gangsters, with their anger and attitude and gluttony and disregard for almost everything. The fear and subordination that previously existed within them was replaced by hatred and vindication—I could see it in their eyes. There was something very cool and comforting about that—comforting, like it *seems* to feel good to not give a shit, to be unhappy and angry and pissed off and to stand up and shout "Fuck it!"; to do whatever you have to do to take care of yourself because nobody else is going to do it. I was completely seduced by their unruly way of life and immediately deemed this archetype as my mentor. Drugs, money, power, women, respect—what more could you want?

2

My first real experience with the drug culture started when I was in the sixth grade. I met this kid, Rico Consuelo, the first day of middle school. We hit it off and ended up becoming pretty tight. Rico was the youngest of five brothers who were all into some kind of shady, quasi-illegal business or another. The Consuelo brothers were pretty well known around town, and nobody fucked with them. They typically weren't all that friendly or inviting, but for some reason they took right to me. Rico was actually pretty timid and kind of kept to himself. His brothers always treated him like a little kid, which drove him crazy, even though he was kind of like a little kid. He wasn't a puss or anything like that, really; he was just kind of shy and quiet and a little insecure—definitely not boisterous or brazen like his brothers. Rico was the only Consuelo brother who had no real desire to get right up in the middle of "the business." I, on the other hand, found it totally and completely fascinating—not just the money, but the way ladies became infatuated with them, like they were some kind of rock stars or something. The Consuelo brothers were feared and respected and actually pretty smart. You may not believe it, but some of the sharpest individuals I've known have been very successful and made loads of cash selling drugs. It's not a dummy's game; it's a business, just like anything else.

Rico's oldest brother, Pablo, taught me about selling weed. They tinkered with all kinds of stuff but only ever let me into the ganja side of things. Even though he and his brothers mostly sold Beast (B grade weed from British Colombia), they knew and dabbled in the various levels and strains of green bud and taught me the weights and different market prices for it all. I was completely mesmerized by the whole game and caught on quickly. Pablo was shocked at how much weed and how fast I could move it for him. It's true; I could move that shit all day long. I had a natural talent and people liked to do business with me.

I never knew exactly how much the Consuelo brothers moved, but it was pounds and pounds and pounds. The basic principles for any product a person is moving are pretty much common sense. You paid 'x' for something and now you want to sell that something and make a profit. Figure out how much you want to make, what the market will hold, and go for it. There were a few more unwritten rules than that, like, we all had a certain responsibility to try and keep the market stable, and, as I mentioned earlier, it was always a better idea not to front your product if you could keep from it. Fronting was okay if it was to someone you could trust because with fronts you can bump up the price, but, regardless of how much more money you *could* make on a front, you always risked getting jacked and losing it all. And then what would you do? File a police report or send them to collections? "Uh, yeah, Mr. Authority Figure? I gave this motherfucker a pound of weed a month ago, and he was supposed to bring me thirty-five hundred bucks later that night, and I haven't seen or heard from him since. Will you help me find that piece of shit and get my money?"

We'd all heard stories of the Consuelo brothers and their crew engaging in violent attacks on anyone dumb enough to fuck with them. I don't think they lived for that type of violence or anything, but it certainly didn't bother them. They just saw it as a part of the process if you wanted to make money and be taken seriously in black-market business. Any show of weakness only ensures defeat. I remember the first truly brutal beating I ever witnessed. One day Jaime (pronounced *High-mee),* the Consuelo brother just two years older than Rico, came home with a huge knot on his head, a fat lip, and bruises where someone had been thumping on him. He'd been down at Saturday Market to meet up with this kid, Wolf, and sell him a quarter-pound of weed. Jaime had worked with Wolf on and off for about six months and never really had a problem with him, but later, he told his brothers that the past couple of times he'd seen Wolf, Wolf had acted a little shady and sketched out. Jaime figured he was probably just a little spun out on something—that was pretty typical in our world, and nobody thought much of it as long as performance was good.

Anyway, on this particular day, Jaime showed up with the ganja at their regular spot, and Wolf was there with two buddies, all three of them looking pretty gacked-out. Wolf didn't have any money for Jaime but still wanted the weed; he told Jaime he would have the money for him later that night. Jaime told Wolf, "No money, no weed." Wolf didn't like that and started to get all up in Jaime's face. Jaime knew it was a bad scene and tried to get out of there, but Wolf lunged forward, grabbed him, and tried to rip his backpack off his shoulders. Jaime fought to defend himself, but Wolf's buddies knocked him to the ground. He struggled to dodge their blows—and then he heard something rip. Wolf and the two other guys ran off, leaving Jaime lying there holding a backpack strap in one hand.

I was there when Jaime got home. "Wolf took my pack," Jaime exclaimed holding up the torn strap. "The fucker got my weed!" Jaime held his hand against his ribs as Pablo silently checked out his lip and then looked at his discolored rib cage, Jaime squirmed when Pablo pressed on it. After deciding Jaime's injuries were not too serious, Pablo walked into the other room and made a couple of phone calls. The next thing I knew, Margarito and Miguel, two more of the Consuelo brothers, were there with some scrappy-looking friend of theirs named Evo. Rico, Jaime, and I all piled into a couple of cars with them and headed down to Saturday Market. We walked around most of the day but never saw Wolf or his buddies. We went back the next weekend but didn't see them then either.

The next Friday night it was cold and raining like hell. Jefe and I were over at Rico's, hanging out and playing video games, when Pablo's phone rang. He talked for a minute, hung up, and made a couple more quick calls. "Evo's over at Marco's house," he told us. "He said a kid named Wolf just walked in. We're going over." A couple of minutes later Margarito and Miguel showed up. Jefe and Jaime got in the car with them, and Rico and I jumped in the car with Pablo. I sat uncomfortably in the awkward silence of the car, listening to the rain's aggressive thumping on the roof. I felt that weird kind of tingly energy, like when you know something unusual is going to happen but you're not quite sure what it is, and you have a kind of sick tickle deep in your gut—a pins-and-needles feeling. I had never really been in a fight up to that point, and I knew we were going after someone. What was I supposed to do? I started to feel like maybe Rico, Jefe, and I should have just stayed at home and let the older brothers and their scrappy-looking friend handle it. But they hadn't really given us an option. "Get in the car," Pablo had instructed. I don't think any of us thought for a second about doing anything except what we were told to do. I glanced over at Rico and could tell by the look on his face that he was thinking and feeling the same way I was.

We circled this one block a couple times and then parked on the side of a dark street and turned the car off. The other car with Miguel, Margarito, Jefe, and Jaime pulled up behind us. Pablo reached in the backseat, under a couple of rumpled shirts on the floor, and pulled out a metal chain about three feet long. We stepped out of the car into the night and walked about half a block down the road, until we were standing in front of a small, rundown apartment complex. I watched as Miguel slid open the magazine of a handgun, checked the cartridges, and then tucked it in the back of his pants. He dialed a number on his cell phone and only talked for a second before he hung up. He nodded at Pablo, and we started walking toward a front door. I couldn't believe I was there; I felt like I might throw up. Pablo looked over at Miguel and Margarito and then softly knocked on the door.

Evo answered, nodded at Pablo, and stood back to let us in.

Pablo took Jaime's arm and pulled him to the front. Wolf was sitting on the couch, counting money on the coffee table. When he looked up at us, his eyes grew wide with fear and disbelief. Pablo's eyes were fiery and fierce, and his voice was sharp and chilling. "You want to fuck with my brother?"

I had never seen this side of Pablo before. A memory flashed through my thoughts of Haas, the 120-pound Rottweiler I'd had as a kid. He was a total love of a dog, big and silly and slobbery, he always just wanted to lick you to death. I used to lie on the couch, and Haas would lie on his back on the floor next to me, driving me crazy always wanting me to rub his stomach non-stop. Well, one night, I ordered a pizza. Thirty to forty-five minutes later, as expected, when the pizza guy arrived, Haas sat up and perked his ears. He watched as this completely unsuspecting man, balancing a bright-red pizza warmer on one hand, strode up the front walk to the front screen door. In less than a second, every hair on Haas's body stood straight up. Teeth I never knew he had flashed, wet and sharp, and a low, blood-curdling growl came from the bowels of his being. And then, Haas went absolutely ballistic. He scared the shit out of me as he bolted up to the glass door, barking demonically. That wasn't Haas; I'm not sure who that animal was, but it was not Haas. Somehow, the pizza guy, innocently going about his business, had conjured Haas's inner hound of hell, and Cujo was released. The poor pizza delivery guy dropped the warmer and started to run ... until he realized Hass was not coming through the glass. I was in shock. Haas had scared the shit out of me too.

So, throughout this fleeting memory, I stood and watched this "other" Pablo, vicious and frightening, that I had heard about but never actually witnessed.

Pablo walked toward Wolf, who sat frozen with terror on the couch, mouth agape in disbelief. "You want to jack my brother and have your bro kick him in the head?" he growled menacingly. Miguel and Margarito followed close behind, and the rest of us stayed back.

"I'm ... I'm sorry. I'll get ... get your cash. Just ... just give me a chance," he stammered. That's when Pablo let loose with the first whip of his chain. Wolf covered his face with his hands and started to ball up on the couch. "No, please!" he cried. "I'm sorry! I'll get it back!"

"Nobody fucks with my family." Pablo lashed him a few more times and then stepped back. Margarito and Miguel stepped in. Miguel pounded on Wolf's head, and Margarito took the chain from Pablo and started whipping Wolf on his back and legs. Miguel pulled the gun from the back of his pants and shoved it into Wolf's cheek.

Wolf's face was draped in fear; I could smell it coming off him. "I'm sorry. It'll never happen again. I'll get your cash, I promise. Just please, don't—"

"You take a minute and look around," Pablo interrupted. "You see the people in this room?" Margarito lashed him again with the chain. "Be smart for once and be afraid of everyone here. Do you hear what I am telling you?"

"Yes." The rough edges of the rusted chain had ripped Wolf's thin Billabong T-shirt in a couple of places, and little bits of blood were starting to seep through.

Miguel and Margarito each placed a hand on one of Wolf's shoulders. Pablo stepped closer. "Take your shoes off," he said to Wolf, who lay paralyzed by fear and pain. His black and gray DC's were loosely tied, and he warily kicked them off, one at a time, exposing dirty, frayed socks. "Take off your shirt," Pablo instructed. Wolf slowly managed to pull himself up and struggled through the pain to lift his arms as he pulled the blood-stained T-shirt over his head, leaving the shirt hanging from his limp arm. His ribcage was peppered with blood and bruises; welts and lash marks were quickly rising up, discoloring and disfiguring his otherwise pale skin. Miguel reached his gun forward and used the barrel to pull Wolf's shirt off his arm, tossing it onto the floor next to his shoes. "Now your pants." Pablo's voice was strong and steady. Wolf hesitated, kind of shaking his head back and forth, but Miguel shoved the gun in his cheek again.

"Do what my brother tells you, asshole." Miguel's eyes looked like black pearls shining with frenzied delight. I saw a flash of the animal in him. I looked at Pablo and Margarito and saw the same thing—even Evo. They all had the same look and feel; nothing that could be faked or mimicked. This was primal pack mentality. I could almost smell the wild pheromones coming from them.

I glanced over at Wolf. He had that sense of prey falling victim to predator that I have seen on Discovery Channel. Miguel still held the gun to Wolf's cheek. "My brother told you to take off your pants, asshole." Wolf slowly and reluctantly moved to unbutton his pants and struggled to pull them down from around his hips. He forced himself to lean forward, pushing them down toward his ankles, and I saw the back of his rib cage, swollen and bruised, with gashes in his skin that exposed the meaty flesh. Finally, he got the pants all the way down and sluggishly kicked them off his feet.

Miguel picked up the pants, reached into a back pocket, and pulled out a wad of cash. He smirked as he stuffed the money into his own back pocket. Then, he leaned over and picked up the cash Wolf had been counting on the table and stuffed that into his pocket as well. Miguel pointed to the bag of weed on the floor. "Whoever bought that, it's yours."

Pablo stood over Wolf's limp body. "If you ever see me or anyone in this room, you put your eyes to the ground, turn in the opposite direction, and don't look back. I don't ever want to see you or hear your name again." Pablo yanked Wolf up off the couch and held him, kind of like a puppet. "Next time, you won't walk away." Pablo nodded to Margarito, who turned off the porch light and opened the front door. An icy wind swept into the warm room, pushing drops of rain in with it, as Pablo pushed Wolf—beaten, bloody, and fragile—out the door in nothing but his boxers. Pablo turned to the three guys who were standing against the wall behind me—I had forgotten they were there. They were still and quiet and scared, but they nodded to Pablo, and Pablo nodded back. Then he handed Evo some money, shook his hand, and we headed out into the rain to get in our cars, drive home, and finish our video games like nothing ever happened.

I remember that when I climbed into the backseat, I was a little shaky and feeling a mixture of nauseated, discombobulated, angry, and amped. What I saw that night was primal and animalistic, like a savage carnivore getting the taste of blood for the first time. Something inside of me was stirred. Even though I wasn't the one who beat on Wolf, I felt the awesome power of dominance tapped inside of me, burning to be unleashed. At the same time, I felt terrible that someone would have to experience something like that. I thought about the people in my life that I truly cared about and pictured their having to go through something like that—it made me feel sick. I tried to make myself stop thinking about it but my mind kept going back to Wolf on the couch, totally consumed with pain and fear and exhaustion.

I've seen plenty of violent, aggressive movies where people get beat on and shot and drugged out and killed and shit like that. I sat through the end of *Casino*, where Nicky and his brother get beat to death with a baseball bat. And *Scarface*, when they chain Tony Montana's buddy to the showerhead in that crappy motel bathroom and make Tony watch as they chainsaw off his limbs until he bleeds to death. But that was the first time I'd actually seen someone fall victim to serious pain and fear and humiliation by another individual, and I felt it. I mean, it actually made me, my ribcage smooth and untouched, physically hurt.

Rico and I didn't talk much that night. His older brothers were sensitive to us and left us alone. They knew we had never seen anything like that—it's probably why they took us along. In spite of all of its fucked-up-ness, it was a valuable lesson that taught me two things:

1) Don't fuck with anybody, and don't let anybody fuck with you.
2) There is power in numbers.

Jefe, on the other hand, was wound up all night long, talking about how cool the whole thing was and how awesome the brothers were to walk in there, all crazy and shit, and how stealth and intimidating they were. He thought beating the hell out of someone and sending him out in the rain all haggard and bloody in nothing but his boxers was absolutely the coolest thing he had ever seen. It was then I first realized a side of Jefe that made me nervous.

Nobody ever saw or heard from Wolf again. I wondered what happened to him that night, all fucked-up-looking and naked in the rain and shit. Part of me worried he would get stopped by a cop and rat us out; the other part worried he might die out there. I wondered if he had anywhere to go or if anybody would miss him if he did die. He took a pretty massive beating. I spent a good part of the night thinking of him, picturing him lying under some bush, bleeding, scared, and on the verge of hypothermia.

3

God, I wanted a drink.

Carrie, the hot little waitress at J. Chill's, walked back to my table with a tray balanced in her right hand that held my burger and fries. "Here you go." She set it on the table in front of me, along with a white paper napkin that was neatly wrapped around a knife, fork, and spoon. The smell of char-broiled flesh with melted cheese and potatoes just out of the deep fryer wafted up to me and stirred the hunger in my belly. "Do you want anything else?"

My eyes went to the neon signs that outlined the bar and the bottles of booze on the small shelves, I immediately zeroed in on the bottle of Jack Daniel's. That was always my drink—Jack and Coke. I couldn't get enough of it; drank it like water. I wanted one—bad! I wanted a fucking drink, just one, just to relax and wind down and celebrate my exodus from jail, rehab, and that fucking halfway house from hell. Goddamn it, I deserved one after all I'd been through. I felt my mouth open. "Could I get a couple of sides of ranch?" I heard myself say.

"Sure, I'll be right back with that." She smiled, and I watched her sweet little ass hurry away once again.

As I sat there, frustrated and jonesing and waiting for my ranch, I began to hear voices in my head—familiar voices, a soft echo from my not-so-distant past. Immediately, I attempted to block them out by focusing more intensely on the Coors Light hottie and her little red half-shirt. But with each passing moment, the voices came louder and clearer. Yep, just what I had suspected. Fuck!

The first voice belonged to Liz, the director of individual inmate counseling in Boulder County Jail, where I spent a simply *wonderful* twelve weeks. "What are you using the drugs to cover up, Kyd? Why don't you want to feel? What are you scared to face?"

Then came Sam, my friend who was a counselor at Willow Winds, the rehab center where I spent another eight weeks in eight-hour-a-day, super-intensive personal therapy. "You're smart, Kyd. You have a magnetic personality. People are drawn to you—I can see it. You just need to focus your energy in a different direction. Trust me, brother, you shine!" God help me, I so wanted to believe all that

Then there was John, one of my roommates at Beacon, the halfway house I lived in for six months after I finished rehab. He was forty-two and had been junked on heroin for years. He claimed to have tried to kick the habit over the past ten years but said it always came back to him. John talked about his addiction to heroin like it was a live person that stalked and found him, no matter what he did or where he went. He referred to it as "that little bitch."

"That little bitch has her hooks in me. She's not letting me go anywhere without her, that little bitch." To watch his struggle made me think of gnarly domestic violence scenes I'd seen on episodes of Cops, where the man and woman beat the shit out of each other, kids are screaming, neighbors in their pajamas are standing on their front lawns watching. And then they make bail, drop all charges, and it happens again tomorrow, or the next day, or the next weekend.

John was on and off the wagon. He was a severely depressed, two-pack-a-day smoker who had been at Beacon for nine months and always swore to kick "that little bitch" but hardly ever came to any of the meetings. He just sat around all day, sulking, with the blinds shut, watching talk shows and smoking his cigarettes, one after the other.

I smoked but not nearly as much as John. Looking at him made me want to quit—the way his teeth were beginning to streak a brownish-yellow, and he wheezed when he spoke, and those flemmy hacks where he coughed up a chunk of something and then swallowed it back down. Fucking gross! John was probably my biggest therapy. Just looking at him made me want to clean up, go to college, and get a real job.

In a flash, Carrie was back with two heaping sides of ranch dressing. "Do you want anything else?" She looked like she knew there was something on the tip of my tongue, desperately trying to fight its way through my teeth. I glanced over at the warm, inviting bottle of Jack Daniel's and had the feeling I was looking in the face of a comforting old friend I had not seen in ages. Carrie, the sweet little thing she was, stood patiently, looking at me with her innocent doe eyes, waiting for a response.

"I'll have a Coke," I heard myself say. *Fuck! Where did that come from?* Those assholes in my head just popped it right out of my mouth. Fuck them, those stupid motherfuckers! I was pissed. I wanted a fucking drink.

"We only have Pepsi. Is that okay?"

"Yeah, sure, that's fine."

I felt the anger welling up inside me, like an ocean at high tide. I just wanted to hit something, beat the shit out of it, rip it to shreds, stomp on it, spit on it, piss on it, drench it with gasoline, light a match, and watch it burn. What the fuck would it really matter if I just had one drink? Who the hell would know? And, fuck 'em even if they did. What the fuck did all those people really know about me anyway? Not a goddamn thing! They didn't really care. They were just doing their jobs. Besides, the chances of my seeing anyone I knew in here were about one in a million. After all I'd been through, I deserved a fucking drink. Fuck that! I deserved to get loaded! What else were you supposed to do at the airport, anyway? Who the fuck cared? I'd be sober enough by the time I got home ... Oh, yeah. Home.

Mom was picking me up at the airport. I couldn't get off the plane reeking of alcohol after all I'd put her through. It would kill her. She's not stupid; she would know. She'd been so cool and supportive of me through this whole deal, doing everything she could for me, but I knew it had torn her up. I knew it embarrassed her that people talked, but she never showed it, and that stung me more than anything. I couldn't hurt her anymore; it made me sick to think about it. But why couldn't I just have one and then brush my teeth? No one would know.

I walked out of the bar, opened my wallet, pulled out the Alcoholics Anonymous card that Sam had given me, and called.

As I boarded the plane, my anger began to ebb and was replaced, quite ironically and to my utter shock, with a new and interesting feeling, a sense of self-satisfaction, possibly even pride, resulting from my decision not to drink. Not so much because I thought I was an alcoholic—maybe I was—but because the decision I made had been based on how it might affect someone else, someone I loved and cared about. I didn't realize I was capable of that. I forgot how it felt.

I kicked back in my seat on the plane. They were showing some taped rerun of *Everybody Loves Raymond*. I put my headphones on and relaxed.

After we landed in Portland, I rode the escalator down to the baggage claim where I was meeting Mom. She was already there, combing the crowd for me. I waved at her. She smiled and waved back.

"Hey, Mom." We hugged and she kissed my cheek.

"Oh, I'm so glad you're here!" She gingerly pushed back a little bit of hair from my eye and gave me another hug. She had a big smile on her face, but I knew it was a veil used to shroud the despondency in her eyes. It was a pretty good veil—it would have been believable to just about anyone but her own flesh and blood. No matter how I tried to forget, I knew the severity of a situation that was not yet over.

I appreciated her stoicism, her valiant attempt to appear calm, tranquil, and unruffled by all that had happened so that I might feel more at ease. Her warrior spirit shone bright; it was the sun of an otherwise infinitely dark and cold universe.

I hadn't seen my mom much over the past year. After my arrest, I spent twelve weeks in jail. My bond was huge, and it was pretty much impossible for anyone to meet all the terms to get me out until they lowered it. Mom visited me while I was there, but I was being held in Colorado, and she lived in Oregon, which made it a little more difficult. She made it to my most important court dates, though—three of them, all bond reduction hearings. My attorney said it helped that she was there. Judges like to see parents who care.

The jail visits were weird—strict and depressing. It was thirty minutes of monitored no-contact that had to be scheduled twenty-four hours in advance. I remember the first time she came in through the metal detectors, so brave, fighting back all the sadness, frustration, and fear of what might happen. I watched her lip quiver as she saw me. My eyes were all fucked up—infected and bloody-looking—because the blood vessels had burst from what the doctor in jail had said was a panic attack I'd had on the day all the shit went down. I was so numb, I never even felt it, never even knew a panic attack was happening, but that first morning, about eight hours after they took me in, I looked like one of Rob Zombie's horror movie creations.

Mom had looked at me, searching for a clue as to what possibly could have happened to her beloved five-year-old who ran through the house in his Spiderman Underoos, wildly brandishing a large plastic knife as he fiercely hunted buffalo and cautiously pioneered a feral land of hallways, bathrooms, bedrooms, and closets. Or her ten-year-old, poised for puberty, in his shoulder pads, thigh pads, shin guards, cleats, and a red Kids Inc. jersey with "13" printed in large white numbers, darting through the house as he desperately searched for his football helmet because he could not be late to practice again.

She sat across from me in a metal chair—we all sat in metal chairs. I was in my light blue BBC jumpsuit and black BBC canvas lace-up low-top sneakers (Converse knock-offs). It was certainly not the most attractive or comfortable outfit, but it was the designated inmate attire, compliments of the Bob Barker Cooperation, hence the BBC labels. Isn't that a trip? That old *Price is Right* fucker making jail and prison garb on the side. I couldn't help but laugh about it. Who would have thought? Maybe if it were Hulk Hogan, Mr. T, Steven Seagal, or even Arnold, I could see it. But Bob fucking Barker? What a riot! I'm sure it was profitable, though, especially these days. That was one thing I understood—the desire for profit. I could really relate to it. It motivated me for years.

We all wore different versions of the BBC jumpsuit, color-coded to indicate which wing of the jail you were in. I was blue—the drug ward. I know Mom hadn't liked seeing me in that jumpsuit, looking like a criminal and all. I could feel her stomach pinch and twist. Her eyes welled up, but no tears rolled down her face. She'd stood strong, like a thousand-year oak braving the turmoil of time, her roots reaching firm and deep through a foundation of endless, unconditional love.

"How was your flight?"

"Fine. I slept most of the way." I heard a loud, unnerving buzz as the luggage carousel began to spin. We stood together waiting for my bags.

It had been a while since I'd been home. When I was

younger, I couldn't wait to get out, and once I did, I'd never really much liked coming back. I tried to avoid it as much as possible. I feel guilty saying that, but it's the truth. I mean, I certainly was never beaten or underfed. I never lacked for anything I needed; in fact, it was probably just the opposite. But for various reasons, when I was growing up, I had just wanted to get the hell out of there. In the past when I came to visit, I always knew I was leaving. I was just there for a few days, a week tops. But this time, I was home for a while—indefinitely. My case wasn't going to be settled for some time. I was still out on bail and technically shouldn't have been able to leave the state of Colorado, but my attorney worked it out with the DA for me to come home and stay at my mom's until the case was settled. That was it, though—I couldn't go anywhere else. Legally, I was bound to Portland, Oregon.

Mom and I walked to the car. It was raining, as usual. I felt my hair and skin soften from the moisture in the air as soon as I stepped out of the airport. It was chilly but nice to smell rain and to feel it—clean, fresh, hopeful, and soothing, like a cool washcloth on a fevered face. It had been so damn hot in Florida and hadn't rained in a while. I was sick of heat and had started to think I'd never feel another drop of rain again.

"Have you eaten dinner?" Mom asked as we headed out of the airport.

"No, not really."

"You want me to stop and get you something?"

"Yeah, sure."

"What would you like?"

"I don't care. Whatever's easiest."

"Well, we are going to pass a Burger World and a Macho Taco on the way home."

"Burger World sounds good."

"Your friends can't wait to see you," she said as we cruised down the highway.

"Really? Like who?"

"Well, Tortoise called as I was leaving for the airport, and Cedar called this morning, and Nico." She hesitated as a more dismal energy fell over her. "And Melissa."

"Really?" My body tensed with a sharp pang of remorse, guilt, and anxiety. I was surprised she'd called. I'd spent the past months trying not to think about her, even though I couldn't stop wondering if I would ever talk to her or see her again.

Mom immediately brightened. "The phone's been ringing all day," she said, clearly thrilled to have me back. "I wrote them all down."

"That's cool."

Throughout the years, I had managed to maintain a pretty tight group of friends in Portland. I talked to a couple of them while I was away, rehabilitating, but phone access had been limited and not encouraged. Still, I couldn't help but wonder how they would act toward me once I got home. Almost everybody I knew had their finger dipped into some part of the black-market pie—not as deep as we did in Colorado but still, enough to count. I was excited to see everybody, but nervous too. There was a group of us who had all known each other since elementary school: Ryan, Tortoise, Cedar, Eric, me, Jefe. We hung out pretty much all the time, played sports together, were in Boy Scouts, went to the stupid school dances, all while simultaneously sharing the fun and awkward growing-up shit we were forced to experience. We discovered ganja in fourth grade and started smoking it daily over at Tortoise's house. He lived with his mom, who worked a lot and spent most of her free time at her boyfriend's place. She typically wasn't home until late, if she came home at all, so we would go over to his house after school, get high, walk over to Burger World, and laugh hysterically as we ate ourselves into oblivion. Then we'd go back to his house, smoke a little more, and veg out in front of the TV or some video game.

A couple of years later, we were selling. Like I learned from the Consuelo brothers, why buy for your head when you can turn a little, make a couple of bucks, and smoke for free? I had the connections and a little bit of working capital. Ounces of weed turned into quarter-pounds, into pounds, into ten packs, into mushrooms, acid, Ecstasy, DMT, cocaine, GHB, 2C-B, and a wide array of pharmaceuticals. After a while we were able to make a damn good living off hanging out and getting loaded all the time. We saw how easy it was, and that was that; we were hooked, especially me. But all that seemed like a lifetime ago, when I was somebody else. A lot had gone down over the past year; everything was different. I wasn't sure who I was anymore, who my friends might be now, or who we would be to each other.

My situation was touchy. No one really knew how to treat me. Eggshells littered the ground around me and I figured people would try to walk, kind of tippie-toe around, without crushing them and making too much noise or slicing their own feet. I understood. It was no secret I was in pretty deep shit, and nobody much likes shit— it's messy and stinks. Anyway, it made me feel good to know they were still calling now that I was back. It said a lot, really.

"They asked if they could come by tonight," Mom was telling me, "but I told them you were up early this morning and would probably be tired."

"Yeah, I'm pretty beat."

"I thought, if you wanted to, maybe we could grill some steaks tomorrow night, and you could have them over for dinner."

"That sounds good."

4

Jefe, Tortoise, and I moved to Boulder pretty much right out of high school. Even though Jefe had dropped out the year before, he stayed around and waited for Tortoise and me to finish. He didn't have anything else to do and had become kind of dependent on me in different ways. It never bothered me, and now, looking back, I can see how I had become kind of dependent on him too. Anyway, the three of us moved to Boulder and got a four-bedroom house with our buddy Cloud, who was this super-cool, crazy, snowboarding, incredibly sick, glass-blowing, third-generation hippie, native Boulder dread that we had met years ago through Cedar.

We had originally planned to live somewhere in the college district of town, where all the Heads ran rampant, and the four of us would just blend in and fade out beautifully. However, because we waited until the absolute last minute to find something, the only four-bedroom house available was in this white-collar neighborhood of suburban Boulder. It was the type of neighborhood where young couples are just starting out, like a cardiologist just out of residency with his 'homemaker' wife, and their 1.5 kids all piled into their Lexus SUV. It was not typical of the type of area where you'd see four heady-looking kids, with their big hairy-ass wolf/malamute mix coming and going at all hours of the day and night. But we stayed to ourselves, kept the music down for the most part, and didn't have loud parties. We made an effort not to call too much attention to ourselves. It worked, and the neighbors seemed fine with us. Although we never really *talked* to any of them, we would all smile and wave and act friendly when we passed each other driving down the street.

Our two-story house was a light sage green with cream-colored trim and a burgundy door. The lawn was fully landscaped, and the interior was nice and clean, with new-looking carpet, some hardwood floors, granite countertops, a dishwasher, and garbage disposal. There were matching brushed-silver plumbing and light fixtures, and can lights that dimmed. It was pretty sick—light and bright, like being at my mom's house. Although it looked nice, none of us liked "light and bright," so we lived with blinds shut and tapestries hung over most the windows, creating more of a cave-like environment, which was much more in tune with our comfort zone. It was a nice freaking house, out of character for the four of us, and we managed to pretty well trash the place within about the first month. We didn't do it on purpose; we just didn't like to clean.

We didn't care much about furniture, so ours was an interesting array of mismatched stuff acquired mostly from Goodwill. We just went around randomly picking up the basics—a couple of chairs here, coffee table there, kitchen table, dishes, glasses, silverware, stuff like that. The only thing I bought new was this pretty sick reclining couch, but as soon as we got it home, Stella—my wolf/malamute mix—chewed the foam out of both of the arms. It looked pretty bad, and I tried to hide it with pillows but she just chewed those too. Man, did she love to chew. We all lost at least a pair of shoes to her and learned the hard way not to leave anything of any real importance on the ground: backpacks, hoodies, books, and papers—it all had to be up where she couldn't reach it.

I soon found that the Boulder black market for illegal drugs was surprisingly soft. It certainly wasn't nonexistent or anything, just some random kids dabbling in little bits of this and that. There were no major players, from what I could tell. Nothing really organized. I saw our opportunity, and it wasn't long before we were raging that town. It was ours for about five years, until we got too carried away with it all, eventually losing all ability to think rationally and completely rejecting the concept of any kind of objective reality. And then, *boom*! Just like that, it all blew up in our faces. Out of nowhere, we were thrown on our asses—heads spinning, ears burning, hearts racing, most likely in some state of Post Traumatic Shock Syndrome—not totally believing all that happened.

Things hadn't changed much back home in P-town. Everybody was still raging pretty hard, from what I'd heard, not dealing too heavy but partying a lot. Tortoise was back at it with a steady pharmaceutical connection and peddling around smaller weights of ganja. Everyone was still hanging out at Stumpy's all the time, the local tavern we had been going to since we were about sixteen. I don't think they'd ever carded anyone, and they made the stiffest drinks of any bar I've ever been to. Lisa, the bartender, pretty much just poured straight alcohol on the rocks, maybe a splash of Coke or tonic or orange juice or something. She was a super-hot, older woman—not too old, though—with long, thick black hair, soft green eyes, a nice tight little ass, and the sweetest set of titties you've ever seen—no shit. I'm pretty sure they were real too. She always wore these low-cut, tight little shirts with some thin little bra, and it was usually a little chilly in there, so you could always see the outline of her hard nipples. Lisa loved to flirt, get us all loaded, and then send us home with a huge hard-on.

It was going be a real pain in the ass bitch to keep out of that shit now that I was home—the drugs, the drinks, her sweet fucking titties. My love and hate for it all were in a constant struggle—pushing, pulling, testing, and taunting. I had gone off the deep end, and scared myself, and some really horrible things happened. I didn't want to be like I was before … but I didn't want someone telling me I couldn't have a fucking drink or smoke a bowl if I wanted to either. It wasn't like my newfound life of sobriety was completely voluntary, but that was my situation, and everyone knew it. I was done dealing and couldn't party, even if I'd wanted to. My case was hypersensitive; the court was trying to fuck with me, to make an example of me, and I was on a short fucking leash.

"What do you want?" Mom asked as we pulled around to order at the Burger World drive-up.

I studied the menu for a minute, like I hadn't ordered the exact same thing every time I'd come here since I was ten; I'm a creature of habit. I leaned across Mom and spoke into the brightly colored boxed sign. "Double cheeseburger, no pickles, large fries, and a chocolate shake." It burbled something back, and we pulled up to the next window.

"So, I talked to Jim, and he said to have you come by Monday morning and talk to him and Mike about a possible work schedule." Mom's voice was intentionally crafted for nonchalance. She didn't want to push too hard, just kind of lay it on the table and give it a little nudge.

"Yeah?" Butterflies danced in my stomach and up toward my throat. "That's cool." Mom had told me about Jim and Mike while I was still in Florida, when it was decided I would stay at her house until my case was settled. They were brothers, attorneys, who shared a well-known and respected law firm in town. Mom had talked to them and had it all set up—they were going to give me a job helping in their office and running errands and stuff like that.

I really was trying to have a good attitude about it. Considering the position I was in and all of its possible consequences, I was willing to do pretty much anything to promote the most positive outcome for myself, and that definitely meant getting a job. The past eleven months I'd spent in Florida, rehab, and jail was the first real stint of sobriety I had experienced since I was probably about twelve. Although the sobriety wasn't necessarily spawned of my own free will, I ended up being grateful for it and realized the whole horrible tragedy, and all of its consequences, ultimately saved my life and made me want to be a better person.

As the therapy sessions increased and the fog in my brain lifted, I began to realize just how fucked up I really was. I had managed to turn myself into a complete sociopath. I don't think I noticed it before because I only surrounded myself with other complete sociopaths who lived the same inebriated, sociopathic reality. I didn't associate with or interact in mainstream society for years—not for my whole adult life, really—until I had to get a job at the halfway house in Florida as part of the program to aid in facilitating our process of re-socialization. It was then I began to realize the true extent of my psychosis.

I had always known I was different from "normal" people, like my mom and her friends, and my friends who went to college right out of high school, and got jobs with salaries and benefits, and got married, and bought houses, and went to back-to-school night with screeching children who had snot crusted to the bottom of their noses and sticky little fingers that grabbed at everything and stuff like that. But I never really worried about it. I always figured they were they fucked-up ones—blind, boring, ignorant, ridiculously submissive, and weak for so freely and eagerly buying into such an oppressive and perverse mechanistic society; one founded on separation, hedonism, and blatant untruths hypocritically masked in our so-called "patriotic, democratic, capitalistic" way of life. Fuck that, dude. I'm no droid. I wasn't just going to bend over, spread my cheeks, and take it up the ass with a big fucking smile on my face, only to sweat, struggle, and squirm inside this heavy masquerade of mandated legitimacy, all the while being taunted, tantalized, and tortured by commercialism, materialism, and advertisement of stuff I want but will never have, because I am nothing more than a slave to the grind, working my ass off, for not nearly enough money, just trying to keep afloat in the ever agitated, rocky, swirling, cold, dark sea of American life.

How many P. Diddys do you know? JLos? Madonnas? Donald Trumps? Yeah, me either. All that shit—the fancy cars, restaurants, clothes, houses, trainers, personal shoppers, vacations—I want it. We all want it. We're programmed to want it. And if you think a freaking minimum wage nine-to-five job or even some random college degree that makes you $40,000 to $50,000 a year is going to afford us the time and the money necessary to properly live out the beautifully grotesque and gluttonous American dream of the twenty-first century than you're fucking wacked. So stop rubbing our fucking nose in it already. Okay, America, you've won. Your process of conditioning has been a success. I am a full blown self-absorbed consumer. I want it all, and I want it now. All of it—the stuff, the time to enjoy it, and the respect and admiration that comes along with having it all. And I don't want to work very hard for any of it. *Blah-bling!* Drug dealer. It just made sense.

It worked well for a while, better than I could have ever imagined, and it might have worked out even longer, but I fucked up. We fucked up—lost respect for it all, for ourselves, for other people, and the universe kicked our ass.

Although I still don't agree with all the different facets of mainstream society, I am beginning to realize that no one, nothing, is really "normal." Everybody exists in their own little bubble of reality and subjectively experiences this objective world from their own little vantage point. Their individual realities consist of their individual worries, happiness, stresses, excitement, and problems. I believe that a good handful of people—possibly even the majority—are honestly trying to make the best decisions, do the best they can, and be the best members of society they can be, which is more than I can say for myself over the past decade.

I did some really fucked-up shit to people when I was all polluted. I hurt people bad, intentionally and unintentionally—physically, mentally, emotionally. It always felt justified at the time. I mean, I never just hurt people for no reason. The people I fucked with had it coming; at least, that's what I thought at the time. They tried to rip me off, fucked with my friends, talked shit, and disrespected me.

I not proud of it now, but that's life in the black market; it carries a price. Looking back, it doesn't even seem real, just like some kind of sick and twisted late-night HBO special. If I could go back and do things differently, I would. I wouldn't let it get so out of hand. I'd just dabble, just making enough so I could live and have fun, where it wouldn't get that out of control, where nothing that bad could happen. But that's a crock of shit, for me anyway... for most people, if they have the opportunity and know how to work it. There is no half-assed; it's all or nothing, entrancing, and all-consuming. It's your bubble, your reality—with tunnel vision; nothing else exists. It's like a predatory animal during a kill, with only one thought, one instinct driving its every move.

There was no "just dabbling" in the black market—not for me anyway. Because if I can launch like a rocket into outer space with all of it, why not do it? It's a total and complete rush. And the thing is, even people who do "just dabble" — just sell so they don't have to buy, just sell to make their car payment, just sell because it keeps them in 'that loop'; you dabble long enough and eventually it's going to catch up with you, one way or another.

But none of that crap makes a shit bit of a difference to me anymore. My damage is done; the worst happened and there's no going back. It got all fucked up. Good people were hurt. People I loved died. And now I have a strike against me, big time. As tempting as it may be, even after all that's happened, to say 'fuck it!' and go back to all of that... if anything happened again, they'd lock me up and drop the key into the deepest, darkest pit of ocean out there. And the thing is, I know I'm better than that. I'm smarter than that. I have something to offer. As hard as it's gonna be and as scary as it already fucking is, I'm gonna step up, because I know eventually, I'll shine.

Although I initially resisted the therapy, yoga, meditation, and tai chi, it became an integral part of my life during the months of incarceration and rehabilitation and started to seep in slowly, adjusting the skewed perception that formerly influenced my thinking. I became painfully aware of the darkness that plagued me for so many years and the negative effects it rendered.

I don't want to be like that anymore—all crazy and shit. I want to balance out, reach my full potential, and be the best person I can be. But just because that is what I want doesn't make it easy. It is a total change of life, of reality, and of identity, and in spite of all the darkness, there still are certain things about my life as a drug dealer that are hard to let go of.

Take a guess.

Blah-motherfucking-bling! The money. It's hard as fuck to let go of that money—C-notes flying all over the place, seeing Bennie's face every time I pulled a wad out of my pocket. Money was never an object. I was making thousands of dollars a month by hanging out and partying. And with the money came respect, power, and women. Just like that. It's true, like Tony Montana says in *Scarface*, "First you get the money, then you get the power, and then you get the women." As twisted as it may be, it's the truth, especially in the drug culture. There is something about it that's sexy, that attracts and fascinates a large portion of our culture a whole hell of a lot more than some rat-cage, minimum-wage nine-to-fiver.

I mean, who can blame them? It seems like such a no-brainer: work really hard for not very much money, only to never have all the stuff you have been conditioned to want, all the while being treated with absolutely no respect, by some egomaniacal, middle-management motherfucker who lives to get off on his self-perceived power and authority over all of the expendable pieces of shit beneath him; *or* barely work at all for quite a bit of cash, get loaded, and hang out with your friends, all the while growing more and more accustomed to the increasing respect, admiration, and dignity from your peers. There's hardly a comparison, and once you're hooked, you're hooked. It's hard to go back after you've gotten a good taste; in fact, it's nearly impossible.

5

In Florida, when I had to get a job as part of Beacon's program for resocialization, I very reluctantly ended up at Fashion Express for Less—discount clothing and accessories, minimum wage, waiting hand and foot on an impatient, outspoken, arrogant, egotistical, and hedonistic general public.

The service industry—talk about a reality check! I had to wear an electric-blue polyester vest that carried a light scent of mothballs, with a white plastic pin-on name tag that had "Kyd" typed in bold white letters across an inch-and-a-half piece of black labeling tape. When I wasn't "taking care of the customer first," I had to sort, tag, hang, and/or fold women's clothing and accessories and put them out on display, all the while enduring crazy headaches caused from working twenty-five to thirty hours a week under the most heinous fluorescent lighting I have ever encountered. It was very surreal, and I just went through the motions stunned, zombie-like. It felt like an out-of-body experience where I hovered above, peering down at my own fucked-up reality. It was pure misery.

I hope I've survived the worst of it at this point—jail, rehab, Fashion Express for Less. Now that I'm back in Oregon, living at home, I'm going to enroll at the community college. And this job Mom has hooked me up with, working in a law office with her friends, doesn't sound so bad.

"I told them that you would be starting school in a couple of months and would only be able to work part-time." Mom's delicately crafted nonchalance was wearing thin as her bona fide excitement pushed through.

"Nice," I said, trying my best to sound genuinely positive and upbeat. After all, it had to be better than Fashion Express.

I didn't really mind "working" all that much. It wasn't that bad; I mean, I've never really thought of myself as a lazy person or anything like that, but I'll tell you what I do have a problem with—authority. I can't stand dumb-ass motherfuckers with some kind of chip on their shoulders and a superiority complex, getting off on telling kids like me what to do, especially when it comes to some lame-ass simpleton job like the Fashion Express that doesn't even pay the bills. "Kyd, I need you to mark down all the women's Jockey bras, and make sure they are sorted according to size and all hanging in their right spots. I don't want to see any smalls in with the mediums. We pride ourselves on that, Kyd. Our customers know that when they come to Fashion Express, the smalls are always in with the smalls, and the mediums are always in with the mediums. Then, when you're done with that, go and clean up the bathrooms. I want you to get in there and really scrub those toilets. I was noticing a lot of brown and yellow crusted splatters around the rim of the bowl and on the underside of the seat. We can't have that. Actually, Kyd, why don't you hold off on the toilet bowl until tomorrow, and you can bring your toothbrush, get in there, and really make it sparkle." You know what, you piece of fuck? Scrub your own goddamn toilet, and mark down your own fucking ladies underwear, because you've been sitting in the office on your fat ass drinking your coffee, eating your fucking doughnuts, and surfing the Net all goddamned week, acting like your Donald fucking Trump or something because you make three dollars an hour more than I do. Yeah, well, let me tell you something, Mr. Manager, Mr. Boss Man. You're no fucking rock star! I hate being bossed around, treated with condescension like I'm some idiotic worthless piece of shit. Fuck you!

People tell me that authority or whatever is just a part of life, but it's been a hard one for me to swallow, especially compared to my previous life—dealing drugs, being the boss, no one to answer to. There was no real authority issue in the drug culture. I mean, pretty much everybody just did what they were supposed to do. You owe someone money, drugs, respect, you give it to them, or they will find you and fuck you up. It was code; it was common sense. You had to be a real dumb-ass to fuck someone over. I mean, people did it, but they were fucking idiots, and almost always, 99 percent of the time, forced to reckon.

Mom pulled into the garage, and I could hear Stella barking, whining, and scratching on the other side of the door into the house.

Mom smiled. "I told her I was going to pick you up and bring you home from the airport. I would look at her and clap my hands and say, 'Kyd! Kyd is coming home!' and she would jump up and down and spin around in circles." She turned off her car and pulled the keys out of the ignition. "She knew what I was saying. She really is so smart."

"Yeah."

I opened the car door to step out and felt my stomach go hollow and twist, and a lump rose in my throat. Suddenly, I was sad and remembered the night all the shit went down—lying on the floor, all bloody and fucked up, and seeing Stella on the other side of the glass slider, barking and growling, trying to get in, and looking at me with panic-stricken eyes. Her muzzle was bloody from her attempts to break through the glass to protect us. Her shoulders were arched up, and the thick fur across the back of her neck stood on end. She looked savage and wild that night, and I could really see the wolf in her. I'd been told she was only a quarter wolf, but she always felt like more wolf than malamute to me. I knew that night had freaked her the fuck out, and I felt horrible about it.

When I first moved to Colorado, I got Stella from this old hippie friend of Cloud's dad. She was just eight weeks old and already extremely smart, very sensitive, and incredibly loyal to me. Within the first two months, she started sleeping right next to my bedroom door, like she was guarding a cave. I think she really only ever half-slept, because her ears would always prick at even the slightest noise. She would be all curled up on the ground with her eyes closed, but those ears were always on alert. She was protective of the whole house but especially of me, and I always made it a point to be the one who fed her. She definitely thought of herself as one of our pack, and it hurt her feelings whenever we left her at home, so I took her almost everywhere we went. Stella always sat next to me, watching everything that was going on around us, keeping guard and constantly evaluating the situation. She would let me know if she didn't like someone or didn't feel good about a situation, and I listened to her—she was always right.

The way Stella watched over me was almost, in a bizarre way, parental or like some kind of guardian angel. She took care of my sorry, loaded ass on several different occasions. I remember this one time we were in Washington at the Gorge for a Phish show. It was completely off the hook, one of the biggest shows I've been to—thirty thousand people, all Heads; it was epic!

My buddy Cedar had just driven up from a visit to the Bay. Jefe and I were kicking it in his 1995 burnt-orange pop-top Westphalia, checking out some of the goods he had brought back with him.

"Dude," Cedar said, pulling a Tylenol bottle out of his

backpack. "You ever eaten any 2C-B?" He looked at me with wide, gleaming eyes, like a kid in a candy store.

"No, but I've heard about it. It's supposed to be some sick-ass psychedelic."

He opened the bottle and shook a few small chalky-white round pills into the palm of his hand. I took one and gave it a closer look.

"Ben has a grip of this shit," Cedar said. "He knows the chemist. The visuals are supposed to be ten times as intense as the best liquid, but you don't get any of that acid head-trip."

"Have you tried it?"

"No." He shrugged his shoulders and shifted his gaze to the pills in his hand. "I don't eat psychedelics."

"Yeah." A few years ago Cedar ate a grip-load of this super shitty blotter and then smoked a bunch of crack. He pretty much lost his shit and climbed a fire escape to the top of this twenty-story building. He was going to jump off and try to fly or something, but the fire department showed up and restrained him. I heard it was pretty bad. They held him in psychiatric for seventy-two hours. He's never really been the same since.

Cedar has never really been "normal." I grew up with the kid, known him since elementary school, and he's just not like everybody else. He went away to a boarding school in the eighth grade, but we stayed tight. We traveled around every summer, going to shows, festivals, gatherings, barter fairs—whatever was going on.

He was an incredibly good guy and would do just about anything for anyone, always picking up the tab for shit—food, drugs, clothes, traveling expenses, whatever. It pissed me off, because I always thought people took advantage of him because he was so generous. Cedar didn't seem to care, though; he was loaded—like millions of dollars kind of loaded. His dad's side of the family owned one of the biggest lumber companies in the Pacific Northwest. Cedar was what some might call a "trustafarian" and would most likely never have to work a day in his life, which is why I never really understood why he risked moving so much ganja. He had this killer Beast connection out of Washington and brought loads and loads of it down to us in Colorado. Don't get me wrong; it made us tons of cash, and I was stoked about that, but the money didn't make a shit bit of a difference in Cedar's life. He wasn't motivated by that part of it. He was just pissed off at the world, like the rest of us. And ultimately, on some level, it was all just one big game between Us and Them. Everyone else was playing.

Cedar had gotten turned on to Hare Krishna some years ago, when he was surfing in Hawaii one winter. He spent most of his time after that in Costa Rica, farming avocados on some kind of Krishna commune. He shaved off all of his hair except for a skinny little ponytail kind of thing that hung from the back of his head, and he took to wearing this long orange robe that was tied around the waist with a rope. He wore several strands of sandalwood beads around his neck and these homemade-looking wrap-around rope sandals. He always carried the Bhagavad-Gita and several other of Krishna Consciousness's pamphlets. He couldn't go five seconds without chanting that damned Krishna mantra—"Krishna, Hare Krishna, Hare Hare, Rama Rama." I hated that blasted chant, and it ended up stuck in my head like some bad TV commercial. I would catch myself subconsciously chanting it under my breath whenever my conscious mind was busy doing something else. Cedar eventually lost the robe and rope sandals but hung on to the shaved head, sandalwood beads, and chanting.

"Ben said you should take a hit of Ecstasy and then when you start to peak, eat four of these 2C-B pills," Cedar instructed.

"Has Ben eaten any?" I asked.

"Yeah, I'm pretty sure."

Jefe sat up. "I'll eat some. What do you want for it?"

"Do you want it with the Ecstasy?" Cedar asked as he fished around inside the Tylenol bottle. He pulled out a couple of gel caps filled a little more than halfway with a dull white powder. "It's super-clean molly."

Jefe checked it out. "Nice. Yeah, man, if that's what Ben said. Come on, Kyd, let's munch some of this shit. I've heard about it. It's supposed to be pretty sick."

I'd always put just about anything in my mouth. I didn't really care. If it was supposed to get me high, I'd do it. After all, that was our motto: Eat it, smoke it, snort it, drink it! But I've got to admit, I was a little hesitant about this 2C-B shit. Not so much because I didn't want to eat it; I did. I had heard about it for a while and wondered why I hadn't seen any yet. It was supposed to be one of the sickest new manufactured psychedelics on the market. I definitely wanted to try it. But Cedar—I mean, I love the kid and all, but he's a fucking wing-nut! Even he knows it; it's just part of what makes him so ... Cedar.

I don't think Cedar would ever intentionally poison me or anything. It's just that I didn't totally trust that he knew what he was talking about. He had all kinds of pills in that Tylenol bottle, and I know how Cedar listened to people—he didn't. Everything about that boy was a mile a fucking minute, a residual effect from his crack-smoking past that ultimately landed him in the hospital and damn near killed him. But that's another story.

Yeah, he knew some kid who knew some chemist down around the Bay; that was true. Cedar first brought us GHB and DMT—now, that was some crazy shit. But he had tried that, drank the GHB like water, smoked grips of DMT right alongside us, and he was fine, relatively speaking. But the 2C-B, I knew we were guinea-pigging that shit. No telling what Ben, his "friend of the chemist," really told him about doses and shit, if he told him anything at all. Cedar would never remember anyway, and it would be like him to just make something up—not in a malicious way but just a Cedar kind of way. After all, the pills were small. You'd have to eat three or four, wouldn't you?

"All right," I agreed. What the hell. I'd eaten a lot of crazy shit, so what was one (or rather, four) more somewhat questionable, ultimately unidentified white pills? "What do you want for it? The Ecstasy too."

Cedar sat there a second, looking over the pills in his hand, his eyebrows scrunched down in a sorry attempt to wear the mask of a shrewd businessman. He was trying to show us he was really thinking, working deals, and making money like the rest of the kids on the lot, but he had no game and plenty of cash already. He probably forgot what he even paid for all that shit anyway, but it didn't matter. "How about eighty bucks for all of it?" He shook the rest of the pills out of the bottle. "I've been getting twenty-five for the E pills all day." I pulled the money out of my pack and handed it to him. He gave us our pills. "You guys should munch that molly right now so you can be flying on the 2C-B when the show starts." He sat there, intently watching us. His arms were wrapped around and crossed in front of his knees, holding them into his chest, as he rocked slightly back and forth.

"Yeah." Jefe popped the gel cap in his mouth, took a swig of water, and handed it to me. We sat there puffing bowls for a while, and when we started to really feel the Ecstasy, we popped the four 2C-B pills and puffed another couple of bowls.

Dogs weren't allowed into the show, so I figured I would take Stella back to our campsite. It wasn't that far. "You want me to go with you?" Jefe asked.

"No, it's cool. I'll be right back." When I stepped out of the bus, it was bright as hell outside, and my eyes were so sensitive to the sunlight that I immediately raised my arm to shield them—a confused vampire, high on drugs, life, and Ecstasy, exiting his cave prematurely.

I stood there for a moment, just outside the door to Cedar's bus, feeling the sun soak into me. I was thinking how I might burst into flames—for real, right there, that very second—and how incredible it would be … a white light, a kind of hyper-spiritual experience that would undoubtedly lead to a transcendence of my body and merging with the raw data strip, the eternal divine fountain of undisturbed, unpolluted truth, love, unity, and oneness. What would that feel like? Pain? Burning? Infinite orgasm? I hoped for the third possibility, obviously. That would be the best. The hurting and burning concept tried to creep back into my conscious thought, but I made myself stop thinking about it by focusing more intensely on the infinite orgasm idea. How could anything, such as divine transcendence, so full of love and light, possibly be painful? Especially burning; that's the worst. I forced the idea out again.

Objects around me were skewed, and they blurred in and out of my vision as I stood there, waiting for my eyes to adjust to the sunlight. Stella was lying on the ground next to the bus. "Come on, girl. Let's go."

It didn't make much difference once my eyes were dialed in with the sunlight, because everything was still incredibly hazy and obscure due to my ingesting the intense psychedelics. It all really hit me as soon as I started walking. I was rolling. I felt nauseated. I found a porta-potty, went inside, and puked—rice and beans from the veggie burrito I got on the lot earlier that afternoon. It was like puking maggots—beautiful maggots, just as much an extension of the divine as any of the rest of us, and it felt sensual in a bizarre, loving, psychedelically harmonious, regurgitative kind of way. It was very Zen, just one big flow—even, steady, and strong, a wave of energy coming up and through from my very essence. I didn't really mind it much, not the way I do when I am loaded on alcohol or have the stomach flu or food poisoning or something like that. I felt better immediately. That's usually all it takes with psychedelics—one good puke when you're first going up, and then it's all good from there, usually.

I walked along Shakedown Street and saw some kids sitting on the side of the road selling ice cold beer, so I bought one. The taste was ultimately refreshing, total bliss, and at that moment it made my world a better place. I swished it around my mouth, and rinsed the remaining chunks of rice and bean from in between my teeth, and then spit it out. I stopped to light a smoke and felt the sun cup my face in a warm, gentle embrace. My heart beat in rhythm with the universe.

I felt Stella against my leg and realized I wasn't holding her leash. I had been walking for a while and completely spaced that she was with me, but there she was, right by my side, her leash dragging on the ground beside her. She had a serious and concerned look on her face, the same look she always had whenever I would get really loaded. I set my hand on the back of her neck to pet and reassure her that everything was okay. "Such a good girl." I had the sensation my hand was sinking deeper and deeper into an ocean of fur, and I jerked it back suddenly because it freaked me out. I thought my hand might get stuck inside her. I told myself it was just the drugs and reached back down, because I could sense that my yanking away had made her a little nervous. I pet her some more, and she relaxed. I started to pull my hand back when I noticed various colors connected from her fur to my fingers. I could pull my hand back and stretch them out and then push it toward her again, condensing them. I pushed and pulled, amusing myself with these interconnected vibrant strings of life, and felt like I was playing an animated accordion whose sound resonated infinitely throughout the color spectrum.

"Kyd!" Stella's ears perked up. I saw Cloud walking over. "What's up?" he asked.

"Taking her back to camp." I watched Cloud's dreads move and squirm like live snakes gently dancing around his head.

He studied my face for a second. "Dude, you're spun."

"Yeah." That was all I could say. I felt myself rapidly losing the ability to form coherent sentences, but I wasn't really freaked out by it. I knew the routine pretty good by now. It was all part of the game, but I still couldn't talk. I watched Cloud's face contort and change color from its usual peachy-brown to a kind of pasty, iridescent, mint green that sparkled as small metallic specks twinkled on and around him. My eyelids were heavy, and I could actually feel my feet growing roots and grounding me into the earth beneath me, sending up a line of energy that ran from the core of the planet, up my legs, into my base chakra, up through my crown chakra and into the sky above, connecting me with all that is. I felt my divine essence of light and love exploding out, expanding in all directions.

"What did you eat?" Cloud's mouth moved so much faster than the words coming from it.

"Molly and some 2C-B."

"2C-B! Where'd you get that shit?"

"Cedar has it." The sound of my voice seemed like it was coming from somewhere else. I felt my mouth move and listened as the words flowed from me ... but who was putting them there? And where were they coming from? I couldn't make any sense of them at all but they kept coming of their own free will.

"Where's Jefe?" Cloud asked.

"Back at Cedar's bus."

"Did they munch some too?"

"Just Jefe."

"You all right?" He squinted his eyes to look at me, to peer into my exposed and vulnerable soul, and then gave my shoulder a friendly squeeze. "You're pretty wrecked."

"Yeah."

"Want me to walk with you to your tent?"

"No, man, I'm cool."

"You sure?"

"Yeah."

"All right. I'm going to go chill with Jefe and Cedar. I want to get some of that 2C-B! Come back to the bus when you're done, and we'll all go into the show together."

"Okay."

"See you in a bit." Cloud took off, and I stood there a minute. Everything was so much more animated, with new dimensions jumping out at me, and then my peripheral vision faded as my depth perception increased. I couldn't see everything all at once; it was a kind of super-deep, fuzzy tunnel vision that warped in and out of cognition, melting and changing from one thing into another. Everything around me—booths, cars, dogs, people—seemed to writhe and breathe and change color as the metallic sparks glittered and flashed, trying to communicate with me. I could actually understand it, not in my brain but somewhere else. And I saw the soft, tightly woven, weblike filaments that ran through it all, ran through me, enveloping me, and I experienced the connection.

I couldn't consciously comprehend all the sounds—people talking, dogs barking, cars running, stereos thumping. It became a bunch of foreign jabberwocky, but somehow, innately, I understood and responded correctly. Colors were deep and rich and alive, in worlds of their own that I sensed I could crawl into and exist—safe, warm, and loved. I could feel it and be it. I *was* color. It was amazing! Ecstatic! Euphoric! I loved it all—the universe, all creation. I loved me.

I watched myself glide with ease through the maze of beautiful pandemonium, feeling fond of everything—a tiny, working, individual part of my immediate collective. I looked up at the clear cobalt-blue sky and watched as hundreds of lighter blue Chinese dragons printed in some kind of funky Asian tribal design moved rapidly across in steady streams. The monochromatic scheme of it all seemed to deepen time and space, add dimension, and open doors. I wiped my forehead and realized I was drenched in sweat; it was starting to soak through my shirt. I felt my stomach in my throat. The sun was starting to go down.

Everything after that became random snapshots in my mind, some kind of bizarre, psychedelic time warp. I was walking around the lot, holding Stella's leash, and I remember feeling like she was leading, kind of dragging me. She kept turning her head to look back at me, as if to say "Just hang in there, Kyd. Follow me. It's all good, brother." I puked again, but it wasn't nearly as euphoric or divine as the first time. I didn't think I had eaten that much rice.

The lot was huge. I don't know how long we walked, but I remember hearing music and seeing colored lights ripping around through the sky above the amphitheater. I knew the show had started and that I was supposed to be in there with my friends, but I wasn't able to think about how to get there. I bought another beer from some kids on the side of the road and sat down.

When the music stopped, the lot got really packed. There were kids everywhere, and I stood up, wanting to walk to my campsite, but I couldn't think about where it was. Everything was complete nonsense, and I started to laugh. It was hysterical and comforting, and it made me feel the slightest bit uneasy as I sailed through it, drifting with no real course, an active, working part of the mania, a factor in the infinite chaotic equation. I felt tears running down my cheeks.

I walked along through the night, feeling that maybe I was in some kind of post-apocalyptic world. There were fires burning in large metal barrels, drum circles, dreadlocks, Mohawks, chains and leather, homemade clothes, and people with tattooed faces and bone and metal rings stuck through their ears, lips, noses, nipples, and cheeks. They were walking around, trading and selling all kinds of stuff—crystals, glass, ganja food, smokes, beer, drugs, candy bars, condoms, incense, clothes, books, trinkets. I was Mad Max in Barter Town, a psychedelic carnival, where all the various subcultures of society came together and set up shop. No rules. Primal and effective. I felt the pulse of unharnessed passion beat through me, connecting me to all these freaks, these beauties, my tribe.

I headed down a street and saw bright lights flashing and heard some funky hip-hop blaring from a large tent. I wandered in and looked up at a big disco ball hanging in the center of the room. People were dancing all around me, and I watched the rainbow-colored tracers that followed their movements. Some chick walked up and handed me this big nitrous balloon. I took the whole thing down in one breath, and it rocked my shit, giving me serious Jell-O legs that nearly knocked me on my ass. The girl laughed and reached out to steady me. Some guy handed me a joint, so I took a puff. It was just what I needed; it took the edge right off. I took a couple more puffs and felt Stella tug on the leash. I had forgotten about her again. She looked up at me, telling me she was ready to go.

We headed down the road. I bought another beer from some kids we passed. I realized I still had that joint in my hand, so I smoked it. I was getting tired and starting to feel funky. I just wanted to find somewhere safe and comfortable to lie down, but nothing was as nearly as familiar or inviting as it had been earlier in the day. The warmth and juice had run off. My head throbbed, and as I leaned over to rest my hands on my thighs for support, I puked again.

Stella barked and growled. It startled me, and I cracked my eyes open. I was lying on the ground, curled up into fetal position. I smelled the earth and felt it, hard and dank, beneath my cheek.

"Stella," I heard someone say. "It's just me." She barked again. "Stella! Chill!" he said. Then he shook my shoulder. "Are you all right?"

"What?" I pushed myself up onto an elbow and looked around. I was in front of my tent, and Stella was leaning into my legs. Cloud was kneeling in front of me.

"What the fuck happened to you last night?" His eyes were wide and layered with fear and concern.

"Huh?"

"You never made it into the show. We looked for you all night. Where'd you go?"

"I don't know." I had come down, mostly, but still felt a little high. *How'd I get here?* I thought. I looked at Stella, sitting straight up, ears perked, aware of everything going on around us. I knew she was the reason I'd made it back to camp. She is so fucking smart. She knew where to go. I rubbed her ears, pulled her down next to me, gave her a hug, and told her thanks.

"Man, I'm glad I found you." The fear and concern began to fade from Cloud's face as mild relief settled in. "We had to find a spot for Jefe to lay down in the show last night. He was so spun, he couldn't even talk—full-on deer-in-the-headlights, man. No kidding; sweat just kept pouring out of him. We were worried. We knew you had eaten the same dose, and nobody saw you all night." He looked intensely at my face. "Fuck, man. Are you okay?" His ran his eyes down my arms, chest, and lower body. "I don't see any blood. Does anything hurt?"

"No." I thought for a second. "Not yet, anyway." I laughed, and Cloud relaxed.

"You got to be freezing." He was right, and that was a good sign. At least I could feel my body now. He unzipped my tent and pulled out my thick fleece hoodie. I put it on and started to feel warm, comfortable, and safe. I just lay there for a second, getting my bearings, and then asked, "Is Jefe all right?"

"Yeah, he's back at Cedar's bus."

"Can he talk yet?" I asked, half joking.

"Yeah, this morning when he started to get his words back, he kept laughing and mumbling, 'Simon says, four plus one equals spun cookies. Simon says, four plus one equals spun cookies.' Over and over again, it was the same thing. 'Simon says, four plus one equals spun cookies.' It started to freak us out a little bit, but at least he was talking."

"What're they doing now?"

"Just hanging out puffing bowls. Cedar ate a couple hits of molly and ended up getting pretty rolled too." Cloud chuckled as he pulled a glass pipe out of pocket, loaded a bowl, and handed it to me.

I started to even out a little and relax as I puffed on it.

"Really?" I passed the pipe back to him. "I thought Cedar didn't eat psychedelics."

"He did last night." Cloud reached back into the tent and fumbled around for a minute. "Here." He handed me a water bottle and a couple of Xanax bars. "Eat this. They'll definitely help." He placed them in my weak, shaky hands, and I gobbled them down.

"Did you eat anything?" I asked. Cloud seemed awfully perky for someone Cedar might have inadvertently given the death dose to.

"I ate some molly and one of those 2C-B pills. Luckily, that was all Cedar had left. I spent the whole fucking night making sure nobody lost it." Cloud still seemed pretty stressed out. "Come on, let's head back over to Cedar's bus."

I didn't really want to go anywhere, but I didn't just want to lie in my tent and come down alone either. "Do you have your keys? I want to get some weed out of the truck."

"Yeah." He pulled them out of his backpack and handed them to me.

I opened the back of my truck, filled my Tupperware with ganja and we headed to Cedar's.

6

efe was in front of me as we walked up some stairs into a house. I couldn't hold my body up; it was too heavy, and I walked kind of sagging and drooped over, having to put a hand on the ground every now and then to keep from falling over. My vision was all distorted, and I felt drugged and heavy and uncoordinated. I heard loud music, and there were people standing around outside, talking and laughing. I knew we were going to a party. I staggered along behind Jefe and saw people standing around inside and sitting on a couch and in some chairs around a big coffee table. Jefe sat down, and I saw his face, blurry and contorted. A big shit-eating grin spread across it like soft butter on warm bread. He patted the spot on the couch next to him, telling me to sit. I nearly fell over on top of him when I sat down. My head was too heavy to lift off of my chest, but I kept trying. The room seemed to spin, and all the faces blended together. I was embarrassed and hoped that no one would notice my lack of coordination. I kept trying to laugh it off and wave my hands around like nothing was wrong. I would lift my head for a second or two, get into the conversation, and then my head would fall to my chest again. I was incredibly frustrated. A huge wave of sadness washed over me, and I started to cry. I heard Jefe's voice calling my name. I felt his hand on my shoulder. My head lifted and felt light for a second; I was looking into his eyes, all shining and full of life.

"Hey, bro, it's cool man," he said, smiling at me. Everything else faded out, and it was just me and him, enveloped in a bright light.

I was crying, and my head dropped onto his shoulder. I couldn't lift it back up; it seemed to melt into him, and a rush of warm energy ran through me. "I'm sorry," I heard myself say—over and over again. "I'm sorry. I'm so sorry. I love you. I'm so sorry."

"It's all good, bro." His voice was strong, alive, peaceful, and secure. "It's all good. It's all good, bro." He kept saying it over and over again. I heard knocking. I continued melting deeper into Jefe's shoulder as the knocking grew louder, and his voice faded out.

I opened my eyes and heard Mom's voice from the doorway behind me. "Honey, are you awake?" She knocked again softly. "Tortoise is on the phone."

"Tell him I'll call him back." I wiped tears from my cheek and lay there feeling paralyzed, with a sharp hollow in my throat.

I had known Jefe the longest of anyone, since kindergarten. We had been friends for so long that I couldn't really remember my life before he was in it. His dad was a big drinker and when they started fighting really bad, in middle school, Jefe pretty much came to live at my house. Mom loved Jefe and always seemed thrilled to have us both around. I was twelve when I bought my very first ounce of weed, and Jefe was the one to help me sell it. We both made money. That was thirteen years ago, and we had worked together, making loads of cash ever since. There was nobody like Jefe. He was a hell of a guy who would do anything in the world for me, but damn, that boy was a loose cannon—as loose as they come.

One afternoon we were at this bar in Boulder, The Black Cat.

It was our favorite place to go, the only place we really hung out besides the Tittie Twister. We were its best "regulars," and everyone there treated us like fucking kings, probably because they knew we pretty much ran the Boulder drug circuit. We liked everyone who worked there and made it a point to hook them up with killer deals on cocaine, ganja, acid, Ecstasy, pharmies—whatever we had our hands on at the moment. The Black Cat, or, The Cat, as it was commonly referred to by locals, was a dark, cave-like place, which is why I think it was so popular with our breed of folks. It made us feel like we could hide. We were never bothered by the burden of sunlight or the objective reality of so-called everyday life. It was totally bizarre and off the wall, with all kinds of random shit hanging from the ceiling—old beat-up bicycles, popcorn machines, tricked-out mannequins, and wagon wheels. The wood-planked walls were like a diary that held secrets about all the people who had carved their names in them over the years. It was an out-of-the-way place like The Cat where people like us, our tribe, would come to feel at home.

On this particular day, Jefe and I were drinking some beers, like usual, and there was this young kid sitting a table near us, outside on the deck. His dirty-blond dreadlocks were pulled back into a loose ponytail that hung down the back of his tattered Sandoz "Exploring minds since 1943" T-shirt. He had this little squirrel skull on a decorated silk scarf that was laid out in the middle of the table. He looked pretty loaded, with his bloodshot eyes hanging at half-mast, and he was talking to some people about how this squirrel skull had some kind of sacred power. He said he carried it with him wherever he went because it was his spirit totem, and he listened to it because it always guided him in the right direction. He said it was a physical manifestation of his intuition, his connection with Spirit. Nobody was really paying much attention to him. I thought it was a little odd but wasn't too concerned with it. The kid seemed harmless enough, and that was just exactly the kind of shit you expected at The Cat—the kind of shit we had seen a million times before.

For whatever reason, Jefe was in one of his moods and walked right over to the harmless little dread and picked his squirrel skull up off the table. "What the fuck is this?" He laughed and turned the skull in his hand for closer inspection. "You pick this shit up off the side of the road?"

The little hippie dread didn't say anything at first. He seemed scared of Jefe, or intimidated (like most people were), and he timidly looked up at him. He meekly attempted to explain the sacred metaphysical importance of this particular squirrel skull.

"I don't want to see your fucking road kill." Jefe threw it over the railing of the deck, and it smashed onto the concrete below. That little dread didn't say anything, but I could tell he was upset. His eyes welled up, but he held it back. I felt bad for him, but what was he going to do? Jefe was a pretty big dude and obviously a little off.

I never knew why Jefe did shit like that. It pissed me off. It wasn't so bad when we were young, but over the past several years, he had developed a nasty, mean streak. He could be so fucking mellow and cool, and then all of a sudden he'd just snap. It happened mostly when he drank. Throw in a handful of Vicodin or a couple rails of blow, and he could be borderline psychotic.

I hated when he called that much attention to us. It wasn't smart, and regardless of the fact that he was my bro, it made him dangerous to be around. Steve, the bouncer, saw Jefe toss the skull over the railing and headed right for us. He was a friend of ours and moved a substantial amount of weed for us. He usually let Jefe get away with shit like that but not today.

"Sorry, man, your gonna have to go." He looked at Jefe and shrugged his shoulders, as if to say it was out of his control. "My boss and his wife are sitting right over there." He quickly flashed a discreet glance toward a table on our left. There was an older man, probably in his fifties, and younger woman, I would guess mid-thirties, giving us the evil eye. The woman's mouth hung open a bit, and her eyes were wide but softened when I looked over at her.

Jefe flared up a little at Steve. "Dude, why you gotta be such a hater?" By the look in Jefe's eyes, I could tell that he was on the verge of going one of two ways—chill or agro.

"Jefe," I said in the tone of voice I used when reminding him he needed to check himself and be cool. It usually worked

Jefe slapped Steve's shoulder and laughed like he was a goddamn comedian. "I was just kidding around." He thought he was hysterical, and I was just relieved it hadn't gotten ugly.

"I'm sorry, Jefe." Steve sounded sincere. "But you are going to have to go for today. You're looking pretty blazed, and I can't serve you, not with him around." He glanced again at the table to our left and then to me with a pleading expression.

"Come on, dude." I said and swilled down the rest of my beer. "We gotta bounce. Nate's probably at the house waiting on us." I got up and started walking toward the door, knowing Jefe would follow.

Steve followed me, speaking softly. "Hey, man, can I call you tomorrow and re-up?"

"You got all my cash?"

"Yeah."

"All right." I gave Steve a kind of half-ass high five and headed out the door.

Jefe stopped at Steve's car in the parking lot on the way out and took a piss all over the left rear quarter panel.

"Dude," I said and shook my head disapprovingly. "Come on, man, let's get out of here."

Jefe laughed as he shook his last few drops of piss at the car. He tucked himself back into his pants, zipped up, and we left.

When Jefe and I got home, Nate was sitting on the couch, drinking a beer and watching Tortoise play Urban Insurgence, the video game he bought three months ago and only stopped playing to eat, sleep, and take an occasional shit. Tortoise was our game-head—he had been since we were kids. He would play for hours, hunched forward in that chair, fingers moving around the control pad like little programmed sausages. Strategic and efficient, he yanked and pulled on the joystick, his eyes all bugged out and dry from staring at the TV screen without blinking.

Like the rest of us, Tortoise had plenty of time on his hands. He was a part-time student at the community college and a part-time drug dealer. The two complemented each other, and he managed to squeak by in his classes with very little effort, while making just enough money selling various drugs to the student body to create a cushy little life for himself.

Tortoise's character in the game, Sux2BU, had just successfully completed a mission to purchase ten kilos of cocaine from a Cuban drug dealer. Things got a little strained during the deal, and Sux2BU pulled out his Uzi and blew the drug dealer away. He also had to off two other guys in the room but managed to grab the cocaine and the buy-money he had brought with him. "Fuckin' A!" Tortoise said as he watched his points accumulate at the top of the screen. "I got the drugs and kept the money. Damn, I'm fucking good!" Sux2BU ran out of the building to a car stopped at a traffic light in the middle of the street. He yanked the lady who was driving out of the car and threw her on the ground. She screamed, and her head bled when it smacked the asphalt. He jumped into the car and sped away, running over anything in his path.

A cop car sped up behind him, lights flashing, sirens blaring, and through a loud speaker the cop repeatedly told him to pull over. Sux2BU, trying to outmaneuver the cop, crashed into another car. He hopped out of the one he was in, pulled out his Uzi, killed the cop, ran a little ways down the road, yanked another civilian driver out of his car, threw him on the ground, shot him, and then jumped into that driver's car and sped away. There were sirens of more cop cars in the distance, but Sux2BU made a couple of strategic moves and out-ran them. He stopped briefly in some alley, pulled out a can of spray paint, and tagged the side of a building. Sux2BU got back in the car and drove along for a second; he crossed a bridge, parked, and walked a couple of blocks to a strip club. Once inside the club, two burly tough guys escorted him to a dimly lit room, where this heavy-set dude in a nice suit, holding a fat cigar and wearing a huge, sparkling gold-and-diamond ring on his pinkie finger, sat behind a big desk. Sux2BU set the cocaine and the money on the desk. The heavy-set guy commended Sux2BU on a job well done, handed him a couple bundles of cash, and told him if he kept working like this, he would move up in no time. Sux2BU walked back out to the bar, ordered a drink, and started talking to this stripper, who was standing there half-naked and hanging out of the little bit of clothes she did have on. (It really is amazing what computer graphics can do these days.) They talked for a second; he bought a lap dance from her and then took her to a back room in the club. Once in the room, Sux2BU closed the door, and the stripper got down on her knees and started giving him head. She sucked his dick for a little bit and then he pulled her up, turned her around, and bent her over the table. It was pretty fucking funny.

"Fuck, yeah!" Tortoise gloated as his points for fucking the stripper begin to rack up again in the top left-hand corner of the screen. You can earn a lot of points in this game for having sex with women. When you start off playing, you can only have prostitutes—you get the least points for them. Then, as you accumulate more points and advance in the game, you get strippers, which win you more points than prostitutes. Finally, when you advance to a certain level, you can meet classy women at dinner parties and the homes of other drug dealers and stuff like that. You get the most points for the classy women, but as you advance in the game and your options increase, you can still fuck the prostitutes too, if you want. They're still worth something.

I walked past Nate and high-fived him on the way into the kitchen. "How's it going?"

"It's going good, man, going good. What have you guys been up to?"

"Just drinking a few beers at The Cat."

Cloud walked into the kitchen from the garage, grabbed a beer, and came in to the living room with us. "You still playing that shit?" he laughed, as he snapped a bottle cap at Tortoise. "You've been in front of that thing for hours."

"Dude, you can play this shit for days," Tortoise said excitedly. "You have to advance from one level to the next. It takes a while." Tortoise was now maneuvering Sux2BU out of the tattoo parlor, where some huge biker-looking tattoo artist put a thick black tribal band around Sux2BU's arm.

"What'd that tattoo cost you?" Cloud asked.

"Two hundred fifty points." There was a cop standing on the sidewalk outside the tattoo parlor, and Tortoise pulled out Sux2BU's Uzi. "Say hello to my little friend," Tortoise said to the TV in his best Cuban drug lord accent as he blew the cop to bits. Points started to accumulate in the top corner of the screen.

Everyone in the house tried to talk like Tony Montana in *Scarface*. I'm sure we sounded ridiculous but it was fun and kind of addictive. We had only seen the movie about a thousand times.

"What did you shoot that cop for?" Cloud asked. "He wasn't after you."

"Yeah." Tortoise's eyes stayed fixed on the screen as his character yanked some lady out of her car, threw her on the ground, and ran over her legs as he sped away. "But cops are worth a lot of points."

"You been blowing much glass today?" I asked Cloud. He had his safety glasses pushed up and resting on the top of his dreads. It's a pretty intense torch he has to stare at.

"Yeah, man. I finished that Sherlock bubbler I've been working on and busted out a few little commercial pieces to fill that order I have going to Chicago."

"Nice. I want to see that Sherlock before you get rid of it."

"Yeah, definitely."

Cloud blew some really incredible glass, some of the sickest shit I've seen. He was a pro and had created quite a name for himself. Cloud's dad was an old hippie glass blower, probably one of the first around, and he started teaching Cloud when he was really young. Cloud had all kinds of people calling him for custom pipes, but he also had quite a demand for regular art-type pieces, like vases and statues and all kinds of other stuff that rich people pay a lot of money for.

I didn't really see Cloud a whole bunch. If he wasn't blowing glass at home, he was on a mountain somewhere, snowboarding. He had been riding professionally for Forum for about two years and traveled quite a bit to various exhibitions and competitions. That boy could shred the half-pipe like no one I'd ever seen. He was insane. The motherfucker had absolutely no fear and no concept of negative consequence. It never entered his mind that he wouldn't pull off some sick trick and land it every time. He just went about everything smooth as silk and confident, like a perpetual positive outcome was simply predestined for him, and therefore made that his reality.

Nate looked at Jefe as though he held the key to Pandora's Box. "So, did you bring us some love from the Bay?"

"Ah, yeah, bro. I'm full of love." Jefe smiled and swilled his beer.

"Sick, dude! Let's see it."

"All right." Jefe walked into his room and came back out with a sweet-breath dropper bottle. He put it on the coffee table.

"That's the shit, huh?" Tortoise asked, pausing the game.

"Yep." Jefe nodded his head. "Czechoslovakian

pharmaceutical grade." He gently shook the bottle, jostling the liquid inside.

"The Czech!" Nate's eyes opened wide. "Have you eaten any?"

"Yeah. We spun on some while I was up there. It's sick—really fucking clean. Definitely the best acid I've ever eaten." That said a lot, coming from Jefe.

"How much did you bring back with you?" Nate asked.

"Fifty vials. But I can get grips of it. We move this, and I'll go get more."

"Dude, we won't have any trouble with this. It won't even be work. It will just move itself. People are jonesing for good psychedelics around here. What do you want for it?"

"I'll give it to you for a hundred fifty bucks a vial. You can get at least two hundred for it."

"Oh, yeah, definitely." Nate was on the edge of his seat. "I heard about the Czech from these old hippies at the Rainbow Gathering last summer. They used to live on Haight back in the late '60s and saw all kinds of super-clean old-school acid. They said the Czech was the closest thing to Dr. Hoffman's LSD-25 they ever had." Nate picked up the bottle off the table and gave it a closer inspection. "My kids are gonna eat this shit up. How much of it can I take?"

"What do you think you can move?" Jefe asked.

"I don't know man. I have ten people lined up who have money and want vials right now. I'm heading out to the Renegade Festival tomorrow and know I can get rid of a grip of it there."

"Yeah." Jefe thought for a second. "You can get cash for ten tonight?"

"I can have it in a couple of hours."

"All right." Jefe walked into his room and when he came back out, he set nine more sweet-breath bottles on the coffee table. "I'll give you ten vials right now. Move those before Renegade, and I'll give you more."

"Cool." Nate stuffed the vials into a pair of socks and stuck them in his backpack. "I'm gonna need to get some more weed from you, too, before Renegade, if that's all right." Nate pulled out a roll of bills held together with a thick blue rubber band. "Here's two thousand for the ganja." He handed it to Jefe. "I'll have the other sixteen hundred for you when I bring you the money for that acid tonight."

Jefe nodded his head as he counted the cash. "Cool."

"Nice." Nate zipped up his pack. "I need to go meet up with a couple of kids. I'll call you in a few of hours."

Nate was a good kid—humble, honest, and had a good head for business. He'd made a good name for himself, and people liked to work with him. He was only seventeen, but he knew how to wheel and deal and could move a lot of just about anything you gave him. Nate had grown up around Boulder too and knew just about everybody who was anybody in the immediate drug culture. He and Cloud had been friends and Rainbow Family to each other since they were little kids. Their parents were both old-school hippies from this area, and they had traveled around on various school buses together, going to festivals and gatherings all their lives. Cloud didn't have any siblings, so he kind of adopted Nate as a little brother. He had been teaching Nate to blow glass and was starting to use some of Nate's pieces to help fill orders. Nate pretty much lived on our couch, but he was cool so I didn't mind.

Nate worked with Jefe for the most part. Technically, he sold my ganja, blow, and pills but did so indirectly, through Jefe. We figured it just worked out better for everyone that way, and Nate didn't ask any questions. He was just happy to have the work, but that acid, the Czech—that was all Jefe's gig. I didn't have any part of that. We met some kids from San Francisco on tour last summer that had a killer acid hook-up, and Jefe jumped on it. I almost jumped on it myself; it truly was some of the best acid I'd ever eaten, but Jefe had been turned on to these kids first. It was a good deal for him, and I wasn't gonna sideswipe it.

I had my hands full with my own shit anyway. I moved ganja,

blow, and pharmaceuticals—Xanax, Valium, and Vicodin, for the most part. Occasionally, I would turn some mushrooms or Ecstasy or something but not so much on a regular basis, just when there was good stuff around. My buddy Cedar's Beast connection was pretty steady, and he would drive down 100 to 150 pounds of it every few months. Nico and I always split it, and I sold most of my half straight up, cash deals, in five and ten packs. Every now and then, I busted down to some smaller weight but not much. I would keep several pounds aside from every crop and take it to Texas, where I knew this kid with some killer blow and cheap pills. I would pay $1,250 for a pound of Beast, take one and a half pounds to Texas, and trade it for a quarter kilo of cocaine that I would take back to Colorado and sell for a thousand dollars an ounce (nine hundred if I was stoking someone), ultimately turning $1,875 into $6,000 or so, easy, just like that. Multiply that by five or so pounds, and that's a pretty good chunk of change. I made a good profit off the Valium, Xanax, and Vicodin too, because I got them so damn cheap, but the real money was in the ganja and the blow. The pills were more for our head than anything; we ate those fuckers like Tic-Tacs. My only financial risk was selling the cocaine before we did it all. We loved that shit and would spin through an ounce and a half ourselves in a weekend, easy.

My other steady gig was with Holmes. I had known Holmes since I was thirteen, when he dated my older sister. He was always super-cool to me. He would pick me up and take me around and let me hang out with him, even when my sister was busy or out of town or something. When life would seem all fucked up, and I'd feel weird and alone and shit, he was always the person I could talk to. I trusted him—always will—and knew he would genuinely listen and give me his honest opinion or advice about stuff, even if it wasn't what I wanted to hear. He would be the first to let me know when I was fucking up or making bad decisions. I would argue with him sometimes—I could be pretty stubborn with the whole "nobody can tell me what to do" thing—but in the end he was usually right, and it sucked! Holmes was the closest thing I ever had to an older brother, and he just happened to grow the most chronic hydroponic ganja of anyone I've ever known. I swear, that man was the Picasso of ganja.

After Holmes and my sister broke up, he and I stayed in touch. When I decided to move to Colorado, he asked if he could bring his weed down and have me move it for him there. He didn't really know anyone but me who could turn his weed into money, and besides, Medical Marijuana had pretty much killed the black market for weed in Oregon anyway. I was happy to move it for him. It was always good to see him, which was every six to eight weeks, and it turned out to be a profitable venture for both of us.

7

M y phone rang. It was Melissa. I'd met her at a party a few
months earlier and we'd pretty much been hanging out
ever since. "What's going on?" she asked.

"Nothing really, just kicking around the house. What are
you up to?"

"Hanging out at home with Becca, looking for something
to do."

"You girls should come over."

"Yeah?"

"Yeah."

I heard her confer with Becca in the background. Then she
said, "All right, we'll be over in a bit."

"Cool."

I went to the kitchen to mix myself a drink. I stopped in my
bedroom on the way back to the den and grabbed a handful
of Vicodin. "Scooby snack," I said as I laid them on the coffee
table.

"Nice!" Tortoise and Jefe reached in.

I raised my eyebrows, looking over at Tortoise. "Melissa and
Becca are coming over."

"Yeah?" He was trying to play it cool but I could tell it made
him a little nervous. Melissa and Becca were roommates and
best friends, and the night I met Melissa, Tortoise met Becca.
They hooked up that night too, and I could tell Tortoise liked

her, but he wasn't exactly the epitome of confidence when it came to the ladies. Becca was a pretty cool chick, as far as I was concerned, and not bad looking either. She had long, straight blonde hair, big green eyes, cute face, and a decent figure. Like Tortoise, she was a little shy and awkward around people she didn't know. They seemed to be a pretty good match, but Tortoise hadn't had very many girlfriends and was always a little nervous with women. Melissa and I just clicked, right from the start. She had pretty much turned into my girlfriend, and we spent the majority of nights together, mostly at my house. Tortoise and Becca's deal hadn't taken off quite so fast, but according to Melissa, Becca wished it would.

The girls showed up pretty quick and brought a fifth of vodka, a bottle of tonic, and some limes. I made everybody a drink and then went to my bedroom and grabbed some more Vicodin. "You guys hungry?" I smirked and laid them on the table.

"Yeah." They each popped one in their mouths and washed it down with a swig of cocktail.

I walked over, set my iPod in the deck of the sound system, and turned on some tunes. Tortoise was still transfixed by the video game he was playing but diverted his attention long enough to make eye contact with Becca. He flashed something that resembled a quick smile and scooted over so she could sit next to him. They had this little cat-and-mouse thing going on and were both a little reserved until you got some alcohol in them. They were still a little weird as a couple when they were sober.

Melissa had no problem showing her affection. She sat down next to me, put her arm around my shoulder, and planted a quick kiss on my cheek. I liked the attention and affection she gave me, and I gave her thigh a gentle squeeze. Like most of us, Melissa's life hadn't been perfect. Her parents divorced when she was young, and her mom had various live-in boyfriends who did everything they could to let Melissa and her younger sister know they were unwelcome and unwanted. Melissa couldn't stand all that bullshit, and when she was sixteen, she dropped out of school, moved out of her mom's house, and lived in and out of various cheap motels with her older, meth-head boyfriend.

Melissa was depressed, and she developed an intense self-loathing, with more and more thoughts of suicide. She realized where she was headed. She woke up one day, looked in the mirror, and said, "I don't need this shit." She dumped the meth-head and got her GED and a job working at a daycare. Melissa definitely had serious strength of character, drive, and ambition, all of which I totally admired and respected. But there was also a little girl side to her that needed to be taken care of, and since I needed to be needed—to be the caretaker—the dynamics worked for us.

Melissa was one of the funniest, most quick-witted people I had ever met. She was confident but humble and had a magnetic personality that just drew people to her. She was beautiful in a very natural, no makeup kind of way, with cascading auburn hair that fell in loose ringlets to the middle of her back. She was by no means fat but embraced her feminine curves and radiated a maternal kind of energy. I liked watching her and listening to her talk. I felt a connection to her that I hadn't experienced before. I could tell she felt it too.

"You killed all the cops yet?" Melissa joked to Tortoise.

"Nah, dude, there's still a few of those fuckers left." Tortoise didn't take his eyes off the screen. "I'm working on it."

"Do you ever play anything else?" Melissa walked over to the entertainment center and thumbed through the video games. "Shaun White 2?"

Cloud burst out in excitement. "That one's the bomb! You can ride gnarly backcountry or bust it tricky-style in the park. Now that's something worth staring at the TV for."

"We go through, like, six-week phases," I said, opening my plastic Tupperware. I pulled a few choice nuggets out and laid them on the metal tray we used to break up ganja and roll joints. "A few of months ago, it was UFC, but we had to put it away after it started making Tortoise puke.

Jefe looked over at Tortoise and rolled his eyes. Tortoise paused the game and pointed at the TV screen, like it was guilty of something. "Dude, I swear. You were sitting right here. You saw me just get up out of nowhere and run to the bathroom that day we were playing. I swear to God, I puked."

"Whatever, dude." Jefe was flicking him shit and enjoying it.

"No man, I swear to God. I had some kind of reaction to it or something." Tortoise's face had a pensive look that meant his mental wheels were turning, searching for an intellectual-sounding verbal comeback that would save him from this mild public humiliation and help salvage his ego. "I think it was some kind of freaked-out subliminal messaging in the game, like MK-Ultra or something."

"MK what?" Jefe laughed

"Project MK-Ultra. CIA mind control. It's fucking for real, dude!" Tortoise was sounding more confident. "They put that shit in everything—movies, TV, video games"—he pointed to the TV screen with the paused video game—"songs, books. They have our heads in the palm of their sadistic little hands."

"How the fuck can they do all that shit?" Even though Jefe was still outwardly defending his position, I could tell he actually had at least some interest in what Tortoise had just said. "How do they get into the studio with Snoop Dogg and say, 'Okay, Snoop, we want you to rap this or play this beat line so it will tell society to buy more Big Macs?" Jefe laughed, feeling more sure now that Tortoise was full of shit.

"Okay, maybe not the Doggie Dog," Tortoise conceded. "But they're the fucking man—the machine. They can do whatever they want."

The mild look of interest momentarily swept back across Jefe's face, but he quickly said, "You're freaked out, dude." Jefe was over all that bizarre, freaky shit. He was enjoying taking a moment to fuck with Tortoise in front of girls. "You played that fucking game for two months straight, nonstop, all fucking day. That's enough to make anyone puke."

"You were playing it too," Tortoise answered defensively.

"Not like you, dude." Jefe laughed, delighted with the rise he was getting out of Tortoise.

"Oh, bullshit, man! You were in here on your sorry fucking ass just as much as I was." Tortoise returned to Urban Insurgence, killing more cops and fucking more prostitutes.

"Then how come I never puked?" Jefe looked at Tortoise, knowing that this question would certainly perplex him.

"I don't know, dude. It's weird. Maybe the subliminal messaging was only geared toward a specific audience or something, an audience of a certain IQ level." He glared at Jefe, but I could tell he was sorry as soon as he'd said it and quickly tried to backtrack. "Whatever it was, it made me sick. Every time I tried to play the game after that first time, I puked. I couldn't even look at the cover of the case without going into cold sweats." He glanced over at Becca, and his cheeks flushed.

"You're fucking wacked!" Jefe said as he pounced on top of him. The next thing I knew it was a full-on wrestle session. Becca scrambled off the couch and out of the way.

"Dude! Pause the game! Somebody pause the fucking game!" Tortoise bellowed as he tried to claw his arm out from under Jefe, who was only twice his size. I made it a point to never wrestle with Jefe. It just wasn't fun; I always ended up getting hurt, or something in the house got broken. Cloud and I looked at each other and shook our heads. He reached down and paused the game, and I took the ganja off the coffee table and moved into the kitchen, where it would be protected from flying arms and sprawling legs.

I finished rolling the joint and sat back to inspect it. It was nice. I gotta say I was a fucking rock star when it came to rolling joints. I liked rolling different types of funky cone joints—they were my favorite. I used five papers on that one and made it like a blossom, with lots of different little ends. When you lit them up, they burned and looked like little petals opening. It was pretty sick.

I walked back into the living room, where Jefe had Tortoise buried underneath him somewhere in the couch. It pissed me off for Jefe to do that shit, especially when we had ladies over. "That's enough, Jefe. Get off him!"

Jefe looked up at me, his expression a mixture of hurt, confusion, and embarrassment.

"You're not on a fucking playground, and I don't want anyone or anything else in here broken." I pointed to the ass-shaped hole in the wall, which was the result of the last time Jefe provoked Tortoise. That had ended up with Jefe holding Tortoise across his back and swinging him around in circles until he stumbled backward, sending Tortoise's ass crashing through the wall. "You with me?"

Jefe climbed off Tortoise, who slowly made his way up. I could tell Jefe had succeeded in humiliating Tortoise—his face was flushed, and he didn't make eye contact with anyone. I glared at Jefe, who smacked Tortoise in the shoulder and then pulled him up to give him a friendly embrace and a quick kiss on the head. He then gently smacked Tortoise in the arm again, intentionally prompting Tortoise to gut-punch him. Jefe leaned over and grabbed his stomach, half-laughing, half-stumbling around like it hurt, offering Tortoise the chance to save a little face.

"Easy ... easy, bro." Jefe kind of half-ass limped, hunched over and laughing, to a chair beside the couch. "I've had enough." He held up his hand for Tortoise to stop. Tortoise sheepishly sat back down on the couch, took the game off pause, and picked up where he left off.

"Come on. dude. We're gonna puff this fine spliff I just rolled," I said, holding it up for all to see, like it was the Holy Grail or something.

"Okay, okay," Tortoise said. "Just let me save the game."

Becca, deeming the situation safe, came back over and resumed her position on the couch next to Tortoise.

I sat down on the armrest of the couch next to Melissa. I lit the joint, puffed on it, and then handed it to Jefe, who was sitting in the chair next to me. I smiled at him, and he smiled back. I loved Jefe, and I never liked having to scold him that way. I didn't have to do it very often, but every now and then, he needed to be reeled in, and he knew it.

Nate sold the ten vials of Czech that Jefe gave him and was back at the house with cash in about three hours.

"Damn, Nate, you weren't kidding." Jefe smiled and sat up to count his money.

"I told you, dude. The kids around here are dying for good psychedelics. There's going to be some seriously spun cookies in this town tonight." Nate smiled, proud of his contribution to such a worthy cause. "Dude, you guys, we should munch some." There were a couple of Vicodin still sitting on the table. Nate picked one up. "Can I have this?" Nate never took anything without asking.

"Go for it," I said and got up to mix myself a drink. "You want a drink?"

"Sure." Nate sat down next to Cloud.

"Munch what?" Melissa perked up.

"Jefe brought back some really nice liquid from San Francisco," I said. "Czechoslovakian pharmaceutical grade. Do you guys want to eat some?"

"Yeah!"

Jefe got a sweet-breath dropper that was about half full from his room. He walked over to Nate and Cloud. "Say ahhh!"

Nate opened his mouth as Jefe squeezed a few drops of the clear liquid under his tongue. Jefe walked around the room squeezing a few drops for the rest of us and then dosing himself.

After we'd all been dosed, the girls decided we should go see this animated movie about some surfing penguins. It was actually one of our favorite things to do—get really spun on psychedelics and go watch cartoon movies. We did it just about every time a new one came out. It was ritual.

We puffed another couple of bowls and then I went into my room to grab a mixed handful of Valium and Xanax. Jefe and Nate climbed into Cloud's truck, and Tortoise, Becca, and Melissa piled into mine with me, and we all headed off to the movie theater. Driving on psychedelics is a very surreal experience, like being in a video game with tunnel vision. You can't really make out anything exactly, and little colored lines, zigzags, and shapes just zip through your peripheral vision, like some kind of rainbowed-out asteroid belt. You are separate from but still connected to your physical body, and your awareness grows from micro to macro. You can feel the butterflies tickling, making you smile, as they dance around inside, and then you know that all you can do is just surrender to the flow. I never really found it all that difficult, though, driving on psychedelics. I always got to where I was going okay; it just took a lot of extra focus, because it was just so tempting to look at everything going on around me. I had to continually remind myself to keep my attention on the road.

As I look back, I realize I was really pretty lucky. A lot of the time I would kind of forget I was driving or zone out on something in the car, and then, after a while, I would remember I was driving and try to focus really fast on the road, wondering how long I had been all spaced out. I always figured I must have some kind of internal psychedelic co-pilot that was mysteriously activated by my subconscious, because there were definitely times where there was just no other explanation for my not having crashed or gotten completely lost or something.

We got on the highway, and I was doing a fine job with the whole focus thing, until this big semi came up and started driving next to us. It was dark out, and there were so many lights on that thing that it immediately caught my gaze. I don't know how long I was staring at it, but it felt like an eternity in another psychotropic time warp. The semi started to melt and change shape. "Look at that microwave oven," I heard myself say.

"What?" Melissa was in the passenger seat and looked over to see what I was talking about.

"That microwave oven," I mumbled, pointing out my window, "with the TV dinner in it." I started laughing hysterically. I couldn't help it.

"What the fuck are you talking about?" She looked past me at the semi next to us. "There's no microwave oven, Kyd. It's a semi." Her words seemed to trail behind and all mix together, like a flow of liquid dialogue dripping in space, somewhere between her mouth and my ears. She had this huge smile on her face that stretched ear to ear. Her teeth looked big and bright. She was the Cheshire Cat, turning all striped and shit, and all I could see was that smile growing and growing, so that it looked like it would soon take over her entire face. I had to look away.

We got to the theater. I garbled something to the lady behind the ticket window, gave her some money, and she handed me tickets. I almost left the change sitting on the counter, but Melissa grabbed it.

I couldn't really understand the movie. The penguins would talk, and it just sounded like some kind of squeaky mouse voice. Then their mouths would grow and swallow their heads, and they would turn into these dancing raisin things. Lots of color, shapes, and squeaking, all swirling together—that's all I really remember about that movie. We laughed our asses off.

Everybody crashed at our house that night, as usual. We got up late the next morning, headed down to the Pancake House for some breakfast, and came home to get Nate packed up for Renegade.

"So how much ganja do you want to take?" Jefe asked.

"I don't know, dude. I can move a pound at the festival, easy, and I've got a friend here in town that wants a half before I go."

"Is he going to have cash for you?"

"No, dude, he'll need a front. But I work with him all the time; he's totally good for it. He'll have it as soon as I get back."

"Why don't you take two. You can give your buddy a half, and you'll have one and a half for Renegade." Jefe and I had already talked about how much we would send with him. Jefe was fronting to Nate, and I was fronting to Jefe so we had come up with a number we could both stand to lose—not that we expected that to happen, or we wouldn't have done it in the first place. Nate ran a relatively tight ship. We didn't worry about him too much, but you just never knew. When playing the front game, you never wanted to put more out there than you could stand to see walk away.

"How much of that Czech do you think you want?"

"I don't know, man. I was thinking I could move, like, fifteen vials or so pretty easy."

Jefe thought for a second. "What else are you taking with you?"

"Not too much." I could tell Nate was taking mental inventory as he rattled off the list. "Just this ganja and the acid you gave me. My buddy Raja may have a little molly with him and maybe some mushrooms and little honey oil, and we might get some hash, but that would just be for our head. That's pretty much it. Oh, and maybe a case of glass, if Cloud has it ready."

"I think he's in the garage, getting it together," I answered. "Have you seen his new bubbler?"

"The Sherlock?" Nate asked.

"Yeah."

"No, not since he finished it."

"He spun some red and gold dichroic through it. It's fucking sick!"

"Nice. Hey, why don't you guys throw a couple things in a bag and come with us?" Nate loved traveling with us, going to shows and stuff like that. I couldn't really blame him; we were a hell of a lot of fun. "Rage is reuniting for it! It's gonna be so fucking killer. Interpol, Arcade Fire, Jesus and Mary Chain, Willie Nelson, the fucking Chili Peppers!. It'll be off the hook!"

"Yeah," I said. "I wish I could. I know it'll be a good time, but I've got Holmes coming to town tonight."

"Sweet!" Nate liked Holmes; we all did. He put up with all of us foolios pretty well. "Dude, save me some, even if it's just a little for my head."

"I will."

Jefe steered us back on course. "So, when are you going to be back from Renegade?"

"Monday, night probably," Nate answered.

Jefe thought for a second. "And you think you could move fifteen vials?"

"Yeah, man." Nate nodded his head, confident with that number.

"All right." Jefe counted out fifteen sweet-breath droppers and set them next to the ganja. "You guys heading out pretty quick?"

"Yeah, I've got to run by my mom's and grab a few things. Raja is picking me up over there." Nate packed the acid carefully into a long, thick sock, folded it inside the match of the long, thick sock, and tucked it gently into the bottom on his backpack. "Hey, can I leave this here while I run home. I'll have Raja bring me back over on our way out of town."

"Yeah, sure." Jefe opened his spiral notebook to adjust Nate's tally. He figured the math and showed Nate the numbers.

Nate nodded his head. "Thanks, man. Tell Cloud I'll be back in an hour or so to pick up that glass."

"All right," Jefe said, still looking down at his notebook,

flipping through the pages, checking out all the debts owed to him from various individuals.

"See you guys later." Nate threw his backpack over his shoulder and headed out the door.

Jefe handed me the two thousand bucks. "I'll have more for you tonight."

"Cool." I walked to my room to get my notebook and came back to the couch. "So where are we at?" I flipped through the pages until I found Jefe's page.

"I think we're at sixty-two right now." Jefe looked in his book. "Minus the two thousand I just gave you. I'll be able to bring it down some more once this acid really starts moving."

"That's cool."

Jefe wasn't very good with money and always owed me a chunk of change, but I never worried about it. He was my bro, and it didn't really make a shit bit of a difference in my life. I figured it would come around eventually.

8

My eyes cracked open. I heard Stella whining and felt her pawing at the edge of my bed. As soon as she heard people up and around in the morning, she'd start itching to get up too. She could be pretty relentless in her attempts to get me out of bed. Her routine procedure started with whining, then barking, pawing the edge of the bed, licking my face, jumping up on the bed, standing over me, and playfully jousting at my face with her damp snout—I really hated that part. Then she would bark right in my face, and I'd push her off the bed. It was all a big game to her. She'd just hop back up and start it all again, a little more forcefully, until I finally got up. Stella was always in more of a hurry than I was to join the rest of our pack.

"Hey, Kyd!" Cloud greeted me. He, Jefe, and Tortoise were rambling around the kitchen, busily putting something together. Cloud pointed out the kitchen window. "Check it out. It's dumping!" He smiled and raised his eyebrows.

"Nice." I wiped some sleep from the corner of my eye, sat down at the table, and watched the huge flakes of snow falling outside. Tortoise poured some whiskey and Bailey's into a coffee mug, topped it off with a splash of coffee, and handed it to me. "Thanks, man," I said. He turned to top off his mug and then lifted it in the air. I toasted him and took a drink. "Whewww-dog!" It was a stout motherfucker and threw me back a little.

"That'll wake you up!" He threw me a playful smirk and nodded his head.

Jefe was standing at the counter, wearing his apron. The front was painted to look like a naked lady, with big titties made of plastic that protruded out, a tiny waist, curvy hips, and pubic hair fashioned to look like a tight landing strip. You could always tell when he was in "cook mode" because he would put on that stupid apron. We all gave him shit about it, but he didn't care; he loved that apron.

He had the waffle iron out and was standing at the counter over a mixing a bowl full of light green batter. He had managed to scatter flour on just about everything in his general vicinity and had a big line of it streaked across his face. Jefe was the only one in the house who cooked. He seemed to really enjoy it and was actually pretty damn good, which always baffled me because it seemed so opposite of his personality.

Jefe held out his mug to Tortoise. "Hook me up, man." Tortoise took the mug, and Jefe started goofing around like he always did when he wore that apron, grabbing the tits, rubbing on them, gently twisting and squeezing the little pinkish-brown rubber nipples, sticking out his tongue, and moving the tip of it up and down like he was giving some lady oral sex. He thought it was a riot and completely cracked himself up. It really was pretty funny.

Tortoise walked over and handed him the refilled mug. Jefe took a swig, and as soon as he set the mug down on the counter, Tortoise started fucking around with him and grabbing at the tits on his apron.

"Fuck off, dude!" Jefe attempted to block Tortoise's advances and tried to turn so Tortoise couldn't reach them.

"Oh, baby, come on, you know you want me," Tortoise said, trying to wrestle past Jefe's blocks and grabbing more fiercely at the protruding plastic breasts. They wrestled around for a minute—Tortoise pushing more and more ferociously with his sexual advances, and Jefe spinning around, back and forth, arms crossed against his chest in a desperate attempt to protect his cherished bosoms. "Oh, shit!" Tortoise abruptly stopped the assault and stood there laughing, his mouth hanging open a bit as he held one of the rubber nipples in his palm.

"Goddamn it!" Jefe grabbed the raisin-like piece from Tortoise's hand and looked at it. "You fucker! You broke my boob! You're such an ass!" he yelled at Tortoise. He turned to me with a mixture of grief and fire in his eyes. "Do we have Super Glue?"

"I don't think so," I said, trying like hell to contain my laughter.

"I've got some duct tape in the garage," Cloud said, cracking up. "A little duct tape, and she'll be good as new." He sputtered through an attempt to hold back his laughter.

"Fuck that!" Jefe was pissed. He walked to his room holding the nipple, his arm extended out in front of him like his was carrying a precious sliver of the philosopher's stone. He came back into the kitchen a minute later, and it was all any of us could do not to fall on the floor in fits of laughter. He glared at Tortoise. "You're fixing it!" he snarled, and then he went back to his mixing bowl.

"What're you making?" I asked, peering into the bowl at the green batter.

"Nothing for *that* fucker," he said, scowling at Tortoise. "But for the rest of us, blueberry ganja waffles, scrambled eggs, and bacon." Jefe's attitude softened, and he poured some frozen blueberries into the waffle mix.

"Nice," I said. We hadn't done ganja waffles in a while. Cloud had made ganja butter the day before and let it simmer for hours. The house still carried the pungent, not-so-great scent of slow-cooking cannabis.

Tortoise looked at Jefe with pleading puppy-dog eyes. "Dude, come on. I want waffles."

"Then fix my nipple, you fuck!" Jefe shook the wooden spoon he was using to mix the batter at Tortoise and a couple of globs hit the floor.

"I promise. I'll fix the nipple." Tortoise smiled sheepishly at Jefe.

"All right." Jefe chucked a frozen blueberry at him. "You can have waffles."

I grabbed a soft pack of Camel Lights off the table and fished around inside of it for a cigarette. It was empty, so I wadded it up and threw it toward the sprawling pile of garbage in the corner of the room. "You guys got a smoke?"

"Yeah." Jefe took one out of his pocket and handed it to me.

"What time do you think Holmes is going to get here?" Cloud asked as he cracked eggs into a bowl for Jefe.

"I'm not sure; sometime later this evening. When I talked to him last night he said the weather was really bad and he was going to stay in Salt Lake instead of pushing all the way through." I called him Holmes, but that wasn't his real name. It kind of started as a joke but ended up sticking. No one but Jefe and me knew Holmes's real name, not even Tortoise.

"Dude, it's got to be sketch to drive with all that weed in the fucking ice and snow," Tortoise said as he topped off my coffee with a little more booze.

"No shit." I took another sip, and the sharp hit of whiskey sent a small shiver up my spine.

Jefe was closely monitoring the bacon that was popping and crackling on the stove. He didn't look up as he asked, "How much is he bringing?"

"Twenty." I leaned back in my seat, watching the kitchen window starting to steam up, blurring the flakes of snow falling outside. I inhaled deeply, savoring the satisfying aroma of coffee brewing and breakfast cooking.

"Nice!" Jefe responded as he carefully poured the first round of batter onto the waffle iron.

I heard my phone ring and walked into my room to get it. It was Nico's roommate, Zack. "Hey, what's up?" he greeted me.

"Just getting up. Jefe's making some breakfast. What's going on with you?"

"Nothing much. I just looked outside and saw it dumping. I was thinking about cruising up to Eldora. You guys wanna go?" Zack and Nico had known each other most their lives, kind of like me and Jefe, except Zack was nowhere near as agro as Jefe. He worked for Nico, helping him with all his deejay stuff and also helped him pedal various illegal substances. Zack liked to ride, especially with Cloud; everybody did.

I tilted the phone away from my mouth and asked Cloud if he was going up. He looked out the window and shook his head. "It'll be a whiteout up there today. Maybe tomorrow."

I moved the phone back to my mouth. "Nah, he says it'll be a whiteout."

"Yeah, he's probably right. I'm not up for that. We had a late fucking night."

"Is Nico up?"

"I doubt it. He was pretty loaded last night."

"Really?" I laughed. "You guys should come over later and play some poker."

"Yeah? When are you going to get started?"

"I don't know. I've got a few things I need to take care of this afternoon. Holmes is coming in tonight."

Zack knew what that meant. "Sick! What time?"

"I don't think it will be too late."

Holmes was cautious about meeting people, but he trusted my judgment, and I had introduced him to Nico and Zack over a year ago.

"Cool man. I'll let Nico know and give you a call later to see where you're at."

"All right. Late."

"Late."

Jefe set a plate in front of me with a piping hot, green

blueberry waffle, heap of scrambled eggs, and five strips of perfectly crisp peppered bacon. He walked back to the counter and grabbed the butter, syrup, and a fork. He raised his eyebrows and nodded his head, pointing to the plate of food in front of me. "That's the shit, bro."

After breakfast we headed into the den to chill around and digest. Cloud put the iPod on shuffle and Outkast's "Southernplayalisticadillacmuzic," came thumping through the speakers. I walked to my room and grabbed my Tupperware of ganja, a small plastic bag of cocaine, the Dead Guy Ale mirror off my wall, and a couple of Phillies. Then I headed back out to the den.

"Look out!" Jefe said, leaning forward on the couch and rubbing his hands together. "Kyd's rollin' up the honey blunts."

"Will you grab the honey?"

"Yeah, man." Jefe stood up. "You want some more coffee?" He grabbed my cup and headed to the kitchen.

I took the first Phillie and held it to my mouth so I could breathe on it a minute to moisten it up. Once it was moist enough, I took a razor blade, sliced it down the middle, and dumped the tobacco out into a paper Pepsi cup that had been sitting on the corner of the coffee table for about two weeks. I took some weed out of the Tupperware and started breaking it up on my mirror into smaller rollable pieces. I mixed some cocaine in with the broken-up ganja and started to load it all into the Phillie. When all of the bigger pieces that I could pick up with my fingers were gone, I took the razor blade and carefully scooped up the remaining ganja and cocaine bits and shook them into the open blunt. Then I took the honey and dripped a small line along the top of my ganja/cocaine mixture and pushed the cigar paper back together to seal the blunt. Once it was all pushed back together, I dripped some more honey along the line I had originally sliced into the cigar to make sure it would hold. I set it to the side to dry while I rolled another one.

I finished rolling the second one, set it aside to dry, and handed the first one to Jefe. I picked the other one up, blew on it a minute to expedite the drying process, put it in my mouth, lit the end, and started to puff. Jefe was puffing tough on his, and it was starting to burn pretty good.

"Nice," Cloud said as I passed him the blunt I had been toking. "Thanks, man."

I nodded at him and tried to smile as I fought back the little coughs of smoke I was trying to hold in my lungs. I passed my blunt to Tortoise, plucked a handful Vicodin out of the Tupperware, and popped one in my mouth. I laid the rest on the table for everyone else. "So who's going to the store to buy some cleaning products?" I asked. They looked at me like I had just asked them to bend over and try sticking their heads up their asses.

"Cleaning products?" Jefe sounded truly confused.

"Yeah, man, cleaning products. You know how Holmes trips on me about the house being dirty. I just don't want to give him any reason to go there. Besides, he's right; our house is a fucking wreck." They were all still looking at me as if I were speaking in tongues.

"Dude, it's not that bad," Jefe said. He looked around sheepishly, intentionally passing his eyes quickly over the most gnarly areas. "I mean, we could stand to pick things up a little, but do you really think actual *cleaning* is necessary?"

"Yes, Jefe, actual cleaning is necessary."

The first time Holmes came to see me, he gave me a bunch of shit about the house being a wreck, telling me I lived like a pig. It kind of pissed me off, and I argued with him about how I was an adult, and it was my house, and I could keep it the way I wanted ... but he was right; it was pretty bad. At that time we had been living there about six months and had not once cleaned anything. The only cleaning product we seemed to be able to keep in the house on some kind of regular basis was dish soap, and we still had loads of dirty dishes always piled up in the sink and stacked on the counter around it. We all smoked cigarettes, and the house was littered with makeshift ashtrays of beer bottles and paper soda cups from various minute markets and fast-food restaurants, the bottom inch filled with some type of a liquid substance and then piled with butts and wadded-up cigarette foil and cellophane and little bits of ganja and stem and seed, which dusted the table tops and floor as well. I don't think we had ever scrubbed a toilet or sink or bathtub; funky dirt rings circled the inside of pretty much everything.

Stella had a thick sable-colored coat, and she shed like crazy. The time of year didn't seem to matter; we were tromping around the house through mounds of dog hair—inches of fur drifts, piled up in the corners of every room and all over the furniture. I never gave her any kind of training so she just ran wild around the house, always up on everything, thinking herself as one of us. There was dog hair collecting thick and deep, interlaced throughout the pile of garbage that flowed from the trash can in the kitchen and spilled over into the breakfast room. We just pushed it up against the wall in the breakfast room: stacks of empty beer bottles, wine bottles, juice bottles, pizza boxes, plastic soda bottles, brown paper bags, aluminum cans, tin cans, and various other materials all intended for garbage or recycle but almost never actually taken out. Dog hair clung to everything in that house; little fine, furry wisps of itchy, annoying adhesive that was a son of a bitch to clean up.

I looked over at Tortoise, relaxing on the couch, enjoying his buzz and the music. I almost felt a little guilty when I said, "We could send Tortoise to the store and then he could get that Super Glue to fix your nipple." I couldn't help cracking up before I even got the last word out of my mouth.

"Oh, yeah, my fucking nipple!" Jefe pointed sternly at Tortoise. "You're going to the store, bitch!"

Tortoise pouted, looking at me with pathetic eyes. "Oh, man!"

"Get some snacks and stuff while you're there," I said. All the various substances swimming around my system began to soften my muscles, giving me the feeling I was melting into the couch. I was going to need some form of sustenance to sop it all up.

"What kind of cleaning products do you want me to get?" he said, reluctantly giving in.

"I don't know. Just get some kind of all-purpose cleaner, like 409 or something, and maybe some Windex, and some sponges that have the one side rough and the other soft."

"And maybe some Pine-Sol," Cloud said, looking at the kitchen floor. "We should mop."

"And some Lysol," Jefe piped in. "And some of those yellow rubber cleaning gloves.

"Do we have a mop?" Cloud's eyes were still scouting the floor.

"I haven't seen one around," I said. "Tortoise, get a mop, too, will ya?"

"Don't get the kind you have to ring out with your hands," Jefe said. He enjoyed sounding like an expert. "Get that kind that has the little thingy on the handle that you pull up, and it squeezes out the water on its own."

"Sounds like I should make a list." Tortoise walked sullenly into the kitchen and fumbled through the random shit drawer. "Do you guys know where a pen is?" He sounded like a frustrated, whining five-year-old that had missed his nap. "Here's a pencil." He sulked back to the couch and started making his list.

"What about a broom?" Cloud asked. "Has anyone seen the broom?"

"The broom is in the garage, but I don't think we have a dustpan." I pulled out my wallet and laid a hundred and fifty dollars in front of Tortoise. "This should cover it."

"All right." Tortoise shoved the list and money in his pocket, put on his coat, and headed out the door.

9

A little while later Tortoise returned with a grocery sack in one hand and a half rack of PBR in the other. He walked into the kitchen and set them down on the counter. "You guys want a beer?" he called to us.

"Hell, yeah." Jefe got up and started rummaging through the grocery sack. "Tostitos and salsa," he said. "Nice!" He walked back into the den, juggling the chips, salsa, and two beers. He handed one to me and took a swig off the other.

Tortoise came in behind him and handed a beer to Cloud. "You guys have to help me carry in the rest of the shit," he said as he fell into the couch.

"What else is there?" Cloud asked.

"Just the mop and a few more sacks," Tortoise said wearily.

I poured some more cocaine out of the baggie onto my Dead Guy mirror, railed up four phat lines, pulled a crisp hundred-dollar bill out of my wallet, and rolled it up. "All right, here's the deal. We only have a few hours to get this place looking decent." I held the rolled bill down to the mirror, snorted my rail, and passed the mirror over to Jefe.

"What do you want me to do?" Jefe took his rail and passed the mirror to Cloud.

"Jefe, you do the dishes and clean the kitchen. Tortoise, you clean the bathrooms—sinks, tubs, toilets, everything. Cloud, would you try and yard all the garbage out of here?"

"What do you want me to do with it?"

"I don't know." I looked over at the sprawling pile. "Just bag it all up and stack it in the garage for now." I looked around at the drifts of dog fur coating everything and shuddered. "I'll vacuum, sweep, mop, and clean up the den." It was an intimidating task. "Whoever finishes first has to pitch in and help someone else." Everyone nodded in agreement and we went to work.

I was carefully sweeping dog hair out of a corner in the kitchen when my phone rang. It was Holmes. He said he'd see me in three or four hours.

We spent the rest of the afternoon cleaning, drinking beer, listening to music, and intermittently snorting rails to keep us motivated. By the time we'd finished, the house looked pretty damn good.

"I talked to Zack earlier today and told him that he and Nico should come over later and play some poker." I said and sat down to rail us up four more lines.

"Cool," Tortoise said as he took the mirror. "I'm down for a little Texas Hold'em." He leaned down to take his.

The mirror went around the circle as I proceeded to roll up some Beast into a couple of phat cone joints. "How's our alcohol situation?"

"We need to go to the store," Jefe said with certainty.

We finished the joints and then all piled into my truck and headed to the liquor store. We picked up a half gallon of Seagram's, a half gallon of Jack Daniel's, some Coca-Cola, Seven-Up, a couple big bags of ice, a case of PBR, and a case of Fat Tire. When we got back to the house, I gave Nico a call. "Did Zack tell you we were playing poker tonight?"

"Yeah, man, you all ready?"

"Hell, yeah, we just stocked the bar."

No sooner had I hung up with Nico than Melissa called. "What are you guys doing tonight?" she asked.

"Nico and Zack are coming over, and we're going to play some poker. You and Becca should come." She agreed.

Holmes had already met Melissa and Becca. I knew he'd be cool with them being there. He thought Becca was pretty hot, but I told him not to go there, because it would fuck with Tortoise, and he already had enough self-confidence issues.

Nico and Zack showed up first, and Cloud went to make each of them a drink.

"Where's Nate?" Nico asked as he sat down at the kitchen table.

"He's at Renegade," Cloud answered and handed him a Seven and Seven.

"Oh, that's right." Nico sipped his drink, and I could tell by the look on his face that it gave him a little bite. We didn't mess around when it came to mixing cocktails. "That's gonna be such a sick show."

"No shit," Cloud said as he poured one for himself. "I wanted to go with him, but I've got way too much to do to get my Chicago order out."

"Yeah." Nico nodded his head sympathetically. "When do you have to ship it?"

"Tuesday."

Melissa and Becca showed up pretty quickly after that with a half gallon of vodka, some tonic water, limes, and a hell of a lot of nitrous cartridges.

"Sick!" Jefe said when he saw the nitrous. He loved that shit.

Melissa donned her mischievous Cheshire-cat grin. "We brought balloons for everybody. Here—you're purple," she said as she handed one to me. Becca passed out the rest.

Melissa grabbed a nitrous cartridge and slipped it inside the brass cracker. She put the mouth of my balloon around the end of the cracker and let it rip. When all the gas from that cartridge had been released into the balloon, she opened the cracker, shook the empty cartridge into the garbage sack and slipped a new cartridge into the brass cracker, which was still attached to my balloon. She screwed the cracker shut forcing the second cartridge to also release its gas into my balloon. "Here," she said, handing me the very full balloon. "Wait for me." She picked up her blue balloon and filled it with two cartridges. "Ready?" We held the balloons to our lips and inhaled as much nitrous as our lungs would hold. Then we pinched off our balloons and held the intoxicating gas in our lungs as long as we could.

I exhaled slowly, feeling my head and body start to tingle. As soon as I completely exhaled, I put the balloon back to my lips, sucked the last of the nitrous into my lungs, held it, and then let it out. At that point I couldn't really lift my head, and my legs felt like two rubber bands. I held on to the counter so I wouldn't go down and saw Melissa's hand on the counter too. My vision blurred, and I felt my whole body pulsate—numb, tingly, euphoric, quasi-orgasmic. "Wa-wa-wa-wa" reverberated throughout my whole body. I started coming back around and heard other cartridges being popped and balloons being filled. I got my bearings, steadied myself, and filled another balloon for Melissa. I had to adjust my fingers a couple of times so I wouldn't burn them on the freezing gas moving from the cartridge into the balloon. After a few more hits of nitrous, I went into my room and got some more cocaine. The Dead Guy mirror was still sitting on the coffee table, so I wiped it off with the inside of my T-shirt, poured some coke out, and railed everyone up a nice-sized line. We hung out for a while, listening to music and getting our fade on. Then we sat down to start our poker game.

Not too long after that, the doorbell rang. I followed Jefe to the door, and as he reached for the knob, I shouted to stop him. "Dude!"

He looked at me like I was being unreasonable. "But we know who it is."

"I don't care," I said, feeling like the parent of an adolescent. "*Always* look out first. You've got to make it a habit, Jefe. You never know who it is, not for sure, until you check."

Jefe sighed in mild disgust and put his eye to the peephole. "It's him. Can I open the door now?"

I ignored his sarcasm and hugged Holmes as he came through the door. "Holmes! What's up? Good to see you, man."

"How the hell are ya, Kyd? It's been a while." He turned to Jefe and gave him a hug.

I felt totally stoked to have my "brother from another mother" in town and was grateful we had made the effort to clean the house. We walked back into the kitchen. "You know everyone here?"

"Yeah." Holmes smiled and nodded, acknowledging everyone around the table.

"You want something to drink?" I asked.

"Hell, yeah! What're you sippin' on?" Holmes pointed to the glass in my hand.

"Jack and Coke."

"Sounds good." Holmes took off his coat and sat down at the table. "Damn, it's good to be here. That was a bitch of a drive."

"Yeah, I bet." I filled his glass mostly full with Jack and threw a splash of Coke on top. "How long have you been on the road?"

"Twelve hours today and twelve yesterday. It was fucking gnarly—ice and snow all the way from Utah."

"You want in this hand?" Cloud asked Holmes as he shuffled the deck of cards.

"What are you playing?"

"Texas Hold'em."

"Nah, dude, I'm just gonna chill for a minute."

I handed Holmes his drink and went into my bedroom to

grab a mixed handful of Vicodin, Valium, and Xanax. I walked back into the kitchen, picked up a glass ashtray off the table, dumped the garbage and butts and shit in the trash, dropped the pills in it, and set it back down in the middle of the table. "Let's eat!" I said and popped one in my mouth.

Everyone reached in and helped themselves.

"This will take the edge off," Holmes said and chased a Valium down with his Jack and Coke.

Cloud called order to the poker game and slid the deck of cards toward me. "All right, a dollar Small Blind, two-dollar Big Blind." I cut the deck. He took it back and dealt my hole cards—ace, jack off suit. Not too bad. I tossed in a chip to even myself with the Big Blind.

"Raise five," Tortoise said, with a huge shit-eating grin on his face. He either had something, or he was trying to bluff— Tortoise was notorious for his bluffs. Nico and Zack dropped out, but everyone else stayed in. Cloud turned the flop, two of diamonds, ace of hearts, and eight of clubs. I looked around the table and saw that Tortoise's smile had faded, and Nico looked pissed that he had folded. Cloud was trying not to look at the flop and shuffled his pile of chips with a stern look on his face. He was my man to beat. Tortoise kept his head down and made a defiant bet of a buck.

"All in!" Jefe shouted and shoved all his chips to the center of the table.

"Dude." Cloud's look of serious concentration shifted to one of serious annoyance. "It's not your fucking turn, asshole," he said and leaned across the table to block Jefe's chips from mixing with those in the pot. Jefe gloated, delighting in his successful attempt to shake things up. I reached over, helped slide Jefe's chips back to the section of table in front of him, and shot him a "chill the fuck out" look.

The game was back on. Cloud raised to five. I called, and Tortoise, trying to save face, followed suit. I loved poker because it didn't matter if the pot was five dollars or five thousand; it wasn't so much about the money. It was about winning, about out-playing the motherfucker across the table, and it nourished my competitive spirit.

Cloud threw down the turn, eight of spades. I kept myself cool and knew there were no flushes out there to beat my two pair. Tortoise chuckled, and Cloud surprised me by looking at his cards a couple of times and then blurting, "All in!"

"All in!" Jefe shouted again. "All in!" He started to shove his chips to the center of the table, but I blocked them just before he created a cluster fuck.

Cloud slammed his cards face-down on the table. "Goddamn it, Jefe! It's not your fucking turn. Why do you wanna fuck shit up all the time?" He shook his head side to side in utter annoyance. "You're not funny, dude. You're an irritating fucking pain in the ass!"

Jefe shot Cloud a wounded look, but then he said, "Dude, I'm just playing. Why do you have to be so serious all the time?" Jefe laughed and leaned back in his chair, almost tipping over backward, but Holmes caught him.

"Mellow out, man," Holmes said as he helped Jefe set his chair on all fours. "You're starting to piss me off, and I'm not even in the game." Holmes looked over at me and rolled his eyes. It was truly aggravating when Jefe got this way—all loaded and belligerent and crazy and shit. Jefe thought he was a riot, but it drove everyone else nuts, including me.

"Hey, motherfucker," I said to him. "I'm about to win a hand here, so will you chill out and let me concentrate already?" I had a small note of humor in my voice, but the look in my eyes told him I wasn't kidding. That's how I always let Jefe save face. He and I communicated more through body language and vibe than anything else. Jefe put his hands in his lap and sat back in his chair, telling me he was ready to be cool.

"All in," Cloud said, clearly annoyed.

Fuck! I thought. I wondered if I missed something. He

couldn't have anything to beat my two pair. "Call," I said, hoping I sounded relaxed. It cost me about seventy-five bucks.

"Fuck you, guys," Tortoise said. His shit-eating grin disappeared as he tossed in his cards.

Cloud and I went heads up. He smiled, and I felt my jaw drop. The two and eight of hearts were sitting in front of him. The motherfucker had a full boat—eights over deuces. Zack was chattering something to Tortoise about how this was just like some World Series Poker hand he'd seen last week on TV. I shot Jefe a look that let him know he shouldn't even think about it. He cast his gaze downward.

It had turned into a pretty intense hand, and everyone was standing around the table watching. "Burn one, turn one," Cloud said and turned over a card. He was the first one to see it and got a look on his face like someone just kicked him in the nuts.

"Ace of spades!" Zack shouted. A wave of relief passed through me, followed by the elation of victory, which I immediately attempted to subdue in an effort to maintain my cool.

"Fuck you, Kyd," Cloud half-heartedly chuckled. "You're a lucky motherfucker!"

"Let's break for a minute," Tortoise said and went to the bathroom.

I lit a smoke and got up to make another drink. "Hey, Melissa," I said. "I think there's still some coke in there on the mirror. Why don't you cut us up some rails?"

"Okay." She headed into the den.

"You want another drink Holmes?" I offered. He handed me his glass. I made our drinks, sat back down at the table, lit a smoke, and then leaned over toward him. "So, let's see your ganja," I said quietly.

"All right." He stood up. "I'll be right back." Holmes walked out to his car and soon came back in with a large Da Kine snowboard duffel bag. We went into my room, where he unzipped the bag and pulled out a food-saver bag full of weed.

When I cut it open, the pungent smell of seriously chronic ganja immediately filled the room. There were big lime-green nuggets with orange hairs interlaced throughout. They looked like they had been dipped in sugar. He pulled one out and smiled as he gently squeezed the center, inhaling its sweet aroma. "You ready to move it?"

"Ah, yeah, man. No problem." I fingered through the bag, checking out perfect buds of all sizes; it was simply beautiful—true art. "This won't even be work." I grabbed a turkey bag and emptied the ganja into it. I pulled out one bud about six inches long and then sucked the air out of the turkey bag, making it tight around the rest of the ganja. Then I tied it off. "Let's go puff some of this." We walked back into the kitchen and I set the bud in the middle of the table.

"Fuck, dude." Jefe's eyes got big as he reached down and picked it up. "This is some seriously sick shit!"

Cloud reached out his arm. "Let me see it, dude."

Jefe attempted to toss the bud to Cloud, but it stuck to his fingers and only went a couple of inches. "Dude, you're holding some of this back for our head, aren't you?" Jefe picked up the bud and gently squeezed the nugget. Then he pressed his fingers onto a piece of paper and gently peeled it off, like it was attached to his fingers by a thin layer of maple syrup or honey or something. He was having a ball with all the attention this demonstration was getting him.

"Hand me that pipe," I said to Tortoise, pointing at one of Cloud's latest creations on the kitchen counter. I motioned for Jefe to hand me the bud. I broke off a good-sized piece and loaded the pipe with the chunk of weed—it heaped out about twice the size of the bowl. I passed it to Melissa.

Holmes tilted his head down and looked up at me from under his brow. He spoke softly. "So, you think this will go as fast as it usually does?"

I nodded my head with complete confidence. "No problem. Give me seventy-two hours."

"Cool."

"You guys want to play another hand?" Cloud asked as he sat down at the table to hit the pipe.

"Yeah," Nico said. He finished his drink and got up to make another. "I haven't won all your money yet, fool."

"Fuck you!" Cloud laughed as he passed the pipe to Tortoise. "Make me one of those while you're up." He handed his glass to Nico.

"This is a sick piece, bro," Zack said, checking out the pipe as he puffed the bowl and then handed it to Cloud.

"Damn straight!" Cloud leaned back in his chair, enjoying a chance to gloat (something he rarely did). "I don't fuck around, yo!"

We played a few more hands, had a few more drinks, did a couple more rails, ate another Vicodin or three, and decided it was time to head on down to the Tittie Twister. Holmes was beat from the drive and just wanted to go to his hotel and chill in the hot tub. I helped him bring the rest of the ganja into the house and told him I would talk to him in the morning.

Melissa loved the tittie bar almost as much as we did, which was just one more reason why I dug her so much. She was just cool like that. She went right up to the stage and got us front row seats, while I went to the bar to order drinks. I high-fived Derek, the bartender. "What's up, man?"

"Same old shit, yo."

"Yeah, I hear ya."

"You want a Jack and Coke?" Derek asked.

"Yeah, and a vodka tonic."

We'd been coming here pretty regularly for the past year or so and had gotten to know everyone pretty well. I sold Derek a lot of blow and pills, and he spread it around the club. They went crazy for that shit.

He handed me the drinks, and I gave him a hundred dollar bill and asked for the change in fives.

"You gonna be around tomorrow?" he asked

"Yeah, I've got some running around to do, but give me a call and we'll work something out."

"Cool."

I took the drinks and went to sit down next to Melissa. Some stripper already was shaking her titties in Melissa's face, and Melissa was loving it. I gave her a handful of fives and put a couple on the stage in front of us. We sat there for a half hour or so, drinking and watching the naked dancing ladies. I watched Melissa's eyes following this one dancer around the bar for a while. She leaned over and whispered in my ear, "I'm gonna get us a table dance." I sat there for a minute, sipping my cocktail, soaking in all the tantalizing, exposed flesh around me, until I felt Melissa tap my shoulder. "You ready?" she asked. She'd donned her Cheshire-cat grin, and we followed the dancer to a semi-secluded table in the back. I handed the half-naked girl twenty-five dollars, and then Melissa and I sat down. This stripper was good; she could really move and was actually pretty hot, with her long blonde hair, sculpted waist, tight bubble ass, and plump, melon-like titties that looked soft, supple, and real. She rubbed around on both of us but paid more attention to Melissa, which I completely loved. Melissa liked the ladies too (if you know what I mean) and was having a great time flirting with this stripper. She leaned her head forward, subtly tilting it to the side so her lips were just an inch away from the stripper's. They would both open their mouths a little, like they were going to kiss, and then the stripper would slowly pull away, running her hand through Melissa's hair and then gently across her face. It was pretty sexy. Melissa would look over at me, smiling. I could tell she was getting even more excited that I was enjoying the whole show. About halfway through the song, Melissa reached over and gently pressed on the crotch of my pants to see if my dick was hard. It was, of course, and with Melissa rubbing on it and the stripper's big titties in my face, I thought I might cum right there in my pants. I could tell Melissa was getting pretty cranked up too. Fun for the whole family—it was great! When the dance was over, Melissa wanted to go to the bathroom and do a line. I slid her a little plastic baggie with some coke in it, and we headed off to find our friends, who were sitting at a big round table near the stage.

I walked up behind them and leaned over between Nico and Jefe. "You guys want to go for a quick rail?"

"Yeah, man." Nico nodded at Zack, while Jefe leaned over and whispered something to Cloud and Tortoise. Cloud sucked down the rest of his drink, and they stood up.

Melissa leaned over and whispered something to Becca, and I reached across to touch her arm and get her attention. "We'll meet you guys back here in a few."

She flashed her Cheshire-cat grin, and we headed off.

We all partied for a while, had a few more drinks, took a few more trips to the bathroom, and then decided to call it a night.

10

I awoke with a start, hearing a knock at my door and Jefe's voice. "Kyd ... Kyd, get up, man." Melissa lay motionless, tucked half in front, half underneath me. My arm was draped over and around her, holding her close to me. "Kyd ..." Jefe said again through the door. Something in his voice made me nervous and I slowly rolled over. He cracked the door open, gently pushing Stella out of the way, and I could see his eyes were wide. It wasn't like Jefe to come into my room in the morning, especially when he knew I had company, so whatever it was must be pretty important.

All the alcohol and drugs from the night before had robbed almost every drop of liquid from mouth, leaving my tongue feeling like a dried-up sponge. My head began to pound, and I pressed my hand firmly against my forehead to relieve some of the pressure. It worked for a second. "What's up?" I spoke softly, trying not to disturb Melissa or further provoke the painful throbbing in my skull.

Jefe's wide eyes were vacant and frozen. "Dude ... Nate was arrested."

"What?" I forgot about my splitting head as Jefe's words ricocheted through me. I saw Nate in my mind's eye—young, naïve, smiling, so good-natured and happy—and Jefe's words didn't immediately register.

"He was arrested last night at Renegade—with everything, all his shit. They got it all." He shook his head back and forth. "His mom just called Cloud. You need to come out here." Jefe stepped back out into the hall and pulled the door shut behind him.

I lay there feeling paralyzed by shock and disbelief as unnerving images raced through my head—Cloud, and how fucked up this was going to be for him. Nate was like his little brother; Nate, who had never been in any trouble before. And this was big; it wasn't like getting popped with an ounce or two or a quarter pound of weed. No, this was fucked. If it wasn't for all that acid ... that acid would fuck him. And the mushrooms, if he still had them. They would fuck with him for all those psychedelics. I knew Jefe was scared shitless; it was his acid. I just had to try to keep everybody calm.

Melissa rolled over and looked at me through eyes swimming with concern. She was no stranger to our world and knew the potential magnitude of this situation. She loved Nate—everybody did. He was witty, charming, and charismatic, and people were drawn to him, but he was young and soft. He had never really been exposed to the dark side of this business. I mean, he had people stiff him for a couple hundred bucks here and there, and he had heard plenty of our stories, but he had never had the 5-0 in his face. Those fucking pigs were trained to be ruthless, especially for something like this. They would crucify him, I knew that, and it would scare the shit out of him. And the fucked-up thing was that if he had even half of what he took to Renegade on him when he got popped, their threats wouldn't be empty. No, it would be for real, and Nate would know that. "It'll be cool," I said to Melissa, not sure which one of us I was trying to convince. "I need to go see what's going on. Come on out whenever you're ready to get up".

I stumbled out of bed, threw on some clothes, and attempted to collect myself as best I could. Stella followed me to the den and sat down next to Jefe on the couch. His elbows were on his knees, and his head was resting in his hands. She nuzzled her snout under Jefe's knee, and he rubbed her behind the ears and patted her shoulders, acknowledging her attempt to comfort him. Cloud was talking on the phone as he paced back and forth behind the couch. Jefe looked up at me, pale and weary-looking. "He's talking to Nate's mom." Jefe's voice was scared, quiet, and humble.

I sat down on the couch next to Jefe. "So what's up?"

"Nate got popped last night."

"Yeah, but what happened?"

"He tried to sell acid to an undercover."

My chest seized with fear. "So where is he now?"

"They're holding him until his mom comes to get him. Since he's a juvie, they'll only release him to her custody. She's flipping out. She needs five thousand dollars to get him out." Jefe looked up at me, his eyes asking for the cash.

"I'll get her the money." I looked around the room, still half asleep and out of it. "Did you wake up Tortoise?"

"No, he went to Becca's last night."

I thought for a second. "Did you call him about this yet?"

"Not yet." Jefe's voice was a monotone.

"Don't—not yet, anyway. No sense freaking him out until we have a better handle on the situation."

Cloud hung up the phone, looking on the verge of tears. The room was heavy with negative energy, and I felt my stomach knot and twist. I knew what this could mean for all of us, but I pushed the thought out of my mind.

"She needs five thousand dollars?" I asked.

Cloud's voice was barely a whisper. "Yeah."

"All right." I went to my room and opened my safe.

Melissa was sitting up in bed, hugging her knees. The blankets were pulled up over her, and her auburn curls cascaded down over them. "Is everything OK?" she asked sleepily.

I pulled five thousand dollars out of my safe as I kept repeating to myself, "Focus, stay calm, take control of the situation." I closed the safe and spun the combination dial, turning to Melissa. "It'll be cool," I said. "Nate's in jail, but it'll be cool. His mom's going to get him." I stuffed the five thousand dollars into a white envelope, wrapped a rubber band around it, and went back to the den.

Cloud and Jefe were sitting silently on the couch. They both looked like they were in a mild state of shock. I laid the envelope on the table in front of Cloud. "So you're gonna take this to Nate's mom," I said, more telling him than asking him.

"Yeah," he said absently. He seemed like he was only half there.

I sat down in the chair across from them. "Here's what we're gonna do." They looked up at me; I had gotten their attention. "Cloud, you take the cash to Nate's mom and tell her not to worry. I'm gonna call Ryan." Ryan was the best defense attorney around and a total ally to the younger street-kid, drug-dealing community. He was a pretty good friend of mine and just happened to be one of my best blow custies. He didn't come cheap but was always down to take our crazy drug- and alcohol-related cases. Ryan was full of energy, a master manipulator and had gotten people out of some crazy shit.

Jefe was beginning to perk up. "Cool."

Melissa walked into the room and sat down in the chair next to me. "Hi," she said, somewhat awkwardly.

I felt like the general of an army, dictating the military strategy for an impending battle. Cloud and Jefe listened closely, hanging on my every word. "Cloud, tell Nate's mom we're gonna get him the best attorney and take care of everything. It'll be okay. Nate's got a clean record."

"Right." I heard life and hope come back to Cloud's voice. "His record's totally clean. I don't think he's ever even had a speeding ticket." Cloud chuckled and Jefe smiled and nodded. I felt the thickness of fear and tension in the air begin to dissipate, and it was easier to breathe.

"Is Nate's mom going to get him today?" I asked.

"Yeah," Cloud answered. "They'll release him as soon as she gets there with his bond. They're gonna put him on house arrest, but at least he'll be out of there."

My phone rang. It was Holmes. I felt a sudden rush of anxiety. I took a deep breath and told myself to relax.

"The sun's shining and the mountain's calling me," Holmes said cheerfully. "Is Cloud going up today?"

"I don't know—he just hopped in the shower," I lied. "You want me to have him call you?" Cloud and Jefe both looked at me, perplexed.

"Yeah, tell him I want to go ride."

"All right." I hung up the phone and turned to Cloud. "It was Holmes. He wants you to ride with him today."

Cloud shook his head. "Dude … I don't know if I'm up for it man."

"We can't let Holmes know anything is wrong," I said. "No need getting him all freaked out. His ganja's already in my bedroom, and I've got people who've put together a lot of cash waiting for me." I could feel Jefe and Cloud growing tense again. "I can move it in a couple of days. It doesn't make sense to put Holmes back on the road to Oregon with it. He doesn't have anyone to move it up there anyway." I needed to calm them down. "We just gotta go along like everything's cool. I'll move the weed, and we'll send Holmes back home with a smile on his face and a car full of cash. Then we'll focus all our energy on Nate's situation."

"You're gonna wait until Holmes leaves before you help Nate?" Cloud words were scared and frustrated.

"No, dude," I said, raising my voice in an effort to regain control of the situation. "I'm gonna call Ryan this morning. Aside from giving Nate's mom the money to get him out, that's all I can do right now." Cloud backed down and nodded his head in agreement. I knew he was scared and worried sick, but I needed him to focus. "I need you to take care of Holmes for me today," I said firmly.

"Dude ..." He shook his head. "I just don't know if I have it in me to go to the mountain today."

"I know everyone's a little freaked out right now, but sitting around here, stressing on it, isn't going to help anything. Come on, man. It'll be good for you to get some fresh air."

Cloud thought for a minute. "All right," he finally said. "You're probably right."

"When am I ever wrong?" I joked and slapped him on the shoulder. He, Jefe, and Melissa all laughed halfheartedly, and I felt the tension break once again.

"So you'll call Holmes?" I said.

"Yeah."

I nodded, trying to push the hectic crap out of my mind so I could focus on what I needed to do. "I've gotta get my shit together and get out of here," I said. "You coming with me, Jefe?"

"Yeah, I'll ride around with you." He followed me into my bedroom, asking, "So how much of this are we taking?"

"Fifteen pounds." I unzipped one of Holmes's duffel bags. He had the ganja weighed out in half-pound increments. I put nine of his food-saver bags, plus the turkey bag I'd filled with the bag of ganja I opened, into a duffel bag and slid it under my bed.

"That's what you're keeping?" Jefe asked.

"Yeah."

I divided the rest of the pot strategically into three large duffel bags, so I could easily carry in five-pound increments at each stop without having the added sketchiness of juggling pot in and out of each house. I opened my safe to take an inventory of my cash. I had just given Cloud five thousand and would need to pull out about ten thousand more to retain Ryan for Nate. I was going to owe Holmes about sixty-five hundred to cover the ganja I was keeping as profit. That would leave me with thirty-five thousand ... plenty to take care of Ryan and Holmes and still leave me with a few bucks. I still had about twenty-five thousand out in fronts but I made it a point never to count on those until I actually had cash in hand.

I made good profit off Holmes's ganja. He gave it to me at twenty-eight hundred a pound, and I turned pounds at thirty-three hundred to everyone except Nico who got a bit of a bro discount at thirty-two hundred. I ultimately traded Holmes my cash profit for the five pounds I was keeping, so I wouldn't really see any of that return until I turned those five pounds. It worked out better for me that way, though, because I broke my five down into smaller weight to capitalize on my highest profit margin. It all worked out, and I ultimately made around twelve G's every time I saw Holmes.

I grabbed my scale and a thousand-dollar bundle and put them in the bottom of my backpack. I put a long-sleeved T-shirt and pair of pants on top of that and stuck my toothbrush, toothpaste, a small plastic bag full of Vicodin and Xanax, and my aluminum bullet filled with cocaine in one of the side pockets. Jefe and I each grabbed two of the duffel bags of ganja and carried them out to my car in the garage. "You ready to go?" I asked him.

"Yeah, I just need to throw a couple of things in a bag."

"All right." I got the last duffel bag of ganja from my room and took it to the car. On the way back in, I stopped by Cloud's room. "You want to puff a quick bowl before we go?" I asked him.

"Yeah, sure, I'll be right there."

I walked into Jefe's room. He was zipping up his pack. I grabbed the glass pipe sitting on his dresser and sat down on the bed. "Nice," he said when he saw me loading the bowl. Cloud walked in and sat down next to me.

I handed him the pipe. "I'm gonna leave Stella here with you guys," I said. "Is that cool?"

"Sure."

"She can hang out in the yard. Just make sure she's got plenty of food and water."

"No worries." Cloud nodded. "We'll take good care of her."

"You talk to Holmes?'" I asked Cloud, trying to use a more gentle tone so he didn't feel too pushed or bossed around. I knew he was freaking out and trying to rise above it all and keep it together.

"Yeah, I'm gonna run this cash to Nate's mom, and then I'll go by Holmes's hotel and pick him up." Cloud seemed to be feeling better, more optimistic. "He's super-stoked to go ride." Cloud smiled. "It's all good. And it'll be good for me to get up there and clear my head a little."

I put my arm around him and gave his shoulder a gentle squeeze. "We just don't want Holmes knowing anything, ya know? I just need to get his business taken care of and get him back on the road to Oregon."

"I know." Cloud was back in the game. "It's cool." We finished the bowl, and Jefe and I got up to get our backpacks. Cloud walked us to the car. "So, you guys will be back tomorrow?"

I nodded. "Yeah, I left you guys a little stash in the Tupperware next to my bed. It should be enough to tide you over until we get back." If everything went smoothly, Jefe and I would be back in about twenty-four hours, but there was probably enough weed and pills in that Tupperware to last Cloud and Tortoise a week. I didn't want my bros going hungry, especially with all the stress at the moment.

"Thanks, bro. Give me a call later on." That was Cloud's way of saying "Check in to let me know everything is cool"—without sounding like some sappy mom.

"We will."

"All right. See ya later."

"Late."

11

I was selling the fifteen pounds in five packs, two at sixteen-thousand five hundred dollars and one, Nico's, at sixteen thousand, so I had three separate stops to make. First we headed about forty-five miles south to C.J.'s house. C.J. was an okay guy—a little full of himself, but pretty harmless for the most part. He was a soft white boy from suburban Denver who thought he was some hard-core gangster right out of Compton, with his phony iced-out (CZ wannabe) Kanye West Jesus pendent hanging on its silver chain. He wore a black velour Sean John track suit, black Supra sneakers, and a black New Era cap, all locked and cocked to the side. He always flashed his hands in front of him when he was trying to talk that gangster talk, and that stupid fucking grill he had—fake as shit but made to look like platinum with diamonds. I hated that fucking thing and was embarrassed for him every time he put it in his mouth. I don't have anything against grills—real grills, that is; the kind the hard-core gangster rappers have that are *really* made of platinum and diamonds. That's their thing, and as far as I know, they started it, so more power to 'em. But some soft, white suburban boy, proudly flashing a bogus one all jacked up with a bunch of attitude because it makes him feel so cool, so tough—I'm sorry; I think it's fucking ridiculous. I feel a little bad saying all this because on the one hand, who am I to judge? But I don't feel too bad, because on the other hand, I'm entitled to a fucking opinion.

Anyway, I put up with him and the grill and all the wigger shit, because I knew the truth: underneath it all, he was harmless kid; plus, he always had cash, and that made him a little easier to take. After all, it was just business.

I called him when we were about fifteen minutes away just to make sure everything was still good and to ask if he had anybody over.

"My bro Tommy's here," he told me, "but he's cool, man; he's cool."

"I told you I didn't want anyone there," I said. "Get rid of him. I'm calling you back in five and if he's still there, I'm turning around."

"Dude, it's all good. Don't go anywhere. I'll get rid of him."

I hung up the phone, and Jefe could tell I was hot. I had a rule, and everyone knew it, that when I delivered, I didn't want anybody there but the person I was delivering to. The fewer people who knew me, the better. That's how people get into trouble—get an ego, want to flaunt it, or just get plain lazy and careless. I had seen it happen too many times.

"Everything okay?" Jefe asked, his eyes beginning to cultivate a 'you want me to kill him?' look.

"Yeah, it's cool. He's just got to get rid of some company."

That was one thing about Jefe—he protective of me, like a fucking pit bull. It didn't take much, and he was ready for the throat.

I called C.J. back in five minutes. "You got company?"

"No, dude, it's just me."

"We'll see you in a few."

C.J met us at the front door. "Right on!" He had a big grin on his face and was rubbing his hands together as I set the duffel bag on the ground.

"You got the cash?" I asked.

"Yeah." He set three bulging envelopes, each wrapped by

a thick rubber band, on the table. I unzipped the duffel and handed him one of the food-saver bags full of ganja. He took out a pair of scissors and sliced it open. The aroma of juicy sweet, organic, hydroponic weed filled the room. "Nice!" He glowed as he fingered through the weed, picking up random buds and holding them close to his nose. He gave them a gentle squeeze.

Jefe and I started counting the money in the envelopes. I sighed heavily as I turned twenties, hundreds, and fifties over and around. "Why don't you face this shit?" I said.

He shrugged his shoulders "I don't know, bro. I guess I just get in a hurry. Sorry."

"It doesn't take any more time to face when you're bundling it up," I snapped at him. I was becoming more agitated as I continued flipping the bills around. "It's just more organized." I had this thing about facing money that some may have considered anal, but whatever, it was my thing. I didn't think it was too much to ask. Everybody was pretty good about it except C.J. He never faced his, no matter how much shit I gave him about it, but he was typically never short, so I tried not to be too big of a prick about it.

There was a time when sitting down to count out that much cash was fun and sexy and cool, but I'll tell ya, after a while, it becomes nothing more than an arduous fucking pain in the ass process. Not that I didn't enjoy reaping the profits and all that, but the stress of driving the shit around, the anxiety of not knowing for sure who may or may not be inside or be watching, and counting out all that fucking money—all that bullshit is what turned dealing drugs into work.

After what seemed like a long fucking time, we finally finished counting. It was all there. Now it was time to weigh out the pot, another arduous process. I always kind of hated weighing out that much pot, but I learned the hard way it was a much better idea to just sit down and do it. You don't want someone calling you later, after you've given him the shit, taken the cash, and left thinking it was all good, only to tell you there's some kind of problem. How do you prove what was there, after the fact? You don't. No matter how tired or ready to get out of there you are, it's always a better idea to count your money and weigh your weed with both parties in the room.

"Is this all you've got?" C.J. asked as I put the money in the duffel bag and rolled it up.

"I've got a little more, but it's all spoken for at this point."

"If something doesn't work out, give me a call."

"All right."

"When are you gonna get some more?"

"Six weeks or so."

"What about that Beast?"

"It should roll through next month."

"Cool."

Jefe and I walked to the front door. "See you later, man."

"Late."

We headed down the road and for a brief moment, I felt a sliver of my incessant tension release. One more drug deal gone good. I would feel even better once we got rid of the other ten pounds in the back of my truck, but I tried not to think about that.

"Dude, are you hungry?" Jefe said as we passed by a Burger World.

"I could eat. You want to stop and grab something?"

"Yeah, I'm starving." Jefe was always -'starving'-.

"There's a Bueno Burrito up here."

"Cool."

There wasn't a drive thru so I pulled up in a parking spot near the front door. "You want to just run in and grab it?" I asked.

"Yeah, sure. What do you want?"

"Just get me a Bueno Burrito Deluxe." I pulled out my wallet and handed him a fifty. "And a Coke."

He jumped out of the car and walked inside. I watched as

several people came and went—laughing, silly, relaxed, just leading their ordinary, legitimate, everyday lives. I thought how these people walking right past me had no idea that I was a drug dealer on a drug run with ten pounds of seriously chronic, homegrown Oregon weed and sixteen-ish thousand illegal dollars in the back of my truck. This thought of society's ignorance to what was really going on right under people's noses made me laugh. I felt powerful and stealth and cool, because I liked being an outlaw, existing outside our fucked-up system that wasn't gonna pin me to some fucking cork board by the collar of a generic, stiff, itchy, ill-fitting blue button-up shirt. Fuck that!

I watched a couple come out with a kid, probably seven or so, all three of them overweight and dressed in worn looking discount clothes, and I thought, *Sheep. Those poor sheep. Just smiling away, oblivious to the slaughterhouse they live in. Oblivious to their will slaughtered daily by a big-business-run government whose intentions are to suck the life force from the masses for the benefit of the few. Mainstream society is nothing more than a slaughterhouse, and I will never give in.*

I sat there genuinely feeling sorry for most of America. They didn't know they were kept blind and full of crap. The Machine had to keep them focused on all the distractions, keep the wheels turning, or it wouldn't work. My scrutiny turned to daydream as I saw myself in a black cape, black pants, black boots, and a black Zorro-type mask. I moved in the night, black as pitch, except for some dark red swirling in the clouds above. I felt a sudden surge of personal power as I walked up to a huge pen holding thousands of sheep, pulled the latch, and threw open the gate. I expected them to all come running out—jumping, kicking and screaming with life—but they didn't come, not one. They just stood there all huddled together, staring at me bleakly, scared and mindless, inching backward in their pen. I was stunned and confused.

As I sat there in my car, wondering why my imaginary sheep would refuse the gift of liberation, I noticed I was holding my breath. I exhaled and thought to myself, *Where the hell did that come from?* I was a little embarrassed and caught off guard by that bizarre daydream and was glad no one could read my thoughts. I looked around to make sure that the one mind-reader in the world wasn't out there, laughing and pointing and ridiculing me for my stupid mental philandering ... and then I saw the black and white car with the red and blue lights mounted on the top.

It pulled into a spot in the back of the parking lot, and two cops got out and started walking toward me. My heart skipped about three beats and then started beating double time, pounding like it wanted to jump out my chest and run for cover. I reached down, picked up my iPod, and started scrolling through it in an attempt to avoid having to make any eye contact with them. In that moment, any shred of self-empowerment I had recently generated from my frivolous daydream went right out the window, and it was abruptly replaced with feelings of anxiety and panic. I felt the cops getting closer and couldn't help looking up as they walked past my car. One of them looked at me with that expressionless face they always have, and I just nodded and forced a smile. I felt a wave of relief until I saw Jefe juggling a Bueno Burrito sack and two sodas, holding the door open as they walked toward him. He stood there like he didn't have a care in the world. He said something as they approached him. One of them responded and actually gave something that resembled a pleasant look as they walked past him and went inside.

"Dude, that sucked!" Jefe laughed as he pulled French fries out of the sack and crammed them into his mouth.

"Fuck!" I was almost pissed at him for not being more freaked out over the whole deal.

"Chill, man, it's just the fucking cops." He smiled at me with that smile that was so genuine and naïve, and I realized, once again, it was all just part of the game.

I scrolled through the list of artists in my iPod and put on some Bob Marley. Even though I was feeling better with my Deluxe Burrito and soda and Jefe sitting next to me like we were untouchable, there was still a hint of anxiety pulsing through me. There was nothing like a little Bob thumping through your speakers, singing "Don't worry ... 'bout a thing ... every little thing's gonna be all right" to make you really believe it.

We drove for a while, eating and not really talking much, and I started to think about Nate. I wondered if he was home yet and thought how scared and fucked up he must feel. Although I hardly let myself think it and didn't dare voice it, I knew how fucked up his situation was. If he got popped with all those psychedelics, even Ryan, our Jedi master defense attorney, could only do so much. Nate's only saving grace was being a juvie and not having any priors. But still, if they really wanted to fuck with him, they would and could. The chances of his getting out of this thing with no time were slim; they would at least stick him with probation, rehab, post-rehab classes, regular drug testing, some fat fucking fines, and a shitload of community service, which would drastically alter life as he knew it.

I had another thought and even though I tried with all my might to push it out of my head, it pushed back and eventually won—the pressure and scare tactics they would use to get him to tell where he got all that shit. I prayed he wouldn't roll on us.

I picked up my phone and called Ryan. After exchanging pleasantries, I told him, "I've got a bro in some trouble and was hoping you would help him out."

"What kind of trouble," Ryan asked

"Drugs. Lots of drugs."

He laughed. "I figured that." Everything was a big joke with him, but he kicked ass with his cases, and that's what mattered.

For Ryan, it was all like a big chess game, and he didn't like to lose.

"I told him I would have you give him a call. He's pretty freaked out and needs some reassurance." I paused, not wanting to say anything even remotely incriminating over the phone, but then went ahead. "It's extra important to me that he is taken care of."

"I hear ya," he said, and I knew he understood my ass was indirectly on the line. "Don't worry, Kyd. I'll call him today and get it handled." His unwavering confidence made me feel better immediately.

Jefe and I were about ten minutes from our next stop. I called Ezra, the kid we were going to meet, and went through the standard procedure. We pulled up, got the ganja out of the back of the truck, went inside, counted the cash, and started weighing out the pot.

"Dude, there's a lot of fucking lumber in this shit," Ezra said. His voice was riddled with attitude.

I threw his attitude back at him. "It's a plant man; that's part of it."

"I can't sell stem, bro."

"Dude, if you don't want it, I'll take it somewhere else." I reached into the duffel and pulled out a turkey bag, ready to dump the opened ganja into it and get the hell out of there.

"It's not that I don't want it. There's just a lot of stem. Can't you cut the price some to make up for it?" Ezra dropped the 'tude when he saw I was serious about leaving.

"The price is the price, and this is what you get," I said. "You're a fucking businessman. Adjust your prices. Pass it along." My day had been too fucked up to jack around with this bullshit. "Why the fuck am I telling you how to run your business?" I said, becoming more heated. "This is the most chronic weed around. There are no special deals. If you don't want it, that's cool. I've got kids begging me for it, but I won't waste my time on you again."

He held a nice nugget in front of his nose, gave it a squeeze, and inhaled its aroma. Then he turned it around, giving it a close inspection.

"Fuck this shit, dude," I said disgustedly. "We're out of here." I looked at Jefe; he grabbed the duffel, and I took the food-saver bag in front of Ezra and started to pour the ganja out of it and into the turkey bag.

"No, dude, I'm sorry. I'll take it."

I looked at Jefe, my eyes telling him to put the duffel bag down, and we would finish the deal.

Minutes later, as we got into the car, Jefe said, "That guy's an ass."

"That's the last time we'll be going to his house."

Jefe smiled and nodded, and we headed to Nico's.

12

A soothing relief settled inside of me as Jefe and I headed to Nico's. He was our last stop and going to his house felt like sliding into home—safe! He and his roommate, Zack, rented a pretty sick three-bedroom house in a secluded area a little outside of Golden. It sat tucked into the trees in the foothills of the mountains and definitely had a cabin-like feel, but it was comfortable and out of the way. That's why when Cedar came down in the motor home with his one hundred or so pounds of Beast, he parked it at Nico's, and we worked from there. There was very little sketch factor at Nico's—much less sketch than at my house in the middle of suburban Boulder or at some motel room.

Nico was cool about letting me leave ganja and money or whatever stashed at his house for a few days if I needed to. He was a total bro and I trusted him completely, which is why I gave him the bro deal on Holmes's ganja. He had the cash and would have liked all fifteen pounds. I briefly considered giving it all to him, but it really is better business to keep several hooks in the water on all sides of the boat. That way, if there's ever a time one side isn't biting, for whatever reason, you've got other hooks, ya know?

I was feeling ready to unwind and let loose a bit and was starting to get pretty stoked about the party Nico was playing that night. It had been a while since I had heard Nico spin, and his shit was always so off the hook. I called him when we were about half an hour out, just to make sure everything was still cool.

We pulled up to Nico's, and he greeted us at the door, holding a cold beer in each hand. "Good to see you guys," he said, handing us the beers.

"It's nice to be here," I said.

We went inside, and I exhaled deeply as I dropped myself down on his couch. I felt like a weight had been lifted from me.

"Been a long day?" Nico asked with a smirk.

"Oh, you know …" I smiled at him, and he nodded.

"Well, you're home free now."

"Yep."

"You want to fuck with this shit now or later?" he said, pointing at the duffel bag.

"Let's get it over with. You want to take it into your room?"

"Sure." Nico grabbed the duffel, and we followed him into his bedroom. We counted the cash and weighed the pot. Nico grabbed one of the nuggets, and we went back to the den.

"Say, fellas," Zack said as he entered the room, "I smelled chronic ganja and figured you all must be here." He smiled and sat down in a chair across from us.

"Your timing's always perfect," Nico laughed. He stuffed a big bud into the pipe and handed it to me.

"You guys need another beer?" Zack asked.

"Hell, yeah, it's hitting the fucking spot!" Jefe answered.

We sat around for a while, puffing bowls, taking hits off my cocaine-filled bullet, drinking beers, and shooting the shit. "So are you guys still feeling up for a little party action?" Nico asked after a while.

"We're always down for some good times," Jefe answered.

"Nice. I need to grab a couple of things, and then we should probably head out pretty quick." Nico got up off the couch. "Help yourself to some more beer; there's plenty in the fridge."

"Thanks."

We sucked down another beer and then Nico walked back into the room. "Ready?"

"Yeah. Should I take my car?" I asked.

"If that's cool. I've got my mixer and turntables and shit packed in mine. It's pretty much loaded."

"No problem."

The party was at Forrest's house. Nico had known him for several years, played a couple of other parties for him, and sold him a decent amount of ganja on a regular basis. Typically, I tended to stay with my core group of friends and was never really a big party kind of guy. I loved going to shows and festivals and stuff like that, but house parties and raves were never really my thing. But I really liked hanging out with Nico, and it had been a while since I'd heard him spin. I was curious about this kid, Forrest, too. Nico had been talking about him for a while now.

Forrest lived in a more rural part of Evergreen, up into the mountains. His place was down a private paved road (which was already lined with cars) that led to a three-story log cabin home, with expansive decks along both the second and third stories and a detached three-car garage. It was still pretty early but already there were probably fifty or sixty people milling around on the decks. I could hear music thumping from the house as we pulled up, and Jefe looked at me with wide eyes, saying, "Dude, this shit's gonna rock!"

Nico walked over to us. "Did you guys bring sleeping bags?"

"Yeah, we're set."

"Cool. There's four bedrooms and several couches, but I'd bet most everyone will crash here tonight, so we might as well bring our shit in now and stash it somewhere." We got our sleeping bags and backpacks and followed Nico over to his truck. "Will you give me a hand with some of this?" He opened the back and pulled out the black case that held his new Rane mixer which he was totally stoked about.

The four of us grabbed his mixer, turntables, and two crates full of records and CD's, and we headed up the drive.

When we walked into the house, it was like old-home week for Nico. Everybody was excited to see him, slapping him high-fives, and patting him on the shoulder. He was like a little celebrity but was seemingly oblivious to all the attention. He introduced me and Jefe to everyone. We went up a flight of stairs and into one of the sickest living room spreads I've ever been in. The ceilings were high and vaulted and seemed a hundred feet away from the hardwood floors beneath them. A wood-burning fire place popped and crackled, glowing from the center of the room, with a wide seating area circling it. The furniture, light fixtures, rugs, wall art, and accessories all matched and had a very modern-type motif. It looked expensive and brand new.

Jefe was impressed and chuckled at the thought of Forrest's obvious "I don't give a fuck" attitude. "Dude, his parents would shit if they knew he was throwing a rager like this up here."

Nico grinned. "It's his house. I don't think his parents are too concerned."

"*His* house?" Jefe repeated in disbelief—and showing a little jealousy.

"Yeah, his. Forrest's. He owns it. Lives here by himself," Nico answered matter-of-factly.

This kid walked up to us. ""Hey Nico. Have you found the kegs yet?"

"No, dude, we just walked in." Nico and the kid shook hands and gave each other a quick hug. "Where're they at?"

"I've got some out on both decks," he answered. Then he turned to Jefe and me. "I'm Forrest." He smiled and stuck out his hand.

"I'm Kyd," I said, reaching out to shake it. "This is Jefe."

"Nice to meet you guys. Nico said he was bringing some

bros" He nodded and smiled at Nico. "There's lots of food set up around the house and a full bar over there." He pointed to an area at one end of the extensive living room. "There's another bar upstairs, and kegs and cups on both the decks." A hottie with dark hair standing behind us was cooing Forrest's name. He turned and held up his index finger signaling he'd be just a second then turned back to us. "Make yourself at home."

"Thanks," I answered.

"You all good to go?" he asked Nico.

"Yeah, I'll just set up like last time, if that's cool."

"Sounds good. Nice to meet you guys." He nodded to me and Jefe.

"Yeah, you, too." And with that, he headed to the sexy brunette.

"What the fuck, dude?" Jefe was unabashed in his astonishment. I knew what he was thinking: how could someone like Forrest—some kid who was just pretty much like us—own a phat spread like this? "He must be rolling harder and faster than any of us," Jefe joked.

"He's a financial advisor," Nico answered as we followed him, still carrying his stuff, to the area where he was going to set up.

"A financial advisor? With Edward Jones, I suppose?" I said with a smirk. I couldn't help it; it just seemed so bizarre. He couldn't have been much older than us.

"Merrill Lynch." Nico was becoming preoccupied with setting up his station, but he looked up at me to show he wasn't kidding. "He's smart as hell. Did the whole college thing; got a MBA from the University of Texas. Hey ..." He pointed to a thick black wire lying inside the case at my feet. "Would you hand me that cable?" I reached down and passed it to him. Nico continued where he'd left off. "His family is pretty loaded too."

"Really?" Jefe seemed less perplexed about the how and why of Forrest, but I could sense his envy thickening.

I gotta admit; I was pretty impressed. And I don't like to admit it, but I was envious too. Forrest—this quasi-preppy, good-looking, obviously charismatic kid—was a financial advisor with Merrill Lynch at age twenty-five or so. And his parents had loads of cash. Fuck him, dude! I started to feel myself resenting him, but then I laughed inside—no sooner had the resentment begun to surface than the words of my now-deceased grandmother rang through my head. It made me feel seven years old again, as I'd been when I'd thrown a righteous fit because my friend Josh got a new bike, and I wanted to get the same one that very second! My mom was not sure how to handle the growing intensity of my tantrum, but my grandmother—Mom's mother—stood strong and spoke to me in a firm but loving voice. "We mustn't envy, Kyd," she said. "Envy is the breeding ground of resentment. Envy breeds resentment, and resentment breeds hate. You mustn't envy others, and you mustn't intentionally give others reason to envy you."

And then, I lapsed into a quick fantasy daydream: Forrest and his should-be-divorced parents—the carousing, alcoholic father and the abused, ignored, taken-for-granted mother who ate Valium like Pez candies and spent all of her time at lunch, the spa, garden club, or shopping, just to eat up the day. And then, there was Forrest—at home in from of the TV, always with the housekeepers and nannies who only kept half an eye on him. It was inevitable; Forrest was headed for some type of narcotic addiction. *Hmmm*, I thought. *I should definitely get his phone number, he'd be a great blow custie.* "You want a beer?" I asked Nico, as I continued to linger in the fleeting daydream, now of me selling mad quantities of cocaine to Forrest.

"Sure."

Jefe, Zack, and I headed out to find the kegs.

We walked out to the lower deck and saw three kegs sitting in large, black plastic trash cans full of ice, along with stacks of red Solo cups. Jefe and Zack each took one, and I took two—one for me and one for Nico. We filled them up and headed back into the house to find him. His turntables and mixer were set up, and he was pulling records out of their crates. The white ceiling lights were now dimmed and strands of soft red and purple lights lined the perimeter of the ceilings. All the lamps had red or purple bulbs as well, and a couple of black lights came on in the main living room where Nico was set up. Pretty soon his music started pumping, and people meandered around, talking, dancing, drinking, passing spliffs, and just having a great time. Jefe, Zack, and I were sipping our beers and puffing on a bowl when Forrest walked up to us. "You guys want to roll?" He opened his hand and showed us six gel caps filled with white powder. "You should eat two. It's on me." He grinned, and I noticed his pupils were dilated. I could tell by the spun-out look in his eyes that he had already eaten some himself.

"Thanks, dude!" Jefe grabbed two and popped them in his mouth. Zack and I looked at each other, shrugged our shoulders, and each took two of the four remaining gel caps from Forrest's hand. We washed them down with a swig of beer.

Nico's rhythms permeated the room as I sat melting into the couch, feeling saturated with the butterfly wings of music as they continuously swept through me. They filled me, lifted me, and held me up to another plane of consciousness—a stream of psychedelic euphoria that made me once again realize the rapture of perfect unity. I watched Jefe in the middle of the room, amped with bliss and dancing with some chick that was all over him. A pleasing warmth passed through me at seeing Jefe look so happy; I wiped at a small tear I felt in the corner of my eye. I was existing in a momentary experience of perfection, and when Zack walked up and handed me a large bottle of water, I felt as though I were complete—that was all I needed, not the warm beer I was holding. I didn't want beer. Water was the source, the heartbeat of life force that nourished all living things. Zack sat down, dissolving into a spot on the couch next to me. We sat there, languid from the relatively intense dose of molly that was coursing through our systems as we cradled our bottles of water, eternally grateful for our source of life. We sipped it and savored it, without talking. We didn't need or want to use words because the energetic wave we were on was communicating a larger, far more awesome connection of perfect contentment.

And then, all of a sudden, this blonde in tight jeans and a sexy black top sat down on the couch between Zack and me. She didn't say anything, but I could tell by the dazed and distant look in her eyes that she was rolling too. She leaned in toward me with a big smile on her face, put her hand on my thigh, and began to laugh as she slid it up toward my crotch. Before I even knew what was happening, she was gently rubbing on my dick, and I could feel it start to get hard. She didn't say anything, but she kept smiling, giggling, and rubbing. And the next thing I knew, she leaned over and was kissing me. I sat there with my eyes closed, in drug-induced paralysis, and started to feel uncomfortable. I saw Melissa in my mind's eye, with her big, bright Cheshire-cat grin and long auburn curls. I didn't like that blonde sitting on me. I didn't like the way she laughed or smelled or the way her lips felt. I started to feel claustrophobic, and I couldn't breathe. The next thing I knew, I was pushing her off. I don't think I meant to, but I must of pushed her pretty hard, because she flew a few feet back and hit the hardwood floor pretty hard. That couldn't have felt good. She sat there a minute, probably a bit dazed, and I watched as she slowly started to sway with the music. In the next minute or two, she was on her hands and knees, crawling back to the couch, only this time toward Zack. She smiled and laughed as she climbed up his legs and then onto his lap. She started rubbing on him and kissing him, and I turned back to watch people dancing and wandering around. I couldn't will myself to move my feet and couldn't think about where to go, even if I'd been able, so I sat there in my Ecstasy high, watching the people dance and feeling the movement next to me where Zack and that crazy blonde were doing whatever it was they were doing.

I woke up in my sleeping bag a few feet away from Jefe. He was tucked into his with the girl he had been dancing with the night before. Their clothes were in a pile next to them on the floor. I rolled over on my back and saw Zack standing up a few feet away from me. He looked a little haggard as he worked at shoving his sleeping bag back into its stuff sack. I rubbed my eyes and slowly pushed myself up on an elbow. "Mornin'!" Nico said as he smiled at me from the corner of the room where he was busy packing up his equipment. He seemed awfully perky as he placed his records back into their crates. I figured he must not have eaten any molly.

Pretty soon Jefe and his new friend were up too. I felt a little bad for her, because I could tell she was embarrassed to be waking up naked in a sleeping bag with some guy whose name she probably couldn't remember. And then to have all of us standing around, trying to act normal, like it wasn't an awkward situation. Of course, Jefe didn't give a fuck and was reaching all around for his underwear and pants, mindlessly throwing the sleeping bag off both of them. She scrambled to pull it up over her until she could get her clothes on, and once she was dressed, there wasn't much of a good-bye between her and Jefe as she scurried out of the room.

We were all pretty bent from the night before and none of us, except Nico, was too talkative as we packed up our shit and helped Nico load his equipment back into his truck. "You guys gotta run by the house before you head back home?" Nico asked, subtly reminding me I had stashed my $49,000 there.

"Yeah, dude, we'll follow you."

"Cool, man, see you in a bit."

When we got to Nico's, we decided to puff a bowl and throw back a quick beer, hoping it would take the edge off the Ecstasy hangover. I pulled out the bag of pharmies I had stashed in the side of my backpack, shook out a few Xanax, chased one down with a swig of beer, and handed one to Jefe. "You want one?" I asked Zack.

"Yeah," he said, and I handed him a couple.

Jefe and I had a couple more beers, puffed a couple more bowls, sat around and bs'd with Nico and Zack a while longer. Then I grabbed my cash, and we headed home. I hadn't talked to Holmes in a while, and I knew he was probably getting anxious to hear from me, so I dialed him up.

"Hey, Kyd!" I heard relief in his voice. "How's it going?"

"Good, good ... it's all good. We're headed your way. Where you at?"

"I'm just chillin' around the hotel room, thinking I'd be hearing from you pretty soon." He laughed. "Guess I was right."

"So, you want us to come there or what?'

"Nah, not here. Why don't I just meet you guys at your house?"

"Okay. We're still an hour or so away."

"All right." He hesitated a moment but then said, "So ... no problems?"

"No problems."

I plugged in my iPod and turned on Slightly Stoopid as Jefe squirmed in the passenger seat, searching out the most comfortable napping position for our ride home.

13

We were about a block from the house when I called Holmes to let him know we were home.

"Nice! I'll head your way."

"Right on, bro, we'll see you soon."

We pulled into the garage and carried all our shit in the house. Cloud was sitting on the couch, flipping through the channels, looking stressed and stiff. "Do you guys need a hand?" he asked as I walked past with my backpack slung over my shoulder and an empty duffel bag in each hand.

"Nah, we got it. Thanks." I walked into my room, threw the duffels in a corner, stashed the backpack full of cash in my closet, and went back to the den. Stella was in the backyard, jumping up like crazy on the glass door, excited to see me home. I let her in and gave her some love.

"Where's Tortoise?" I asked Cloud. I had expected to walk into yet another intense session of Tortoise playing Urban Insurgence.

"He ran to deliver some weed."

I sat down on the couch next to Cloud. "So, what's going on with Nate?"

He's home, so I guess that's good," Cloud said, sarcasm lining his voice.

"Has he talked to Ryan?"

"Yeah, they have an appointment Tuesday morning."

"Ryan's the fucking bomb, bro. There's nobody better. He'll take care of it."

"Yeah." Cloud was distant and distracted. "The cops are really fucking with him, though. They are telling him twenty-five years unless he tells them where he got all the shit."

"Dude, there's no way." I really didn't want to think about all this right now. I knew they'd use scare tactics to get Nate to point the finger, and it made me nervous as hell. "He's a juvie with no priors. They're just fucking with him."

"Yeah, I know." Cloud shook his head. "But it's working. They've got him scared and depressed as hell."

"What do you mean, it's working?" I snapped.

"Dude, he's not gonna roll!" Cloud snapped back. "They've just got him freaked the fuck out, that's all."

I took a deep breath and counted to five while Cloud was talking. Emotions were running high, and I had to remind myself not to fall victim to that. I had to set the pace, mentally and emotionally, for this situation. I thought for a minute. "I should talk to him."

Cloud gave me a sideways look. "You can't talk to him. What are you gonna do? Go over there? You know they've gotta be watching him, and I'm sure they've fucked with his phone by now."

"Do you know any of his other bros very well?"

"Yeah, most of them." Cloud narrowed his eyes. "Why?"

"I've got an idea." I pulled my phone out of my pocket to call Melissa. "Who do trust to take him a phone?"

"River," Cloud said. He knew what I was thinking. "Definitely River; he's as solid as they come."

"All right, give him a call and ask him if he'll come by."

When I called Melissa, she sounded thrilled to hear from me, like she always did. "Are you back?" she asked.

"Yeah, we just rolled in a few minutes ago."

"Awesome." She was just as relieved as the rest of us. "So, what's up?"

"I have a favor to ask. Can you swing by?"

"I'm on my way." She didn't even question it.

Cloud was watching me like a hawk. I looked him straight in the eye, demonstrating strength and confidence. "I want River to take Melissa's phone to Nate and have him call me on it."

"All right." Cloud sat forward on the edge of the couch. "Dude, I think this is the best idea. Nate really needs talk to you."

"I know." I thought for a second. "Here's the thing, though—Holmes can't know about any of this. It'll trip him out."

"Yeah, I know."

"He's gonna be here any minute. When Melissa gets here, I'm gonna take her in the other room and tell her what's going on. She can give you her phone, and you give it to River when he gets here. He just needs to hang out with Nate while I talk to him and then bring the phone back later today. You got it?'

"Yeah, I got it."

Holmes knocked at the door, and Jefe went to let him in. "Hey, Kyd!" Holmes came bouncing in with a half rack of Fat Tire under his arm, knowing he had tens of thousands dollars waiting for him in my bedroom.

"Everything work out?" he asked, already knowing the answer.

"Yeah, no problems."

"You ready for some brews?"

"Sure."

He walked into the kitchen, took four beers out of the box, and stuck the rest in the fridge. He came back into the den and handed one to each of us. "Cheers!" He held up his beer, and we all clanked bottles. "So, you want to get this over with?" he asked, referring to the tedious yet necessary money-counting mission.

"Might as well," I said.

Jefe, Holmes, and I went into my room and shut the door. I

pulled my backpack out of the closet and dumped bundles and bundles of cash onto the floor.

Holmes's face lit up. "Fuck, yeah. Nice run, Kyd!"

"Not so bad," I agreed. I picked up one of the bundles and pulled off the rubber band. "They're thousand-dollar bundles. I figure we'll just do this like we always do— count the bundles, make sure they're a solid grand, and then stack them over there." I pointed to the corner of my room. "Then we'll count the bundles."

"Sounds good to me." Holmes and Jefe each grabbed a bundle and slid the rubber band off and onto their wrists.

We had only been counting a few minutes when Cloud knocked on my bedroom door and stuck his head in. "Hey, Kyd. Melissa's here. You want me to tell her to come back in a little bit?"

"Nah, I'll be right out." I set my bundle down. "You guys keep counting. I'll be back." I walked into the den, where Melissa was sitting in a chair across from Cloud. She jumped up and gave me a huge hug; I kissed her head.

I spoke softly so they couldn't hear me in the other room. "Did Cloud tell you what's going on?"

"No." A look of concern spread across her face as she sat back down on the couch.

"It's all good," I said, trying to put her at ease. "I need to borrow your phone for a little while."

She looked a little confused but was willing to do whatever I asked.

"I need to talk to Nate," I explained, "and it's not safe to call him from my phone or anyone else's here. I'm gonna have someone take your phone to him, so he can call me from it."

"O ... kay," she said tentatively.

I could tell she was a little nervous. I took her hand and gave it a gentle squeeze. "It's all right. I just need to calm him down and let him know everything is cool."

She pulled the phone out of her purse and handed it to me. "Whatever you need."

"I'll have it back for you tonight. You can use mine today if you need to."

"I won't need it."

I looked at Cloud and then Melissa. "And let's keep this to ourselves. No need to cause everyone more angst than they already have."

Melissa nodded and stood up, saying she had errands to run. "Can I come back by in a couple of hours?" she asked.

"Of course." God, she was sweet. "We'll probably go out to dinner later. You want to come with us?"

"Sure."

"Bring Becca, if you want." Becca didn't bother me, and I knew Tortoise wouldn't mind. But most of all, if I were Melissa I would probably feel a little more comfortable having another girl around. Collectively, our pack could be a lot of testosterone to deal with.

"Okay."

I walked her to the door, gave her a kiss, and told her I would see her later. Then I handed her phone to Cloud. "When River gets here, just give him this phone and tell him the plan. Nate can call me any time. I'll just step out and talk to him."

Jefe and Holmes were sitting on the floor, Indian-style, when I walked back into my room. On one side of each of them was a huge pile of cash.

"Hey, grab us another beer while you're up." Holmes instructed.

I went into the kitchen and took three more beers out of the half rack. "You want another beer?" I shouted to Cloud, who was back in front of the TV in the den.

"Sure."

I took one more out and walked in to hand it to Cloud. "When's River supposed to be here?"

"He's on his way."

"You wanna make a beer run when he leaves?"

"Sure."

"Just get whatever you want." I handed him fifty bucks.

About fifteen minutes later I heard the doorbell. Jefe and Holmes looked at me questioningly. "Cloud's buddy is stopping by," I said. "It's cool." That put them at ease, and we went back to counting money. Not too long after that, Cloud knocked on my bedroom door. "Tortoise and I are gonna run to the store for some beer," he said, poking his head into the room. "You guys want anything else?"

"Would you grab me some smokes?" Holmes reached in his pocket and pulled out a twenty. "Camel Lights."

"Sure."

"Grab some for me too." I gave him another twenty. "Why don't you just pick up a carton."

"All right." He stuffed the money in his pocket. "I'll be right back."

We sat there for a while, absorbed in our counting session. When my phone rang, "Melissa" came up on the caller ID so I knew it was Nate. "Hello."

"Hey, it's me."

"Hey, man," I said brightly. "Just a second, bro." I stood and said to Jefe and Holmes, "I gotta take this call—it's business. I'll be right back." I stepped outside and shut the bedroom door behind me. "How ya doin'?" I asked Nate.

I heard him sigh, and when he spoke, he sounded tired and fragile. "Not so good, man. I'm pretty fucked. Unless I tell them where I got all that shit, they're gonna try me as an adult. They say I'll be a felon and go to prison for a long time."

"They're just trying to scare you, Nate." I tried to sound as confident and strong as I possibly could. I needed to be just as convincing as the cops. "You're a juvenile, and you don't have any priors. They can't do that."

"I'm seventeen, man. I'm right on the line. They said that

with everything I had on me, they will most likely try me as an adult."

"Ryan's working on it, and he's the best. He's a fucking miracle worker. I've seen him get people off for some insane shit—way more intense than what you've got going on." I was nervous about it too, but I couldn't let him sense that. "Hang in there, man. It's always the worst right in the beginning, but it'll cool down. Trust me; it'll cool down. Just hang tough. What did Ryan tell you?"

"He told me to hang in there; he said that in situations like this, time was your best friend. He said that next month they'll be focusing on someone or something else. He told me to try not to worry."

"I told you—Ryan is good. He doesn't fuck around."

"Yeah, I know. I just ..." His voice started to crack and tremble, and I could tell he was starting to cry. "I just love you guys. I never wanted to do anything to hurt you. I'm scared. They're really fucking with me. I'm sorry."

"Hey, man, listen ... you didn't do anything wrong. I know you love us; we love you too. We're family. But we all play this game, and we all know the potential consequences. You just took a stumble, that's all. And I'm gonna help you get back up, okay? It's gonna be all right, Nate; I promise." I couldn't believe I just promised him something I had no way of controlling. I didn't mean to lie, but I could picture him sitting on the edge of his bed, scared and crying, counting on me to make it all better. The truth of the matter was, I was just as scared. It was fucked up, and there was no guarantee he would come out of it without some pretty harsh consequences, but I couldn't let him sink into that darkness. I had to do everything in my power to hold him up. "You just gotta hang tough, buddy. Meet with Ryan on Tuesday, and I'll figure out a way to get a phone to you so we can talk that afternoon. I'm gonna call him tomorrow and make sure everything is rolling smoothly, all right?" Nate didn't answer. He was crying softly on the other end. I used the softest, most calming voice I could pull up. "All right?"

"All right," he finally whispered. "I just love you guys ... and miss you."

"We love you too." I felt a lump rising in my throat. I just wanted to give him a hug, to rescue him, and to pop a cap in that motherfucking pig of a cop that busted him. "We're not going anywhere, bro." I hoped I sounded upbeat, positive, and confident. "You'll be over here drinking beers in no time, okay?"

"Okay." His voice was flat and didn't sound the least bit convinced. He was just answering my prompts and telling me what I wanted to hear.

I got off the phone feeling completely depressed and anxious. I walked into the bathroom, thinking I might throw up. I splashed some cold water on my face, sat down on the lid of the toilet for a minute, and tried to collect myself. I knew if I didn't get back to Jefe and Holmes soon, they would start to wonder what was going on. I heard Cloud and Tortoise come in the front door, and then Jefe and Holmes in the den, talking with them. I took a couple of deep breaths, trying to center myself, and then went out to join the pack.

"Yeah, I see how you are," Holmes joked as I walked in. "Hiding out in the bathroom, leaving us to do all the shit work."

"Sorry, man," I said sheepishly. "I've been waiting for that call."

"I'm just fucking with you, bro." He slapped me on the shoulder and gave me a beer. "Jefe and I've been doing all right in there, but we're not done."

Jefe rolled his eyes and nodded his head. "Let's bust this shit out," he said, leaning backward to stretch his back. "Get it over with."

The three of us went back to my bedroom and started back in on the bundles.

I heard the doorbell a little while later. A couple of minutes after that, Cloud knocked at my bedroom door and poked his head inside. "River stopped by to see you, but I told him you were in the middle of something," he said, cueing me that he had Melissa's phone back. "He said he would give you a call later."

"Cool." I didn't look up; I just kept flipping through cash.

"I gotta break for a minute," Jefe said. He leaned his head back to stretch his neck.

"Let's take five," I said. My eyes were starting to cross, and my knees were stiff and felt stuck in their crossed-over position. I stood and followed Jefe into the kitchen for a beer.

There was a knock at the front door, and I knew it was Melissa but looked out the peephole anyway. She was standing there with Becca, and I opened the door feeling excited that she was back. "Hey," she said, flashed her broad grin. "Are you still busy?"

"We're just about done."

"Hey," Tortoise called to Becca, and I could tell he was excited she had come along.

"You two want to hang out in here with Cloud and Tortoise while we finish up? There's plenty of beer in the fridge, and I've got some vodka and tonic."

"Sure."

Cloud walked over to Melissa and discreetly laid her phone on the coffee table. She looked at it and smiled.

"I'm starving!" Jefe said as he opened and closed kitchen cabinet doors, nosing around for something to eat. "We never have any food around here!" His blood sugar was dropping, and he was getting cranky.

"Let's get this over with and go get some dinner," I said as I stuck a phat nugget in the pipe and handed it to Melissa.

"Sounds good to me," Holmes said. He had already pounded his beer and was reaching in the fridge for another one. "Anyone else want one?"

We sucked down the ones we had and each grabbed one more for our cash-counting finale.

"Make yourself at home." I handed Melissa a lighter. "There's ice in the freezer. We won't be long." I laid some Vicodin, Valium, and another nugget in the middle of the coffee table.

Holmes eyed the money that was stacked in front of us. "Forty-nine thousand. Not a bad run, huh, Kyd?" He looked like a child let loose in Wonka's chocolate factory. "So you're keeping that five pounds toward your profit?"

"Yeah," I said, walking to my safe. "So I owe you seven thousand, right?"

"Forty-nine and seven is fifty-six thousand," Holmes said, scribbling the numbers on a piece of paper to make sure.

I gave him the seven thousand dollars, and he began stacking the bundles of cash inside one of his duffels.

Jefe rubbed his eyes and shook his head like there was something loose in there he was trying to jar back into place. "Dude, I'm glad we're done, because there is no way I could possibly count any more fucking money." He stood up slowly, and his knees popped as they went into standing position. "And I'm fucking starving."

"We're almost done." I said calmly, feeling like the mother of a fussy child. "Why don't you go tell Cloud and Tortoise to get ready if they want to go eat."

He walked into the other room, and I heard him deliver my message.

Holmes finished stacking all the cash into his duffel. "Nice fucking job, Kyd!" He smiled and gave me a high-five. "Not such a bad business we're in."

14

Tortoise was playing Urban Insurgence again, and everyone was watching. "Check this out," he said, as his character, Sux2BU, walked through the strip club, past naked ladies swinging off poles, and into a dark room where the boss, Uncle Smiley, sat on the far side of a large oval table, with three men in dark suits standing behind him.

"You are doing very well in this business." Uncle Smiley leaned back, resting his elbows on the arms of his chair. He clasped his hands in front of his chest, gently interlacing his fingers. "I hear you know many people and have been doing your own jobs on the side."

"It doesn't interfere with the work I do for you," Sux2BU answered defensively.

"It's unacceptable!" Uncle Smiley leaned forward, dropping his hands down. "All jobs must be run through me. I am the boss! You work for me!"

The incredibly lifelike cartoon character, Sux2BU, raised his voice in defiance. "I make you plenty of money. What's the problem with me making a couple of bucks on the side? It's not hurting you."

"I am the boss!" Uncle Smiley stood up and pounded his fist on the table. "I give the orders, and you obey them".

Sux2BU reached inside his coat and took out his Uzi. "Not anymore." He gunned Smiley down.

Tortoise was hooting and hollering at the boss he had just gunned down, who was lying in a pool of blood, face down on the table. "Who's your daddy now, bitch? You sorry motherfucker!"

Sux2BU turned and walked out of the room. On his way back through the strip club, he grabbed the hand of some topless chick and led her into a small room. He sat down in a chair, unzipped his pants, and she kneeled down in front of him. He leaned back in the chair as her head bobbed up and down in his lap.

"How do you like that, bitch?" Tortoise yelled in frenzied excitement. The rest of the boys were laughing and chiming in with lewd comments.

Becca smiled, but I could tell it made her uncomfortable. A little twinge of feeling bad for her shot through me. "Watch your fucking talk around the ladies," I said sternly to Tortoise.

"Sorry," he answered and looked at Becca apologetically.

"Come on, kids." I stood up to grab my hoodie. "Jefe's about to starve to death. Let's go eat." I walked over to the sliding glass door, and put Stella in the backyard.

"All right," Tortoise said, his eyes still glued to the screen. "Where're we going?"

"Luigi's," I answered.

"Sick!"

I knew everyone would be stoked. Luigi's was the bomb.

"Dude, I'm fucking pimpin', yo," Tortoise gloated. Cloud held up the TV remote with his finger on the power button. "No! I gotta save this shit, yo," Tortoise exclaimed as he quickly pushed buttons before Cloud had a chance to destroy his alter ego, SUX2BU, and the make-believe world that accompanied it.

"I'm gonna turn it off. Ten, nine, eight ..." Cloud counted down.

"All right, all right, just a second." Tortoise saved his game, and Cloud turned off the TV.

Jefe, Melissa, Holmes, and I piled into my car. Cloud, Tortoise, and Becca climbed into Cloud's truck. I called Luigi on the way and asked him if he would hold our table.

"Yes, Kyd, of course," he said, in his thick Old-World Italian accent. "It will be so good to see you."

"Yeah, you, too. Thanks."

Luigi was a super guy. He grew up in Italy and only had moved to the States about ten years ago. He bought this very cool, older one-story house near downtown Boulder and turned it into a totally authentic mom-and-pop type of Italian restaurant. His wife did the cooking, and he was the was face man, always out on the floor, greeting and seating customers, visiting, and making sure everyone had everything they wanted. Anytime you went to Luigi's, he made you feel like a king.

I loved the feel of Luigi's with its deep-red walls, plush red velvet chairs, Las Vegas-style carpet, and heavy drapes. He had some overhead lighting but kept it very dim so as not to interrupt the ambiance generated by the myriad candles burning throughout the restaurant. Their flames danced to the soft violin music that always sounded a little crackly and scratchy, like it was being played through some old Victrola.

"Welcome, welcome," Luigi greeted us. He sat us at our regular table back in the corner of the restaurant. He gave us each a menu, disappeared into the kitchen, and came back with four baskets of breadsticks. "Some wine for my friends?" He looked at me, his face beaming with delight. "I have a very good Chianti I know you would like."

"Sounds good, Luigi," I said. "Why don't you bring us a few bottles."

"Very good!" he said and disappeared into the kitchen again. A younger kid walked out holding a tray with several glasses of water. He set one in front of each of us. I opened my menu and looked at it, even though I ordered the same thing every time.

"What do you like?" Melissa asked as she rested her hand on my thigh.

"Chicken Parmesan." I closed my menu and laid it on the table. "It's the bomb!" The young kid came back with wine glasses, and Luigi followed close behind with three bottles of wine. He opened one and poured a little into my glass. I swirled it around, held the glass to my nose, inhaling the smoky, sweet aroma, took a sip, and nodded approval to Luigi. He filled my glass and then walked around the table, pouring wine for everyone else. He opened the other two bottles and set them in the middle of the table.

"Are you ready to order? Or should I give you a little more time?" Luigi stood at the end of the table, looking over us. "I think I know what Kyd will be having," he said, smiling at me.

I smiled back at him. "Chicken Parmesan."

"Very good!" He went around the table taking everyone else's order and then disappeared back into the kitchen.

Being at Luigi's always made me feel like mafioso, and I loved that. I looked around the table at my crew, all smiling, happy, and carefree. I thought about Jefe and me, delivering all that weed and picking up all that cash, and what a party it all was—what a rush, the ultimate high. I thought about how I would take some ganja to Texas in a few weeks and trade it for blow, and bring the blow back to Colorado and make even more money, profiting on both sides of the deal—*cha-ching!* I thought about Tony Montana and Tony Soprano, and I felt a surge of power. My ego expanded as I thought about how smart I was, and how lucky I was, and how careful I had to be, living the life of an outlaw. I wondered how anyone could possibly ever be happy working for the man, slaving away for their ten or twelve bucks an hour or thirty-five or forty thousand a year. Holmes had just made sixty thousand in two days off of about six weeks' work, with relatively low overhead, and he was headed back to Oregon to snowboard and chill and wait another six weeks for his next harvest, followed by his next trip to see me and his next sixty grand. I loved living outside the law and felt eternally grateful to Rico Consuelo and his brothers for teaching me how to sell drugs.

This is what it was all about—hustling hard for a few days, making a quick ten, twenty, fifty-six thousand dollars and then taking your bros to a nice dinner with as many bottles of red wine as you could drink. And with Luigi, his white dishtowel draped over his shoulder, waving you in, smiling and asking if there was anything else you wanted. I leaned back in my seat and delighted in the satisfaction I felt at having my primal need for comfort and security met.

We polished off dinner, and the young boy came over and started clearing our plates. "Everything good?" Luigi asked as he walked up to our table.

"Delicious, as always," I answered.

"Will you all be moving to the cigar room?" Luigi knew our tradition.

"Yes, and could we get a few more bottles of wine?"

"Of course. I'll bring them in." Luigi was heading back to the kitchen, but Holmes stopped him and whispered something. Luigi nodded and went on his way.

With our bellies full and with a warm red-wine buzz, we walked down the hallway to a dimly lit room with a large dark-mahogany humidor in the corner. It held various brands of cigars, some Sherman cigarettes, and a little pipe tobacco. Aside from the humidor, there were two plush red-velvet couches and four large matching chairs. There was a large oval dark-mahogany coffee table in the center of the room and various other little end tables on the sides of the couch and chairs. All the tables had glass tops that were perfect for railing out phat lines of cocaine while you sipped a little more red wine and let your stuffed belly start to digest. The room didn't have any windows, but Luigi had a killer ventilation system in there, so the smoke was never really a problem. We made ourselves comfortable, and then Luigi knocked on the other side of the large wooden door—he always knocked and then waited a few seconds before he came in. He carried in three more bottles of wine, opened them, and set them in the center of the coffee table. "Montecristo?" he asked me and smiled.

"Yes, thank you."

He unlocked the humidor and passed one around to each of us. "I will be back in a little bit to see if you need anything else."

Holmes rested his hand on his stomach as he lay his head on the back of the chair. "Damn, that was some good shit!"

"Fuck, yeah!" Cloud said. He filled a glass with wine and passed it to Tortoise.

I took the other bottle and filled glasses for Melissa, Jefe, and me. I cut the end off my cigar, lit it, and reached into my pocket for the bag of cocaine—it was part of the tradition. Melissa smiled as she watched me pull it out.

"Nice!" Tortoise said when he saw it.

I poured a little pile onto the glass tabletop and railed out seven lines. I rolled up a hundred-dollar bill, took a line, and handed the bill to Melissa. She snorted hers and then everybody else took turns, coming around for theirs.

"Dude, I don't know ..." Holmes said, his head still resting on the back of the chair. "I'm already feeling pretty bombed. I gotta get up and drive tomorrow."

"A little bit will probably make you feel better," Tortoise said sincerely.

Holmes somewhat reluctantly stood and came over to take his line.

We drank our wine, took a couple more rails, wiped the cocaine remnants off the glass tabletop, and were puffing on our cigars when there was another knock at the door. A few seconds later Luigi cracked it open and poked his head through. "Is everything good?" he asked as he walked in the room.

"Yeah, Luigi, everything's fine." I was just about to ask for the check, but he walked over to Holmes and handed him the small black book.

"I was gonna get that," I said and reached my hand toward him.

Luigi smiled at us as we argued over the check. "I'll be back to take care of that in a couple of minutes."

Holmes held up his hand, palm facing me, giving me the "back off" hand signal. "I got it," he said as he pulled a wad of cash out of his pocket. He laid several hundred dollars inside the book.

"Thanks, man," I said.

"Thanks, Holmes," everyone else echoed.

Holmes gave a modest nod and said, "I'm gonna head back to the room. I gotta hit the road early." Holmes wasn't used to our style of kicking it.

"Yeah, I'm feeling pretty beat too," I said. We finished our wine, paid Luigi, and headed out to the parking lot. "Call me along the way, Holmes."

"Yeah, I will." He gave me a hug. "See you in six weeks." He smiled and climbed into his car.

15

I couldn't believe it—I'd forgotten how to count. I had all this money in front of me, a whole pile of it, and I couldn't remember what I was supposed to do with it. I kept picking it up, holding it, and flipping through it. I hoped it would come to me, so the guys sitting across from me, watching, wouldn't think I was a freak. I tried to take my eyes off the money and give them a very chill 'I'm just checkin' it all out' look, but my head was heavy, and I couldn't lift it up. I started to feel anxious and panicky and just wanted to gather the pile up in my arms and go. But my vision was all discombobulated, and I couldn't stand up. I kept trying to gather the money, to remember how to count ... and then I heard Tortoise.

"Kyd? Kyd?"

I tried to look behind me, because I knew he was there, but my head was too heavy, like a bowling ball, and I couldn't lift or turn it. My surroundings began to fade, and I felt myself detaching, like I was being sucked into a tunnel. I felt a hand on my shoulder, gently shaking me. My eyes opened with a jump, and I saw Melissa.

"Shhh." She knew I was startled and comforted me with her soft voice and reassuring touch. "It's okay," she whispered. "Tortoise is at the door."

He knocked again. "Kyd?"

"What's up?" I called to him.

He cracked open the door, gently pushing Stella out of the way, and poked his head in. His eyes were wide and vacant; he looked dazed.

Something wasn't right, and I felt a knot tie in my gut. "What's wrong?" I asked him.

He stood there for a second, silently, looking dazed and confused. His mouth opened, but it took him a few seconds before the words came out. "Nate's dead."

"Wha-at?" My psyche immediately slammed the door on such a possibility.

"Cloud just got off the phone with his mom." He spoke softly and in a monotone. "He killed himself."

I was stunned. I felt like someone had just punched me in the stomach. Every muscle in my body tightened, and the knot in my gut turned into a burning hole. "What ... do you mean?" is all I could get out.

Tortoise's eyes welled with tears. "She found him in the bathtub," he whispered, as the tears began to stream down his cheeks.

I couldn't respond. I didn't want to believe it. I saw Nate's face in my mind's eye, happy, smiling, joking around, looking up at all of us with such respect, love, and admiration. He'd just wanted our approval, just wanted to be included, to be a part of us. This couldn't be right; it had to be a mistake. Nate couldn't be dead. He was so young and full of life. Melissa gently squeezed my arm. "Where's ... Cloud?" I asked.

"I don't know." Tortoise wiped his eyes—eyes that pleaded with me for some direction. "He took off right after he told me." Tortoise lowered his eyes and shook his head. When he looked back up at me, and my heart sank into the hollow of my gut, and I was consumed by the fear and sadness I saw on his face. "Cloud's fucked up, dude."

"Let me put some clothes on," I said, starting to function on autopilot. "I'll be right out." I hopped out of bed and grabbed the first pair of pants and shirt I saw laying on the floor.

Melissa looked at me, her face pale, tears filling her eyes and spilling down her cheeks. "Oh my god." I knew she didn't know what to say, and neither did I.

I sat down on the bed next to her and gave her hand a gentle squeeze. "This is fucked up," I whispered. It was all I could manage to say. I grabbed my phone and walked into the den.

Tortoise was sitting on the couch, hunched over, with his head in his hands. Becca sat next to him, teary-eyed, gently rubbing his back. "Where's Jefe?" I asked.

"I just got him up," he said without looking up at me. I opened my cell phone and called Cloud.

He answered, sobbing. "This is so fucked! It's fucking wrong!"

"Dude, I know." I didn't know what to say. I knew I needed to talk him down, but my mind went blank. "You gotta come home, man. We should all be together right now."

"What the fuck do you know?" Cloud demanded. "You didn't know him! You didn't care about him!"

"You gotta get home, bro," I said gently as I listened to his heaving sobs on the other end of the phone. "I'm so sorry. Please ... I'm afraid you're gonna do something stupid, and that's not gonna help anything right now."

"You didn't care about him! He was protecting you!" he screamed. "You motherfucker!"

"I did care about him. I know I wasn't as close to him as you were, but I loved him too." I sat there taking the daggers Cloud threw, feeling them stab into my heart and slowly slip down, tearing it open. But I knew he was hurting. "Please come home. We need you here."

"Fuck you! You stupid motherfucker!" He hung up.

Jefe was sitting on the couch next to Tortoise, looking like a lost child. I sat down next to him, put my head in my hands, and started to cry. Nobody said anything, but I felt Jefe's hand gently patting my back. I know it freaked out him and Tortoise to see me break like that, because it never happened. I was always the calm, centered one. I was the rock, but what Cloud said had hurt me. It hurt because it was the truth. Nate died to protect us, and I knew that. I would have done whatever was in my power to take care of him. I mean, I would have paid his fines, and even if he had to do some time or probation or community service or classes, at some point it would have been over. But it just got to him. *They* got to him. I just wished I could have talked to him again, one more time, to reassure him that it wasn't the end of the world.

Melissa came out and sat in the chair across from me. She didn't say anything; she just looked at me through pain-ridden eyes. It was devastating and awful and painful for all of us. There are no words.

Nate was cremated. He loved being outdoors—snowboarding, hiking, camping, and kayaking—and his mother scattered his ashes in some of his favorite spots. Cloud took some to the top of the mountain and although I doubt he'll ever totally get over Nate's death, I think it helped him gain some closure. Nate's mom had a memorial service at her sister's house. It was a beautiful spring day, with birds chirping, bees buzzing, flowers budding—the energy and zest of life all around us. We sat around all afternoon, talking about him, sharing funny and touching stories, toasting champagne, and celebrating his life. I know his mother suspected that we had something to do with the reason for his death, and I could feel some tension as she tried to struggle past that and into the space where she knew we loved him. She was an old hippie from the '70s, who grew pot, followed The Dead, was a member of the Rainbow Family, pickled her brain with myriad drugs, and continued to be antiestablishment. She knew.

Nate's suicide seemed very surreal, and it was hard to let go of the feeling that at any minute, he was going to come bouncing back through the door with a gleaming smile and excited eyes, looking up at us with such love and admiration. I couldn't help but wonder if I would be punished with infinite feelings of depression and doom for having let him down in some way, for not doing enough to protect and save him. But then my hard, rational side would step in and say, "Kyd, Nate was an adult, and you never forced him into anything. He grew up in and around the business, and if he wasn't hanging out and getting shit from you guys, then he would have been hanging out and getting shit from someone else."

He always seemed to get plenty of shit from other people anyway—people we didn't even know. Nate sought out the business of his own accord. He wanted it; he was good at it. And anyone who steps into it knows there are consequences. They might choose not to think about them or they might push those unsavory thoughts down to the tips of their toes, but on some level, they know.

My attempts to excuse myself from responsibility for Nate's death made me feel mean and cold, and I actually harbored guilt for those thoughts. But I had to find a way to objectively rationalize the situation, to talk myself out of its somehow being my fault. It fucked with my head. It fucked with all our heads—but no one as much as Cloud. My heart bled for him. He walked around the house for weeks like a zombie, hardly speaking to any of us. He told us Nate's death wasn't our fault, but we knew he didn't really mean it. He wanted to believe it; he wanted that to be his truth. But it was not, and the heated energy that continued to emanate from him and vibe in our direction was confirmation of it. Cloud was pissed—pissed at Nate dying; pissed at the heartless, vengeful universe for taking him; pissed at life for being so unjustly mean and cruel; and pissed at us. I think that on a rational level, Cloud told himself all of the same things that I told myself to justify the situation, but he needed something to be mad at—somewhere to put all his sorrow, anger, and negativity. I wasn't surprised when he told us he was moving to Utah. He said he needed a complete change of environment and he really loved Brighton. I was sad to see him go and felt that his leaving us signified an unraveling of things, and that made me feel anxious, uneasy, and moderately depressed.

Throughout the months that followed, I too felt I needed a change, but I struggled to push the idea out of my mind, because I didn't like the change I was sensing. A hollow, quiet throbbing told me things weren't right. After Nate's death, I felt like there was probably some heat on us, and my instincts that told me to get out of the business were unsettling, because it made me think—if I wasn't selling drugs, what would I do? Who would I be? I never could imagine being "normal," enjoying some mundane, black-and-white life, stumbling through a less-than-average existence. I am programmed, on some level, to want the luxuries of time, money, respect, and freedom.

I couldn't imagine working at some minimum wage job. And what if I ever wanted to raise a family? It would be a recipe for disaster. It takes both parents working to support a family these days, and the kids are raising themselves. Then, the parents divorce, the kids are now from a broken home, and still raising themselves. Unless you're one of the few upper-class families, and then the nannies and housekeepers raise the kids, while you golf and enjoy garden club. I've never understood why any of us try to be 'normal' when there really is no such thing. The truth of the matter is, you're damned if you do and damned if you don't.

In spite of trying to rationalize my existence in the drug culture, the dull ache in my gut persisted and grew in intensity—it was like the universe was sending a 911 signal. Most people in the drug culture are quick to write off any paranoia about the business. You never let yourself believe that the universe is actually sending you messages to get *out*; instead, you say, "I'm just being paranoid" and push it out as quickly as it came. Still, it sits there, hauntingly pulsing at the very top of your subconscious. I put up a good fight, trying to exorcize my paranoia, but it was strong and determined, and after a few months, it started to wear me down. I was teetering on the edge of throwing up my hands and actually entertaining the idea of thinking of something else to do ... and then my buddy Cedar called.

"I'm thinking about coming down with some friends for a party," he said. That was code for "I came across some Beast, and I was hoping you could move it for me."

"How many people are supposed to be there?" I asked.

"A hundred or so."

"Yeah? What's it cost to get in?"

"The usual."

"Let me make some calls and see if anybody wants to go with me." I told Cedar.

"I already talked to Nico. He's down."

Our regular gig with Cedar wasn't supposed to happen for a few more weeks, but occasionally random shit like this popped up. "You still planning on coming back down in a month or so?" I asked.

"Yeah."

I thought for a second. "Sure, man, sounds like fun."

"Nice!" Cedar sounded stoked. "I'll probably pull out of here tomorrow morning. I doubt I'll push all the way through, but I'll definitely see you by Thursday."

"Sounds good. Give me a call along the way."

"All right. Hey, are you guys going to see Further at Red Rocks this weekend?"

"We talked about it, but haven't bought any tickets yet."

"Why not?" Cedar had seemed disgusted with my recent apathetic attitude toward almost everything. "Get tickets for everybody, and I'll pay you for them when I see you. It's gonna be epic. We can't miss it, bro!"

Cedar's genuine excitement traveled through the phone and started to permeate my body. What was wrong with me? What was I thinking? I couldn't miss Further. Fuck that! "Do Nico and Zack have tickets yet?" I asked.

"I don't think so, but I told him they were going."

"I'll call him and pull it all together."

"So, we're going to the show? You'll handle it?"

"Of course we're going to the show!" I said. "Like we'd miss Further at Red Rocks?" I laughed, lightening the mood. "Don't worry. I have it all worked out by the time you get here."

"You're the man!"

"Drive safe and we'll see you in a couple of days."

I hung up the phone and the warning signals in my gut flared up again at the thought of Cedar's coming to town and my having to scramble to move fifty pounds of Beast on the fly. I tried desperately to drown it out by turning on Sublime and another attempt at rationalizing my "paranoia." I caught myself making a quick promise to the universe that if it would just watch my back a little longer, I really would start to think more seriously about my exit from the drug culture.

16

When I got home, Jefe and Tortoise were in the den watching *Blow*. Stella was lying on the ground next to them but jumped up and ran over to greet me as soon as I opened the door. She never liked it when I left without taking her with me. It hurt her feelings, and she'd just kind of sulk around the house but was always very forgiving and happy to see me when I got back. "You guys want a beer?" I asked as I carried a half rack into the kitchen.

"Yeah!" they answered in unison.

I walked back into the den, handed one to each of them, and sat down on the couch. Jefe opened his and immediately flicked the cap at Tortoise, hitting him in the side of the head.

"Fuck you, dude!" I'm not sure what pissed Tortoise off more—getting smacked in the head with a beer cap or Jefe's laughing his ass off at it. "That shit fucking hurts, asshole!"

Jefe could flick a beer cap like nobody else. It went with amazing force and speed, and he put some kind of spin on it so it made this whizzing, whistling sound as it tore across the room. His caps had left numerous dings in our walls, and on more than one occasion I had seen them break skin.

"Don't be such a pussy," Jefe taunted. He got great enjoyment out of provoking Tortoise.

"Cedar's coming to town," I said, attempting to divert their potential wrestling match.

"Really?" Jefe was surprised. "I thought he wasn't gonna be back for a few more weeks."

"Something came up."

"Is everything okay?" Tortoise sounded concerned, and there was a hint of panic in his voice. Since Nate, we'd all become a little head-shy.

"Yeah, everything's fine. I guess he just came across some more Beast."

"When's he gonna be here?" Jefe asked.

"Thursday. He wants to see Further at Red Rocks this weekend."

"Ah, yeah, man." Jefe was always on board for a show. "We should definitely go!"

"I'm a little strapped right now." Tortoise hung his head, a little embarrassed. It wasn't a huge surprise; he was always broke.

"I'll get the tickets," I said.

"Nice! Thanks, man."

I appreciated his effort at sounding surprised and excited by my offer to pay, even though it was really nothing new. I funded most of our adventures, but it never bothered me. They were my bros, and few extra bucks here and there didn't make a difference in my life.

My phone rang—it was Melissa. She always sounded so excited to talk to me. I asked her to come over.

"Do you need anything?" she asked.

"Nah ... just you." I felt a little stupid saying that, but I really liked her.

"Okay," she said. I could almost feel her blushing through the phone. "See you in a few."

"So, what's he got?" Tortoise asked as I hung up.

"Hmm?" I was preoccupied, thinking of who I needed to call to move the fifty pounds of Beast that would be here in two days.

"Cedar!" Tortoise said, irritated with my spacing off. "What's he bringing?"

"A hundred."

"Can you get rid of it this quick?" Jefe seemed doubtful.

"Nico's taking fifty. It won't be a problem." I always said that, even when I wasn't sure. It was more of a mind-over-matter thing with me. I convinced myself and therefore created that reality.

Cedar gave me pounds of Beast at twelve hundred and fifty dollars each and I sold ten packs at fifteen thousand. Out of the fifty I was getting, I would keep ten pounds myself some of which I would take to Texas for trade. The weed I traded in Texas for cocaine and pills was ultimately my best profit margin, but there was always that trick of actually selling it, especially the coke, before we took it all to the head. I knew the kids in Texas always had plenty of cocaine, pills and cash but were always hurting for ganja. I could probably dump all of it on them if I had to, but I felt pretty sure that my kids around here would be stoked to have some B-grade weed to move too. If I absolutely had to, I could cover the cost for all of it myself, but that would take up the majority of my cash, and I hated tying up all my capital.

I went into my room to count the cash in my safe, and a couple of minutes later Melissa knocked on my bedroom door and poked her head in.

"Hey, come in," I told her. She sat down on the bed and watched quietly as I finished counting my cash. Then I sat down next to her and gave her a hug. She giggled as I kissed her and pushed a piece of hair back from her face, tucking it behind her ear. "Cedar's coming to town," I said.

"When?"

"He should be here Thursday." I had recently sensed that Melissa wasn't totally down with the level of my involvement in our drug culture. She never came out and said anything, but I could tell that the more she grew to like me, the more nervous it made her. I understood; it made me nervous too, but I just pushed those feelings down and ignored them as best I could. "He wants to go to Further this weekend at Red Rocks."

"Oh. Really?"

I was a little surprised by her lack of enthusiasm. She always loved going to shows and was usually the one to jump in, take charge, and plan the whole thing. "Why don't you see if Becca's into it. It'll be fun for the whole family!"

She sat there a second, looking confused and a little sad. "I think I'll skip out on this one," she said reluctantly.

"What's wrong?" I wasn't sure what exactly I was sensing from her, but it made me uncomfortable. She was spacing off, gazing at the floor, and I could see tears welling in her eyes. I put my arm around her. "What's up?" Her long pause was awkward and I felt myself tensing up.

She looked up at me, hesitating, and a single tear rolled down her cheek. "I'm ... late." My chest seized up as the word "late" hung suspended in the air around me. "I should have started my period over a week ago." She looked at the floor, and I knew this was not the time for me to freak out. I put my arms around her and pulled her head into my chest. "I don't want to party until I know something for sure or not," she mumbled through her hair. "And if I go to the show and don't party, then everyone will wonder what's wrong, and I don't want a bunch of questions. Not until I know ... I mean, even if I know, even if I am, it doesn't mean anything. I mean, it doesn't mean I would have it. I mean, if you—"

"It's gonna be okay." I stroked her hair and held her close to me, desperately searching for the right thing to say.

"I don't want you to worry. If I am, we don't have to ..." Her silent tears had turned into soft little sobs that moistened the front of my shirt. "I mean, if you don't ... we can always ..." She didn't look up. "I'd understand."

Stella was lying in the corner of the room. She could sense

that something was wrong and lifted her head, cocked it to one side, and looked at me with those big sympathetic eyes.

The whole situation tugged at me emotionally, and I sat utterly dumbfounded, mechanically stroking her hair, not knowing quite what to do. "Do you think you are?" I tried to ask in my most loving, compassionate voice.

"I don't know." She lifted her head to look at me. The crying was louder now and muddling her words. "I've never been pregnant. I don't know. My period's never late. My boobs are really sore." Her head was buried against my chest again, and she had her right hand tenderly pressed underneath her left breast.

I kissed her head and rubbed her back. "It'll be okay," I whispered. "Just relax. It's gonna be all right." I hoped I was doing a good job of convincing her because on the inside, I was freaking the fuck out. I felt all my internal sensors shut down, not wanting to deal with a potential reality of such intensity. I mean, if she was pregnant, what did that mean to life as I knew it? I pushed that thought out of my head and focused on being the rock I knew she needed right now.

"Don't tell anybody," she said. She looked up and wiped the tears from her eyes and off her cheeks. "Not until we know."

"Okay." I took her hand and wondered what exactly her last statement had meant. "Until we know" ... what? If she was pregnant? If we were gonna keep it? My gut wrenched at the thought of not keeping it, and that surprised me and made me nervous. I had never thought that I wanted a kid, but now, with Melissa possibly being pregnant with my child, the idea actually made me feel warm and fuzzy and hopeful. I hoped she *was* pregnant. Oh fuck! Was I going to be a dad? I had simultaneous feelings of wanting to celebrate and wanting to hurl.

The next day was miserable. All day long I tried like crazy to stay focused, to call all the people I needed to call to get this whole thing with Cedar worked out. That part of everything was going well. My boys in Texas were stoked and had plenty of coke and pills, which I figured they would, and my kids here were hungry and excited, pushing to pull it all together in forty-eight hours. I should've been more excited about Cedar coming to town, but I wasn't. All I could think about was how incredibly fucked up I was. My lifestyle was fine when it was just me, not giving a fuck about anything, but now I might be a dad, and I was actually excited about it.

I loved her. I kept having these little fantasy daydreams of me carrying some kid around with Melissa's auburn curls and Cheshire-cat grin and my hazel color-changing eyes; feeding it; dressing it in baby Etnies, tiny Bob Marley T-shirts, and little zip-up hoodies; gently tossing it up over my head; and it laughing like crazy, having a great time. I started to think I could be a pretty good dad, and maybe this was just what I needed to finally give myself an excuse to get out of the business. But then what?

And my fantasy would come crashing down, and I would be back to the same fucked-up sociopath that I was before. It was a terribly vicious cycle that tantalized and tormented me all day long. I went to sleep that night with a smile on my face from visions of Melissa with a beautiful glow, gently rubbing her growing belly.

Although I continued to experience "paranoid" feelings regarding my involvement in the drug culture, I couldn't wait for Cedar's call to say he was rolling into town. There was something about the game of drug dealing that did offer a comforting distraction, and right now, I needed that. I wanted to get my mind off life for a second.

He finally called on Thursday afternoon, sounding awfully perky for someone who had been on the road with a hundred pounds of ganja for two days, and I welcomed the wave of relief his call brought to me. I'd told Cedar to head to Nico's, but I got there before Cedar did.

Nico grabbed three beers out of the fridge. "He just called and said he's about twenty minutes out."

I sat down on the couch and watched Zack play Tony Hawk. "Watch this, bro!" Zack said. He had his character tie one trick into another for 190,000 points. "That's so fucking sick!" he gloated as his computer-generated skateboarding savant went sailing on.

"You remember Forrest?" Nico asked as he sat down next to me.

"That kid you deejayed for?"

"Yeah. He's got a nice hook on some killer molly out of Switzerland— pure MDMA."

"How much?"

"I think he's letting it go for $2,500 an ounce."

"Is it the same shit we rolled on at his party?"

"Yeah."

"That was pretty sick. Sure, sign me up for an ounce." I knew I could move that in no time. "Is his connection pretty steady?" I wondered if I should get more.

"Ah, yeah, he can get it loads of it any time he wants."

"Nice!" It had been a while since I had a steady molly connect.

A couple minutes later we heard Cedar's motor home pulling in Nico's drive. Nico grabbed a beer out of the fridge for him and we walked outside. "What's up!" Cedar called to us as he jumped out and gave us all a hug.

We shot the shit for a minute and then walked into the motor home to check out the ganja. It was packaged like usual, in medium-sized cardboard boxes filled with ten pounds each. Because Beast was a considerably less expensive, more commercial form of ganja, it was expected to be packed down more than, say, Holmes's chronic weed. People knew not to bitch; that was just the way it came. I asked Nico if I could leave thirty of my fifty pounds at his house overnight. I was planning on taking the twenty pounds home with me, but didn't really feel like trying to pile the entire fifty into my truck. That would mean piling boxes on top of boxes, completely filling the back end, and that seemed a little sketch, especially with all the weird gut feelings I'd been having lately. I hadn't been able to shake my paranoia and was still feeling a little uneasy.

He didn't mind hanging on to it; he said I could leave it there as long as I wanted. Nico had a couple of people waiting on him and needed to get going, so we decided to meet back at my place in a couple of hours. We unloaded the rest of the ganja into his house and made sure everything was locked up. Cedar jumped in the car with Nico and Zack, and we headed in our different directions.

17

Nico, Zack and Cedar showed up at the house a little later and Jefe grabbed at a chance to shine by immediately boasting to Cedar about the Czech. "Yeah, man, this shit is the bomb." Jefe held one of the small sweet-breath droppers to the light, checking to see how much liquid was left inside. "People are chomping for it. I can hardly keep it around."

"Are you sure this shit is coming from the Bay?" Cedar asked skeptically. "My buddy Ben has been up there for years and knows a ton of kids but hasn't been able get his hands on any." Although he was trying to play it cool, Cedar was noticeably perplexed, and we all knew why. He had always bragged how Ben was some kind of ninja drug lord who had ties to everyone who was anyone in the northern California drug culture and could get his hands on anything he wanted. He didn't like the idea that we small-town Colorado foolios might actually be privy to something from that area that his Jedi master Ben couldn't manage to track down. "I want to take a vile back to him." Cedar seemed determined to somehow prove us wrong— that it was not from the Bay, that it was not the Czech, that we didn't really know what we were talking about. Whatever. Like I gave a shit. The whole thing cracked me up.

"I can hook you up," Jefe said, loving his opportunity to be the man.

"What do you want for it?" Cedar's tone and body language, like most everyone else, changed when talking business.

"I've been getting two hundred bucks for it, but for you?" Jefe thought for a minute, reveling in his moment to act like a cunning, scrutinizing businessman. "How 'bout a hundred and twenty five? If you want more than one, I'll need to get one fifty." Cedar raised his eyebrows, maintaining his game face, like he was expecting a better deal. "I'm paying a hundred bucks a vial," Jefe lied and shrugged his shoulders. Nobody ever told the truth about what they paid for something, which is why I never understood why people threw numbers like that around in the first place. Anyone who had half a brain knew that everybody lied, but it happened all the time, like we were all fooling each other or something. It was hysterical to watch, and it cracked me up every time, even when I was the one doing the bullshitting.

"All right," Cedar said reluctantly. He dug a buck twenty-five out of his back pocket. "You guys want to eat some?" Cedar's eyes lit up. The room fell silent, and we all just looked at each other, not knowing exactly how to respond. We all knew that Cedar's track record with psychedelics wasn't the greatest. It was not totally appealing to go into something like that fully aware that you would most likely have to engage in some degree of babysitting while mentally impaired.

"I don't care." Jefe shrugged his shoulders and looked sheepishly around at the rest of us.

I decided to quickly put the suggestion to bed. "I'm not really up for it tonight. I gotta get up early and move that Beast if I'm gonna make it to Further."

"Yeah." Nico followed me up, and I felt a wave of relief. "I've got some more driving around to do tomorrow too."

Cedar shrugged his shoulders and stuck the sweet-breath bottle in his backpack.

"Let's go down to The Cat and shoot some stick," Jefe

suggested. "I think Vanessa's working tonight." He raised his eyebrows with interest.

"Who's Vanessa?" Cedar asked.

"This bartender at The Cat that Jefe's got the hots for," I said, chuckling.

"Dude, she's fucking bomb!" Jefe said defensively. He was right; she was pretty hot and perfect for Jefe—she liked to party. She was a fire-dancer with lots of tattoos and piercings. A little rough around the edges, she was your basic tough girl who didn't take any shit from anyone. Jefe needed a chick like that, someone to put him in his place every now and then. He'd walk all over some mild-mannered meek thing.

"We better go before she falls in love with someone else." Nico laughed, grabbed his hoodie, and we headed out.

I woke up the next morning feeling a little dazed and confused. I held my throbbing head as I stumbled over Stella and into the kitchen, desperate for water to moisten the dry sponge of a tongue that lay swollen and lifeless in my desert-like mouth. I rounded the corner and jumped back in surprise, not having expected to see Vanessa. She was holding a cold beer in one hand as she rifled through our cabinets with the other, and she was wearing nothing but one of Jefe's old T-shirts that barely covered her ass.

"I'm so hungry!" she didn't seem the least bit embarrassed by my presence, so I walked in but made a conscious effort not to gawk at her exposed long, lean, muscular, golden-brown legs that led up to the bottom half of her perfectly cupped ass. Goddamn! Jefe was right. She was smoking. I wasn't attracted to her in a way that I wanted to fuck her right there—or anywhere else, for that matter—but I couldn't help notice her nicely sculpted figure; her long, thick, straight and shiny obsidian hair; her supple skin; her cat-like eyes; and the fact that she wasn't wearing a bra. Jefe's thin T-shirt draped beautifully, perfectly outlining the firm, tight silhouette of her seemingly flawless breasts, profiling their hard little nipples that seemed to be taunting me. "You got any chips or anything?" she said, completely unfazed.

"I think there are some Doritos in there." I pointed to an upper cabinet on her left. She reached, and I tried with all my might not to look at her ass.

"Nice!" She pulled the Doritos out of the cabinet and turned back around to catch me in a losing battle against my will. "You want some?" She smiled coyly and reached toward me holding out the bag of chips.

I felt myself blush and turned my head in the other direction. "No, thanks." I had a flash of how Melissa would not be down with this scenario. Vanessa sucked down the rest of her beer and then opened the fridge and grabbed two more. She tucked the Doritos under her arm and headed back to Jefe's room.

I grabbed a cup out of the cabinet, feeling even more dazed and confused than before, and pounded two glasses of water. I filled it up a third time and went back to my room to masturbate.

It was only about eight o'clock, so I lay there for a while, with a knot in my gut, thinking of Melissa and my possible child and my whole fucked-up reality. I tried to go back to sleep. After tossing and turning for about an hour, I decided I'd better get a move on if I was gonna get Cedar's Beast peddled around town before we headed out for Red Rocks, so I reluctantly pulled my ass out of bed and headed for the shower.

Jefe was going to ride around with me, like usual, so I walked toward his room to make sure he was up and getting his shit together. By the primordial grunts I heard coming from the other side of the door, I figured Vanessa had already taken care of it—at least the "getting up" part anyway. I got out of the shower, went back to my room, got dressed, and called Melissa.

"How are you?" I asked.

"Okay ... I guess." There was hesitation in her voice.

"Okay?" I asked. "What do you mean?"

"I don't know, I got sick this morning."

I felt my chest seize up the same way it did when she told me her period was late. "You threw up?" I knew what she meant. I think I was just clarifying it to myself in some way.

"Yeah. But I feel better now."

"When?"

"Early this morning."

"Are you okay?"

"Yeah. I don't know. Who knows? Maybe it was just something I ate." I was quiet for a second. We both knew that was a bunch of shit. "I'm going to get a pregnancy test today."

"At the doctor?"

"No, just one from the store."

"When?"

"I don't know. Later. I'll call you."

"Do those things work?"

"I've never taken one. My friend Michelle has though."

"Was her's right?"

"Yeah."

"Was she pregnant?"

She hesitated. "Yeah."

Jefe emerged from his chamber of love. "Hey, bro!" He cracked opened the door to my bedroom and poked his flushed face through. "We gonna go sell some weed today or what?" The adrenaline generated from his wild lovemaking fest had manifested into an obvious attitude of male dominance.

"I'm shit, showered, and shaved, bro. Just waiting on you."

"I'll be ready in a few."

Cedar had stayed the night over at Nico and Zack's so I called to see what they were up too. "You guys up?"

"Yeah." Nico sounded like he was hurting a little. "We're gonna go grab some breakfast and then head out to make the rounds. What about you guys?"

"I'm up. Jefe's in the shower, and then I thought we'd swing by your house, so I could pick up those CDs I left last night."

"Cool. If we're not here, you know where the key is?"

"Yeah. Jefe and I have some running around to do, but I should be done by about three or so. I figured we'd just take off for Red Rocks then."

"Sounds good."

A few minutes later there was a knock at my door, and Jefe's face pushed through the crack. "I'm ready."

"Cool." I grabbed my backpack, tucked my scale inside under an old T-shirt, and pulled three larger-sized duffel bags out of my closet. I grabbed some cash out of my safe, stuck it in my pocket, and walked out into the den.

Vanessa was dressed, sitting on the couch, smoking a cigarette, and sucking down another cold beer. Her obsidian hair was tousled and a faint smell of sex and pheromones emanated from her, giving me about half a chub. "You guys are going to Further tonight?"

"Yeah, you should come with us." As soon as I said it I hoped Jefe wouldn't mind my inviting her along.

"I wish I could, but I've got to work all weekend."

"That's too bad." I was relieved she didn't jump on the invitation.

Jefe came bouncing into the room. "You ready?"

"Yeah, we better get a move on."

We took Vanessa home and headed to Nico's. Once we got to Nico's I found the hide-a-key under the rock in the backyard. Jefe and I went in, opened the cardboard boxes filled with Beast, and loaded ten pounds into each of the duffels I had brought. Although it really was the lesser of two evils, a couple of suspicious-looking "heady" kids carrying large duffel bags in and out of houses in the middle of the day seemed less sketch than trying to juggle awkward cardboard boxes. I called the kids we were delivering to and let them know I was on my way.

Jefe and I made our runs and thankfully, it was pretty much hassle-free. We headed back to the house to pick up Tortoise and get our stuff together for Red Rocks. When we got home, we sat down and started to weigh out some of the Beast into half ounces, quarters, and eighths that he wanted to try to get rid of at the show. "You think I should take any Czech?" Jefe asked.

I wasn't stoked about cruising around with a bunch of psychedelics, but he could most likely move them and make a few bucks. "You could probably get rid of a few vials," I answered reluctantly.

"Yeah," he said excitedly and scurried out.

Tortoise walked into my room. "Are you about ready?"

"I just gotta finish breaking up this pound."

"You want some help?"

"Yeah, you want to bag it?" I never asked but always appreciated some help when breaking weight down to smaller quantities. It was a pretty tedious task and moved quite a bit faster if you had one person weighing and one bagging it up.

"Sure." He sat down Indian-style in front of me, and we proceeded with our little assembly line. I'd put the Tupperware on the scale, tare it out, fill it up to the appropriate weight, pass it over to him to stuff in a baggie, put another Tupperware back on the scale, and do it all again.

Once we bagged up all the pot, I went to the kitchen and got a brown paper grocery bag. I went back into my room to make sure I had all the cash I owed Cedar for the Beast. First, I thumbed through all the thousands, checking to see that they were all faced and bundled in brown rubber bands. Then, I bundled ten thousands, stuffing them in white legal-size envelopes, also held together by large brown rubber bands.

After I double-checked, making sure it was all there, I started to load the ten-thousand-dollar white envelopes into the brown paper bag. I was right on and had plenty of my own capital left—just the way I liked it.

I grabbed my backpack, a couple of shirts, a hoodie, an extra pair of pants, a glass pipe, and my Tupperware full of ganja and pharmies. I filled my bullet with cocaine and carefully stuffed it all in.

Tortoise and Jefe already had my truck loaded with all our camping gear and were sitting on the couch, drinking a beer, waiting for me. "You guys ready?" I asked, already knowing the answer.

"Fuck, yeah!" Tortoise jumped up and headed for the garage.

"You ready?" I looked at Stella and clapped my hands. She jumped around in a circle, excited because she knew we were headed on another adventure.

"We need to stop and get some beer." Jefe was diligent about taking responsibility for the most important things.

"We will. Let's just get to Nico's first, okay?"

"All right." He grabbed the last few beers out of the fridge, and we all piled into my rig.

We pulled up to Nico's, where Cedar was busy loading gear into to the motor home. "I thought we'd all just ride together," he said as he carried two small propane bottles up the steps. Jefe, Tortoise, and I all looked at each other and shrugged our shoulders.

"All right," Jefe said. He walked around to the back of my truck, opened it, and started pulling out our stuff.

"Dude, I'll take care of it." Cedar was serious and very focused on his important task at hand. "I've got a system."

Jefe raised his hands, backing off and giving Cedar the green light to take control.

"Where's Zack and Nico?" I asked

"In the garage, looking for the big cooler." Cedar was like a soldier marching forward with his mission, not stopping to engage in frivolous conversation.

I reached into the back end of the truck and dug out the brown paper sack with his sixty-two thousand five hundred dollars. "Here you go, bro.'" I trailed behind him to the motor home and tried handing it to him.

"What's that?" he asked with half interest.

"It's your cash."

"Oh." He carried a tent and backpack onto the motor home and came back out. "Thanks, bro." He glanced at it and headed back to my truck. "Just set it down."

Even though it was typical Cedar behavior to not really be all that concerned with something like a sixty-two thousand five hundred dollars in a brown paper bag, I was still surprised by his nonchalance. "Don't you think you should put this up somewhere?"

"Would you take it in and ask Nico to stash it somewhere for me?" He continued forging ahead, dutifully loading the motor home.

"All right," I agreed. I knew he'd probably never even count it and not just because it was from me—that was just Cedar. He'd been very lucky.

I walked around the side of the house. Zack was holding the cooler open at a tilt as Nico sprayed out the inside of it. They both looked up as I approached. "Hey, man," Nico said, continuing to spray the cooler. "I guess you saw that Cedar decided we're taking the motor home.

"Yeah, he's getting it all packed up."

Nico laughed and shook his head. "Yeah, just stay out of his way. He's got it all figured out."

"He told me to give this to you to stash." I held out the paper sack. Nico knew what it was. He finished spraying the cooler and tilted it upside down with the lid propped open so the water could drip out.

"Did he even look at it?" Nico asked.

"What do you think?"

Nico rolled his eyes, took the sack, and disappeared into the house. He returned a couple of minutes later with three beers and a towel over his shoulder.

"You should call Forrest. He's looking for some coke," Nico said.

"Really?" I was excited that the prospect of my earlier fantasy about making loads of cash selling mad quantities of cocaine to Forrest might actually come to fruition.

"Yeah. He was asking me if I knew where he could get any. He's got that molly connect, and I figured you guys could do some business together."

"Nice!"

"I haven't said anything to him yet. I wanted to talk to you first."

"Cool."

"You want his number?"

"Sure."

Nico pulled out his cell phone and read me the number as I programmed it into mine. "I'll let him know you're gonna give him a call," Nico said.

"Thanks."

Zack wiped the cooler down, and we carried it around the house to the motor home.

Jefe couldn't help himself. He was having a ball taunting Cedar by telling him he was doing it all wrong. "Dude, if you put the tents and sleeping bags in first, then you're gonna have to set the coolers on top. It'll crush everything and get it all wet when the coolers sweat.

"And leak," Tortoise chimed in. "They always do."

"I'm not putting the coolers on top," Cedar snapped. I could tell he was frustrated because he honestly hadn't thought of that. "We're gonna line them down the middle and stuff the sleeping bags behind them." It was the best on-the-fly attempt of intentional packing logic he could come up with.

"If we put them in the middle, how will we fit our legs in when we sit down?" There were two long bench seats that faced each other and ran down either side of the interior. I could tell that the conundrum of where our legs would go if the coolers sat in the space between the bench seats had not only genuinely piqued Jefe's curiosity, but it was mildly upsetting to him.

"Your legs will rest on top," Cedar replied with confidence.

"But what about when we need to open them to get beer or something?"

Cedar thought for a minute. "Well, how would you open it if there were a bunch of tents and sleeping bags piled on top?"

Jefe scrunched his eyebrows and pursed his lips in defeat. Cedar, knowing he had won a battle of wills, bounced along victoriously, happily completing his mission. I didn't dare bring up the fact that the easiest thing to do would've been to pack the large coolers under the tents and sleeping bags and shit, and stock the smaller cooler, which would fit perfectly in the space between the driver seat and the sitting bench that ran along behind it, with the beer we'd need for the drive. It definitely wasn't worth bringing it up.

Once the motor home was loaded, Nico locked up his house, and we all piled in and headed to the store for food and beer. When we got there, Tortoise grabbed a cart and started pushing it toward the walk-in beer cooler.

"Back off, bro." Jefe stepped in front of Tortoise, taking command of the cart.

"Dude, come on." Tortoise's feelings were a little hurt and his ego a bit bruised by Jefe's show of dominance. His head hung with resentment as he stepped aside and let Jefe proceed with the cart. We stocked up with copious amounts of beer, grabbed a few loaves of bread, some peanut butter, jelly, chips, salsa, several gallons of water, and Cedar's sole source of sustenance—chocolate chunk cookies.

"Anything else?" Jefe asked as he proceeded toward the checkout line.

"Did you guys bring the dog food?" I looked at Jefe; I'd ask him to be sure to put the dog food in the truck before we left the house. He stood, staring blankly at me, shamefully shaking his head.

"Sorry, bro, I completely spaced it." I sensed Jefe feeling a mild twinge of failure which, as far as I was concerned, was good for him on occasion. He rarely encountered an opportunity to dance with the sobering slap of humility. We picked up a sack of dog food and a cheap Tupperware for Stella to use as a water bowl and headed to the checkout.

18

We were a little way out of Morrison; I absolutely could not believe all the people. I had been to shows at Red Rocks before, and I knew it would be pretty crazy, but I hadn't imagined it would be as nuts as it was. First of all, it took us over an hour to drive the last twenty miles into town because of the long line of traffic: cars, VW buses, campers, tricked-out school buses, all just part of one big cluster fuck trying to get in and find a place to set up camp. We finally made it to Morrison, and I was stunned by all the people—hippies everywhere, with their dogs and kids and surplus duffel bags and hemp clothes and necklaces that hung with various-sized wrapped crystals and blown glass pendents. There were more of the new breed, with their dread locks and leather and crazy tattoos and oo gauge plugs in their ears, looking like the anarchists they were. I wondered where all these people were the rest of the time. Where did they all come from? What rocks did they all crawl out from under to attend events like this? I loved it. I felt euphoric and elated and full of myself for having the intelligence, the balls, and the truth to be a part of our underworld—the subculture that soon would take it all over. Another generation, maybe two, and the world would be ours. To my surprise, there was some part of that thought that made me shudder.

We had gotten there late, so by the time we finally pulled

into the lot and found a place to park and call home for the next couple of days, the show was about to start. We boogied over to Will Call to get our tickets. As usual, dogs weren't allowed into the amphitheater, so we headed back to camp to check on Stella one more time and make sure she was cool.

"Do you guys want to spin or what?" Cedar was eager and excited to try the Czech, but I pretended not to hear him as I filled Stella's bowl with water and set some food out for her. Stella was pretty used to this routine. She had been going to shows with us all her life. I usually did what all the other hippies did—tied her up at camp, giving her plenty of slack, and made sure she had plenty of food and water. I told her to watch over everything, and we would be back soon. She was cool with it and just chilled around, doing what she loved to do, protecting her domain until we returned.

"Let's eat some acid." Cedar's initial question had turned into a definitive statement.

Nico and I looked at each other and rolled our eyes. "I thought you didn't eat psychedelics." Nico's comment sounded authoritative, like a half-annoyed older brother.

"Ben says I should be fine," Cedar said, coming to his own defense. "If it really *is* the Czech." He shot Jefe a dubious glance. "Ben says the Czech's so clean, there's no way you can really head-trip."

I found his last statement a bit ironic considering its source, Ben, who had never even eaten any Czech. The truth of the matter was that psychedelics were psychedelics—there was always the possibility that one might completely lose their shit.

"It's the fucking Czech!" Jefe was offended by his doubting Thomas.

"So, let's eat some." Cedar disappeared into the motor home and came back a couple minutes later with the vial he bought from Jefe.

"You sure you're cool?" I asked, trying not to sound too condescending.

"I've eaten molly, and that was fine." Cedar made another attempt to settle any doubts, although I had a feeling they were more his than ours.

"All right," I reluctantly gave in. I wasn't so much worried about Cedar's freaking out as I was worried about myself. I really didn't feel like tripping under my current circumstances, with Melissa's probably being pregnant and my instincts about my life in the business slapping me in the face with big, bright red flags, telling me to pull my head out of my ass already. I had a lot on my mind, and lately I'd felt like it was all I could do to hold it together while relatively sober, without the intervention of mind-altering psychedelics to really churn things up, making me more aware and vulnerable. It's not that I didn't want to trip and party with everybody else, especially at Red Rocks seeing Further—typically, I would be stoked and have a blast! It's just that I already felt so emotionally spent and on edge. Don't get me wrong; it's not that I was completely bummed about the prospect of a new life. I could get excited when I really thought about having a kid to look up to me and follow me around; and I was really starting to feel like I loved Melissa. I didn't like to think about her not being in my life and knew she would be a great mom. I thought I could be a pretty good dad too, but what would that mean? I couldn't raise a kid being a drug dealer, not on the level I was at now. It was fine when it was just me, not caring about anything and not having anything or anyone else to be responsible for, but if I had a kid, it just wouldn't be right. Besides, kids aren't stupid. If I managed to stay out of jail, at some point the kid would figure it out. And what if someone ever left something lying around? What if the kid ever got a hold of a mushroom chocolate or Vicodin or bag of cocaine or a foil of molly. No matter how careful you are, you just never know. All it takes is one fuck up, and that's something I could never live with. But what if I didn't deal? Then what? I don't want to work graveyard at the 7-Eleven for minimum wage the rest of my life. I don't want to raise a kid and try to support a family that way either. Fuck!

"Here, you do it." Cedar handed the vial to Jefe.

"We should probably go inside," Nico said and led the procession into the motor home.

"All right." Jefe was standing in front of Cedar, holding up the sweet-breath bottle. "Say ahh ..."

Cedar opened his mouth and held his tongue back. Jefe squeezed out a few drops and then worked his way around the group, squeezing drops of Czech under everyone's tongue. He got to me, and my palms started to sweat. I felt like saying, "No thanks, bro. I think I'll just puff a couple bowls, drinks some beers, and enjoy the show mellow-style tonight. You guys go ahead and have fun." But instead, my mouth opened—a programmed response—and he dosed me.

We sat around the motor home puffing bowls and shooting the shit, while Nico rolled us some joints to take into the show. There was a backpack check when you went into the amphitheater, so you had to be a little careful about how you took shit in. They were pretty cool, for the most part, primarily just making sure no one was taking in glass bottles or obvious weapons and shit like that. There were plenty of booths inside that sold food and beer and all kinds of other stuff; it was just a little more expensive, that's all. But 80 percent of the kids in there probably had a phat wad of illegally earned dollars in their pockets, so it wasn't like they really gave a shit.

I could tell when the acid started to kick in, because our laughing and talking slowly began to subside, and we all sat there staring at each other, with that look that said, "I am entering another dimension in which normal comprehension, understanding, and communication do not exist. Be back later."

"We should go," I heard myself mumble. Nobody said anything, but everyone started to gather their shit and stand up. Nico handed each of us a few joints, and I passed around some pills. We filed off the motor home. I made sure Stella was cool and told her to chill and guard her den and that we'd be back later. She lay down on the ground next to the door of the motor home, ready to man her post.

We walked to the amphitheater, along with thousands of other people, and when we got close to the entrance, the moving wall of people started to slow and ultimately come to a complete stop. It took a minute for the people working the show to stop each person, quickly go through their stuff, confiscate whatever they deemed necessary, and send them on through. The acid we had eaten was in full effect, and I could tell it was not comfortable for any of us to be stuck in the middle of a stagnant crowd of people, most of whom were probably high on something too. It was claustrophobic and made me start to feel anxious and weird. I looked over at Nico and Jefe and could tell they were just trying to breathe their way through this little hiccup, so I decided to do the same. Deep breaths, one at a time. It certainly wouldn't do any good to lose my shit in the middle of this huge crowd. There was no escaping now. Deep breaths. We'd be inside soon. Just about the time I started to feel like we were all just animals stuffed into a pen, waiting our turn to be run through a shoot, I heard mooing sounds coming from somebody across the crowd. It was funny and lightened things up a bit, and pretty soon we were all mooing like the herd of livestock we seemed to be. We were trying to have fun with it, and pretty soon we were moving forward again.

I felt relief wash over me as I walked inside. Stepping into a show, festival or rainbow gathering always felt like entering another dimension—the booths, the vendors, the pinwheel hats. All the freak flags were raised and flying high. It felt so secluded, excluded from all our modern bullshit, and was completely awesome! We went to one of the booths and bought some bottles of water. Nobody was quite ready for beer. When you're high on psychedelics, your body tends to have an aversion to alcohol. All you want is water—clean, cool and rejuvenating.

It was getting dark. We got our water and went down toward the stage and found our spot to hang out and watch the show. The band wasn't on stage yet, but they already had their incredibly elaborate light show going, and it was mesmerizing to watch all the flashing colors bouncing off the rocks and into the sky. Pretty soon, the band walked on stage, and I felt a shift in our shared energetic field, generated from all the people, as the crowd went wild with excitement. The incredible psychedelic light show, combined with the crazy acoustics created by the sound waves of music bouncing around all the rock surroundings of the natural amphitheater generated a very high vibration, and I felt like I might lift and float up off the ground. I wished I had something to hold on to, to make sure I wouldn't go drifting into outer space.

A few minutes later, Jefe nudged me and pointed to a shadow running around on top of the rocks. Some kid was up there, most likely tried to scale the rocks and sneak in, which happened on a pretty regular basis at Red Rocks. The bitch of it was, they were some shear-ass motherfucking cliffs, and it was a hell of a lot easier to get up those rocks than to get back down. I felt bad for the kid, even though it was his own damn fault. All you could see was a shadow, but he was running around, back and forth, most likely starting to freak out a little and desperately looking for a way down into the show with the rest of us. That had to suck. It had to be fucking cold and dark up there. Before long, everyone around us was watching and pointing up to him, talking about it. Poor kid. At least he could hear the music. I watched him running around up there and hoped he wasn't all spun out or anything. That'd be fucking intense!

The band finished their first set of songs, and Phil Lesh talked to the audience. "Hey! How's everybody doing out there tonight?" The crowd roared with excitement. "We're excited to be here at Red Rocks tonight and glad all of you could make it to be here with us!" The crowd roared again. Then he pointed up at the rocks and said. "And we just want to say hello to that guy up there on the rocks. Be careful up there, man." The crowd went wild. Everyone could see his shadow scampering around up there, and although you couldn't help but feel a little bad and concerned for him, we were all just glad it wasn't us.

I was watching the band and dancing to the music, when Jefe tapped me on the arm. I looked over at him, and he showed me he was holding a little sweet-breath dropper. He raised his eyebrows, as if to suggest I should have some more. I was already flying but having a great time, so I figured why not. I extended my hand toward Jefe, and he squeezed a puddle of the liquid onto my palm. I held it to my mouth and licked it off. Not too long after that, I was spun cookies but still having a blast, playing with the tracers from my body and the lights and the music that felt like a different kind of liquid sacrament, absorbing into my essence.

As I danced, I became mesmerized by this beautiful gypsy-looking girl with long dark dreads and a flowing hippie skirt. She was dancing next to me, and her dance was tribal and God-like and felt like a direct extension of the divine. As I watched her, I noticed a bulge in her lower belly and could tell that she was probably in the early stages of pregnancy. I looked away and felt myself grow warm, and then a chill ran up my spine, making me shiver. I looked over at her again and the shape of her face started to shift. It made me a little anxious, so I intentionally redirected my gaze to the ground. After a minute or two, I looked back, expecting her face to be normal again, but instead, her face had shifted even more, ultimately morphing into what looked like the face of a sheep. I quickly looked back down again and decided to drink some water, which always seemed to be comforting and grounding in times like this. I drank my water and reluctantly looked back over at her. She was still a sheep, a sheep with long dark dreads, a flowing hippie skirt, and human body. I looked over at Jefe, and he was a sheep too. Nico, Tortoise, Zack, Cedar—sheep. I scanned the crowd around us—all sheep. My heart beat faster, and I could feel beads of sweat forming on my brow. I started to think again about having a kid, being a dad, and what all that meant for my life. I kept dancing because I didn't know what else to do. I didn't want to stand still, because I felt like something might get me if I quit moving.

Then, all of a sudden, out of nowhere, I was back in that daydream—the one I had that day Jefe and I were running around peddling Holmes's weed, and I was sitting in the car waiting for him outside of Bueno Burrito; the one about the sheep in the pen, and the dark swirling clouds, and my very heroic attempt to liberate them. I felt scared and cold but kept dancing. I tried to fight it back, push it out, but it kept creeping back. Again I was seeing the sheep in my mind's eye—in their pen, confined and scared and huddled together for safety, warmth, and protection. I couldn't pull myself out of that fucked-up daydream, and I felt like I was on the verge of some kind of panic attack, but then, I saw one smiling at me. It was a smaller sheep, a lamb, and I felt a connection to it. Another larger sheep—I sensed it was the mother of the lamb—smiled at me too. I slowly looked around at the rest of the sheep in the pen, and they were all smiling at me. The next thing I knew, I started to feel totally relaxed and warm and the dark clouds churning above their pen began to break, and a ray of light shone through. Soon the clouds were gone, and the sheep weren't crouched together anymore. They were walking around their pen, grazing, comfortable, content just being sheep. I stepped out of my daydream with ease and looked back over at Jefe. He was still a sheep, and so was everyone else, but I wasn't so freaked out anymore. They seemed happy, tender, and calm. I started to feel a certain comfort and serenity with all the sheep, and as soon as I surrendered to them, they began to fade away, and their human faces returned.

We danced and laughed and had a great time for the rest of the show. As soon as it was over and everyone started filing out and heading back to the all-night lot party, we saw a helicopter coming in to get that kid off the rocks.

Because we hadn't taken the time to set up our tents before the show, we all crashed in the motor home that night, which was terribly uncomfortable for everyone. I was lucky enough to get one of the long bench seats but had to share it with Tortoise, so I had his crusty socks and stinky-ass feet in my face all night. Somehow, we had managed to get the coolers stacked up, so Cedar slept on the floor in the aisle between the bench seats and woke up bitching because his sleeping bag was drenched with beer. We slept with the door open and had Stella stationed right outside to guard, which totally nurtured her pack mentality instincts. But even with that door and a couple of windows open, it was not enough to properly ventilate the putrid stink of Jefe's all-night fart fest.

We got up, puffed a few bowls, popped a couple Xanax, got our bearings as best we could, and decided to set up the tents.

"I need food," Jefe said, walking toward one of the coolers. "You guys want me to make some sandwiches?"

"Sure," we answered. It was sometime late morning, and I hadn't even realized how low my blood sugar was until Jefe mentioned food.

"Dude, did anyone bring a knife?" Jefe asked, digging around the cooler and then through the brown paper grocery sacks.

We all looked blankly at each other. "Oh, wait a minute ..." Tortoise said. He dug an old rusted pocket knife out of his backpack. "You can use this." He opened it up and attempted to clean off the blade by wiping it across his dirty pants.

Sluggishly, we worked to set up our tents, while Cedar draped his sleeping bag over the motor home to dry out. I was in my tent, arranging my sleeping bag and pillow, when I heard Cedar and Nico outside talking to some guy who was speaking very emphatically about something. I poked my head out the door of my tent and saw an older guy, probably in his late forties, with straggly salt-and-pepper pseudo-dreads, a beaded hemp necklace, a worn-out tie-dyed T-shirt, and a pair of army-green cargo shorts that looked like they'd never been washed.

"Dude, it's not right!" He wore a very concerned look on his face and was shaking his finger to exaggerate a point. "It's fucking oppression, man!"

I crawled out of my tent and stood up. "What's going on?"

"They're running us out of the town. They've got cops everywhere, brought 'em in from all over the place. They're arresting people, hassling us for no reason." He shook his head. "They don't even want us in the town store. How are we supposed to eat? Where are we supposed to buy food? We're just trying to live our lives, man. We're not hurting anybody." He spoke to us like we were an innate part of the "we" he was talking about. I guess, in some way, we were. "It's not fair, man," he went on. "It's the fucking man, the fucking machine, trying to keep us down. We need to rise up, band together, and fight! We have a fucking right to life, man!" His head hung sullenly as he shook it from side to side. I thought he might either break down in convulsing, hysterical sobs or just freak out and start randomly shooting people right there. He started to raise his head, and Nico and I looked at each other, not knowing quite what to expect. He looked at us dismally, but then his expression changed. "Hey, you kids want some 'shrooms? I've got some killer stuff. Picked 'em myself."

Nico shot Cedar a "keep your mouth shut" glance.

"Nah, bro, we're cool."

"You sure?" He held out a sack of highly questionable, sad-looking mushrooms.

"No, thanks," I said firmly and decisively. I hoped he would get the drift that not only did we not want any of his sad and highly questionable hand-picked mushrooms, but that it was time for him to mosey on down the road. It worked, and he was on to the next pack of kids, ranting about the same story.

"It's Us and Them, man. Us and Them," Nico laughed. "You gotta fight for your right, bro!"

"I don't know." Cedar shook his head, seeming a bit distraught. "It doesn't seem right to me either."

"What? We were only kidding," Nico said.

"They shouldn't oppress people just because they're different."

"I agree." I felt myself becoming impassioned with a belief I wasn't previously aware I had. "I don't condone blatant, abusive oppression of the masses either. But oppression is one thing; controlling total mayhem is another. If people are using oppression as an excuse because they want to be able to run amok and not extend the basic courtesy of respect for the people around them, than that's bullshit too!"

"We've got a right to eat acid and freak out in the general store!" Nico laughed, trying to lighten things up.

"We've got a right to get drunk and swim naked in the town's fountain with our dogs!" I chimed in.

Tortoise laughed. "You guys want a beer?" he asked as he walked to the cooler, attempting to divert any further argument.

"Hell, yeah, it's almost noon for Christ's sake." Jefe smiled and slapped me on the shoulder, and we went about our task of finally setting up camp.

Our emphatic visitor was right—about all the chaos, anyway. There was word on the lot all day of what was going on in the little town of Morrison—complete pandemonium. The hippies had overrun the town, and the town had pulled in all kinds of authorities, trying to control them. The more crowd control they attempted to enforce, the more the hippies rebelled, ultimately leading to full-on riots. We debated whether or not we should just pack it up and get out of there before shit really hit the fan, and they pulled up with paddy wagons to haul us all off to some hippie Alcatraz somewhere, but ultimately, we decided to stay put, keep our heads down, forget about peddling all our illicit shit around the lot, and try to enjoy the last night of the show.

We were all still reeling a bit from our late night of psychedelic, frenzied partying and were completely content to hang around camp, eating Xanax, drinking beer, and puffing bowls. Nico and Tortoise were napping in their tents. Jefe, Zack and Cedar were sitting around the little table in the motor home playing cards, so I took the opportunity to sneak off and call Melissa.

"I've been thinking about you and just thought I'd call and say hi," I told her. She'd really been on my mind.

"I'm glad you did. How's it going?"

"The show last night was killer. Jefe's buddy from the Bay showed up, and we were up all night partying with him." She knew I was talking about the Czech.

"Cedar too?"

"Yeah, him too."

"How was that?"

"Surprisingly, he was fine."

"That's good."

"How are you?"

"I'm okay." She sounded tired, not like her normal bubbly self.

"Just okay?" I felt my stomach start to knot. "What's going on?" It was a stupid question but a conditioned response to someone I cared about telling me she was okay in a not-so-okay voice.

She hesitated. "I wasn't gonna talk to you about this until you got back. I want you to have a good time with your friends."

I knew what was coming but said, "Well, now you gotta tell me."

"Well," she said, "I took that pregnancy test."

"Yeah?" My stomach was now in my throat.

"It came out positive."

"Positive, meaning you're pregnant?"

"Yes."

It was a very surreal moment for me. Everything around me just kind of stopped. I felt like someone had replaced my blood with low-voltage electricity and it was now pumping through me, making me shocked and disoriented. I had goose bumps, and the hair on my arms was standing up. "Don't worry." I tried to sound as calm as I possibly could. "It'll be okay. Just try to relax until I get back."

She was softly crying on the other end of the phone. It broke my heart. "You know," I said, "I think this could be a good thing." I couldn't believe I'd said that. Even though I believed it, I couldn't believe it came out of my mouth.

I heard her sniffle and could tell she was trying to suppress the excitement in her voice. It didn't totally work. "Really?"

"Yeah, really. We'll talk about it when I get home."

"Okay." She sounded relieved.

"Let's not tell anyone else about this yet, okay?"

"Okay. I love you."

"I love you too." I hung up the phone, still shocked and reeling from what I knew was about to be my new reality. I went back to camp, took another Xanax, got a beer, and crawled into my tent to pretend to take a nap. I lay there thinking through it all, experiencing a plethora of emotions. Ultimately, what it all came down to was that I loved her. I loved her, and I wanted to be a dad. My life didn't have to change overnight. I had friends who worked as much as I did, who played the game at the same level as I did, and some of them had kids of all different ages. I didn't have to stop dealing now, but I would slowly work my way out of it. I would make that my intention. Maybe I would go to school. My mom had been on me about that for years. I'd just deal until I graduated and bank a shitload of cash. That wouldn't be so bad.

"Are you alive in there?" Cedar stuck his head into my

tent. He was holding a bag of Tostitos and dropping little chip crumbs everywhere.

"Huh?" I was super groggy. I slowly propped myself up on an elbow and rubbed my eyes.

"Come on, bro, it's time to go to the show."

I didn't remember falling asleep, and I lay back down for a second in an attempt to come back to earth.

Cedar handed me a jug of water. "Here. Chug on that for a minute. You're dehydrated." Cedar, the self-proclaimed expert on everything, was right. I pounded about half a gallon of water and sluggishly crawled out of my tent.

We went to the show that night on a much mellower note than the night before. There had been a little talk of the Czech, but I certainly wasn't into it, and Cedar wanted to head back to the West Coast as soon as we got back to town the next day. We ate a bunch of pills, rolled some spliffs, and spent the evening listening to music and going back and forth to the beer garden. It was chill and awesome and just what I needed.

The next morning we packed up early to try to beat the inevitable mass exodus of Heads that was sure to be a traffic nightmare. It worked; with Cedar acting as group motivator, we were one of the first ones out. Although we were a little groggy, we were on the road headed home by about ten o'clock. I popped another Xanax and relaxed, surprised by the excitement and newfound feeling of hope I was experiencing as I thought of my impending new life.

19

"How was your day?" My mom beamed with delight at my working a real job for her attorney friends, Jim and Mike. I felt some sadness, knowing that my having an actual "get up and go to work like everybody else" kind of job—something that it is thought to be so trivial and expected in our society—thrilled her so completely. You would have thought I was the president of the Unites States or something. After all I had put her through over the past months, I really wanted to please her and make her happy. I wanted to let her know that it was all going to be okay, but it was hard, because I absolutely hated it.

I reached deep within myself and silently struggled to conjure up the best happy voice I could as I answered her. "It was all right." Because it was a blatant lie, I don't think it was terribly convincing. I saw her enthusiasm waver for just a second but then the shining smile was back.

"What did you do?" Her beaming had paled and was replaced by apprehension because she knew I hated to be prodded into talking about things I didn't really want to talk about, which was pretty much everything these days. But she couldn't help herself, and her genuine curiosity won out, putting her on the front lines of my potential to lash out at her.

Instead of taking my frustrations out on her with an intentionally hurtful stream of verbal abuse, I took a breath, like Sam had told me to do, and tried to respond as civilly as possible. "I boxed up a bunch of files and documents for a trial they have tomorrow." I could hear a tone of agitated sarcasm beginning to line my voice, because the uncanny irony of my day had been unnerving.

"What kind of a trial?"

I knew she would ask. "A drug case." I didn't feel like going into it and knew my abrupt answer would let her know it was time to talk about something else.

There was only a hint of her being taken back, and then she said, "Well, they just went on and on about you. They said you just did a wonderful job and that you are very sharp and caught on very quickly."

I had a real love/hate relationship with her incredibly genuine attempts to boost my self-confidence and offer immeasurable support. I was eternally grateful for and appreciative of the fact that even after all that happened, she still loved me, stuck by me, and would do anything in her power to help me through this mess. I loved her optimism as much as I despised it, and although a large part of me wanted to believe it, I knew it was a lie. I was not good. I was not smart. I was fucked up and angry and pissed off that she had ever brought me into this world to struggle and suffer, like I was living through some bad joke. I wasn't normal, for some reason. I was just fucked up. I wondered if I was born fucked up or if it was just something that happened over time, some kind of perverted fate thing. After that first day working for Jim and Mike, my gut wrenched as I realized there was a very good chance that I might never be able to successfully function in mainstream society.

I was disappointed and upset because underneath it all, there was a big part of me that wanted to be normal, to live a clean, happy life, and to be successful and have a house and wife and kids and a Labrador bouncing around and all that shit you see in the Kodak ads. But after today, I just knew it wasn't gonna happen. Jim and Mike were nice enough guys, but I felt uncomfortable and self-conscious all day long. I was riddled with feelings of paranoia, guilt, and self-loathing, and I felt constricted and claustrophobic, like a caged animal. I just wanted out, to be in the fresh air and wearing comfortable clothes, and not have to worry about breaks and taking lunch. I had been on the verge of a panic attack all day long and was now feeling the insidious depression attempting to consume me.

Mom looked over and smiled gently at me. The hairs on my arms prickled as I had the sensation she could read my mind. "You want to get some dinner?"

"Sure."

"What sounds good?"

"I don't care. Whatever you want."

"How about Senor Charlies?"

"That fine."

We drove along, her talking on her cell phone and me gazing out the window. I watched the people driving past, walking down the sidewalk, and riding their bicycles, and I thought how we were all experiencing the same weather, the same day, the same time and place of Earth, but all our individual realities were completely different—our own sets of worries, problems, fears, hopes, dreams. We drove past a guy pumping gas into a Mercedes, and I felt a surge of resentment, thinking, *I want to be the guy in the Mercedes. I want to have cash and time. I want to be carefree and confident, exempt from so many of the typical confines of life. I'm never gonna be able to have all that, stuck in Middle America.* But the thing that I knew was that if I was to become the guy in the Mercedes by selling drugs, then what? How would I clean up the cash and live with the constant paranoia that at any moment, the whole thing would be yanked out from under my feet. Even if you have the best intentions, at some point the dark side of it gets a hold of you, and then it's just a matter of time before the universe raises her hand and spanks the shit out of you. The truth about the drug business—and everybody knows it—is that it's not a matter of *if*; it's a matter of *when*. If the cops don't get you, the gangsters will.

And I know.

My "when" was October of last year.

Melissa was officially pregnant, already through her first trimester. It was a big adjustment for both of us, and although I was a little freaked at first, I found myself becoming more and more excited about my impending life as a dad. Melissa hadn't technically "moved in," because Becca couldn't hold the lease on their place by herself. She needed Melissa's name on the paper and needed me to pay half of the rent (Melissa had stop working) until she found another roommate. But most all of Melissa's clothes were in my closet, and she spent every day and night with me.

Initially, Jefe had a difficult time adjusting to it all; Stella did too. They had a hard enough time sharing me with each other, so to bring another person into the mix was challenging. Stella couldn't sleep in the bed with me whenever she wanted anymore, because space was limited, and Melissa wasn't down with dog hair all over the pillows and blankets. Jefe had to make a general effort to control himself, his disrespectful talk, his careless rambunctiousness, and his incessant burping and farting. Melissa was nesting—maternal instinct was swinging into full effect, and with it came her subtle determination to polish ol' Jefe up a bit. She would kindly remind him to throw his trash into the garbage can, keep his dirty clothes in his room with the door shut, and to please put his dirty dishes in the sink. Melissa would wash them; she just wanted them in the sink. Jefe might have retaliated against her valiant efforts a little more if she hadn't been so gracious and loving about it all. She saw him and Stella as part of our little family. She was even more than willing to do his laundry, if Jefe had it sorted and ready, and to clean up after him a little. Stella was getting monthly baths and was brushed outside on a regular basis. I couldn't believe how much of a difference it made with the dog hair all over the house thing. And I felt a twinge of guilt for not having not done it myself when I saw how much Stella loved it. Melissa had definitely turned into the mama of our little house and ultimately, everyone seemed pleased and content.

Tortoise moved out pretty soon after we told everyone Melissa was pregnant, and she started basically living with us. His move wasn't motivated because he was pissed off or angry about the situation or anything like that; he just sensed that we were going to need some more space, and he saw change on the horizon and took the initiative. We all knew Jefe wasn't going anywhere. Melissa knew the depth of my relationship with Jefe, and she and I mutually understood that Jefe might be with us forever—our eternal adolescent—and she was okay with that. Tortoise, Nico, and Zack got a place together, and although I was touched by his genuine sensitivity to our situation and his ability to be proactive about the inevitable by moving, it became obvious that he did not really want to go. We had all been together a long time. It takes some time to fully gain closure after transitions, changes, and endings of an era. Tortoise had a hard time cutting the cord. He had moved his stuff and was paying rent somewhere else, but was still at our house all the time, constantly popping by, eating dinner, grabbing beers out of the fridge, crashing nights on the couch—almost like nothing had changed. It didn't bother us, really. Tortoise was a pretty mellow guy, respectful and easy to get along with. Nobody asked him to go, and he probably could have stayed until the baby was born, but I think "moving" and then kind of pretending he hadn't was just his way of slowly acclimating to the new reality.

We were still dealing drugs as hard-core as ever, if not more so. I had Cedar and Holmes coming to see me on a regular basis and was still making my runs to Texas for blow and pills. My business relationship with Forrest had proven to be quite profitable as he was now my biggest blow custie and had an endless supply of bomb-ass molly. Jefe had become semi-famous for his Czech, and the demand for it had gone through the roof, especially with the college kids. He was spinning through mass quantities of it and making lots of cash. Life was good on that end, but Jefe knew of my plan to quit, and he was cool with it.

Somewhat to my surprise, I had actually enrolled in school, and much to my surprise, I actually liked it, I was good at it. I wasn't going to the university, just community college, but I could get all the same core classes I needed there and for about half the cost. My new life plan—the first legitimate life plan I'd ever had—was to do my first two years at community college, transfer into the university for the last two, and continue selling drugs in the interim. Then, after I graduated, I'd quit dealing and get a "real job"—the kind that's boring and ultimately sucks and doesn't pay much. I would keep the suck-ass job while I worked on my master's degree and then, I hoped, I would move up the ladder of financial legitimacy.

That was my plan in a nutshell, and my mother was thrilled about my decision to go to college. I was thrilled that it wasn't completely miserable, and I could see myself gaining a little self-esteem and hopefulness toward life in general as I started to prove to myself and others that I was actually a pretty sharp guy and possibly had a little worth after all. Of course, I gravitated toward business. I liked the preliminary classes; the whole theory of it came naturally to me and resonated with me, so that's what I decided I'd major in. I started to have little fantasies of myself: "Kyd ... Wharton MBA ... CFO ... Berkshire Hathaway" Who knows? Maybe Warren and I would become best buds, and he would see all of my potential and take great pleasure in mentoring me and shaping me into the stealth businessman I was born to be. It could happen. Anything is possible if you just set your intention and work hard enough, right?

Melissa and I were in the kitchen. She had just put Stella

outside to eat and go to the bathroom and was standing over the stove, stirring her spaghetti sauce. I was sitting at the kitchen table, completely immersed and somewhat aggravated by a calculus problem that was giving me some grief, when there was a knock at the front door. I had my brain so twisted around that stupid problem that I didn't even hear it. I only knew because I heard Melissa yell, "Jefe, can you get that?"

"Huh?" I looked up, knowing I had heard her say something but not sure if it was directed at me.

"Tortoise is just in time for dinner." She smiled and chuckled, rubbing her belly as she stirred her sauce. "Jefe!" she shouted again. After another second or two with no response, she sighed, set down the large wooden spoon, and walked toward the den. I heard the front door open, and then Melissa screamed—not loud, like a blood-curdling scream or anything; more like a scared surprise and then a loud thump. A sick sense that something was terribly wrong twisted my gut, and the hairs on the back of my neck rose. I jumped up to see what was going on.

About that same time I heard Jefe say, "What the fuck!" I ran in, and the first thing I saw were three guys in ski masks. The only one that really stuck out in my mind at that moment was the one with the gun pointed at me as soon as I entered the room. Jefe was standing at the hallway entrance and the gun went from me to Jefe and back to me.

"Where's the fucking drugs, Kyd? Where's the fucking drugs?"

I looked over and saw Melissa curled up in a ball on the floor, and one of the guys in a ski mask was standing over her holding a bat.

"She's fucking pregnant!" I yelled. I knew he had hit her and at that moment, I saw red. Everything just blurred and my rational thinking went away. I saw Jefe leap over the couch, heading for the guys, and I went for them too. Before Jefe could get to the guy with the bat, he swung it and smacked Jefe in the head. It was a hard hit and dropped Jefe to the floor. The next thing I knew, the other guy was swinging a bat at me, pounding me in the arms and ribs. I was on the floor.

"Where's your fucking money, Kyd?" The guy with the gun was leaning over me, pressing the hollow barrel into my cheek. "We're not fucking around, yo. Where is it?"

I heard Jefe mumbling curses and could see him trying to get back up and fight. The guy standing over him pounded him with the bat a few more times in the ribs. *Thud, thud, thud.* It was terrible. Jefe tried to get back up again, and the guy cracked him over the head. It was the worst sound I've ever heard, like a watermelon being dropped onto concrete from a second-story window. I was reeling. I didn't know what was going on. It all happened so fast. "Motherfucker!" I think I was yelling, screaming, over and over again. "Goddamn you!" I could feel tears of rage and sadness streaming down my cheeks. I tried to push myself up. I just wanted to see about Melissa and Jefe. I just wanted to kill those fuckers!

I started to get up, and the bat came down on me again, across my back and kidneys. It knocked the breath out of me for a minute, and I heard Melissa crying, "No! Don't! Please!" I looked over and she had pushed herself up to her knees. "Don't hurt him. We'll give you what you want." She held her stomach as she pleaded with them, and I watched as they smacked her across the belly one more time. She doubled forward, and they smacked her across the back of her shoulders, and I watched her go down. I know this may sound crazy, but it wasn't until I heard Melissa say, "We'll give you what you want," that I realized we were being robbed—that they were there for the drugs and money.

The whole situation was very surreal, like watching a movie, like something spinning around outside of me. Everything happened in about two minutes, maybe less, and I couldn't believe it. It literally wouldn't register. It was like all rational comprehension and understanding no longer existed, like everything was just happening around me, and I was just there—stunned and dazed, suspended at the mercy of it all.

"Where are the drugs, Kyd? Where are the drugs?" I felt the cold steel barrel press harder against my cheek, and then it lifted and the butt of the gun smacked hard across my forehead. And then, another smack across my forehead. I hardly felt it, just the jolt of my head toward the ground. "Where's your fucking money, Kyd? Where's your fucking money?" He said everything twice. I remember that. And he wasn't yelling. It was more like a firm whisper that sent a kind of sick static electricity down my spine. I realized I was being raised off the ground. One of the guys had my arms behind my back and was lifting me up. The guy with the gun held it to the back of my head, down low, in that hollow point where the back of your head meets your neck.

A sense of calm came over me. "Don't hurt anyone. I'll get you whatever you want." My right eye burned. I couldn't see out of it, and I realized it was because of the blood. They stood me up, kind of holding me with my hands behind my back, and I started toward my bedroom. As soon as I was up, I looked over at Jefe and Melissa. Melissa was curled in fetal position, and I could hear her sobbing softly. And Jefe ... part of me died when I saw Jefe lying on the ground, kind of rolled on one side, with his face covered in blood. My soul, my energy, my life force, whatever you want to call it, left me at that point. I felt it go. I had failed them, failed to protect them, and my will was gone. I heard growling, barking, thumping, and scratching and looked over at the back sliding glass door at Stella, who could see everything going on and was killing herself trying to get in and protect us. I remember seeing blood on the glass from where she must have busted her lip or something trying so hard to break through. I hadn't heard her before that, but she must have been going crazy the whole time. I was walking—it felt more like a pushed glide—back to my bedroom when I heard the sirens.

"Fuck!" I heard one of the guys say. "It's the fucking 5-0!" They dropped me, and I fell to the ground. "Get the fuck outta here!" I heard hurried footsteps leaving the room.

Both my eyes were burned from blood. I tried to wipe it out and crawled, still disoriented, back into the den to check on Melissa and Jefe. I went to Melissa first. She was lying on her side, rolled up tight and still moaning. "I love you," I whispered as I held onto her. "I'm so sorry. I'm so sorry." Then I looked over at Jefe. He didn't move. He was lying on his right side, facing me, with his left arm and leg hanging limp, draped down over his body. The floor underneath his head was saturated in blood. There was a huge split in his forehead and blood continued to stream out. His eyes were wide open and vacant, and I saw blood dripping in a small but steady stream down out of his ear.

I knew. Not on a conscious level at the time, but some part of me knew. I buried my bloody head in Melissa's back and screamed, "No! God, no! Please!" Over and over again, I begged with God, like he just might change his mind and turn back time, and give us another chance—give me another chance to keep this from happening. "No! Please! God!" And then I heard the voices and walkie-talkies behind me. I didn't look up, didn't move. I just kept holding on to Melissa. Someone was trying to talk to me, but I didn't understand them. My head was still buried in Melissa's back. They were pulling me off. I held on tight but felt more than one set of hands pulling at me. I heard someone on a walkie-talkie saying our address. They rolled me on my back next to Jefe. "Don't move him," I heard someone say. "The paramedics are on their way." I remember feeling like I was out of my body but aware, on some objective level, that I was shaking and shivering uncontrollably. And then someone wrapped a blanket around me.

20

We were taken to the hospital, and they searched the house that night. I was treated, held in the hospital overnight, and then booked into Boulder County Jail on eleven felony charges:

- Schedule I Controlled Substance (Seven pounds of weed – two separate charges: possession and intent)
- Schedule I Controlled Substance (Five vials of acid (Jefe's Czech) – two separate charges: possession and intent)
- Schedule I Controlled Substance (An ounce of MDMA- two separate charges: possession and intent)
- Schedule III Controlled Substance (250 Vicodin – two separate charges: possession and intent)
- Schedule IV Controlled Substance (100 Xanax – two separate charges: possession and intent)
- Felony 2 Special Offender (for Jefe's 1911 Colt. 45)

I hadn't been charged with the $57,000 they took from my safe, but it wasn't helping anything.

My motion of discovery was over two inches thick. I was

in "intake" at Boulder County Jail for one week in maximum security, with twenty-three-hour lockdown in a freezing-cold cell, with no visitors and no contact with the outside world except a few phone calls with Ryan, my attorney, who told me Melissa had lost the baby and Jefe was dead. Maybe you can imagine how I felt; maybe you can't. I wished I was the one who was dead. They had me on suicide watch.

I was deemed "high-flight risk" and the bond that was initially set for my bail was two million dollars. There was no way anyone in my family could meet all the criteria to get me out immediately, so I had to sit there and wait. My story was all over the local newspapers, and everyone in jail knew who I was, like a little criminal celebrity. The old-school bros, who were pros at this shit, always in and out, were preparing me for prison, because that's where everyone, including me, thought I was headed.

I remember this one guy we called Mikey Mumbles. He got his name because he had smoked so much meth throughout his life that it had permanently fucked up his speech, and he talked so fast, in kind of half-word, muddled-up sentences, that no one could ever totally understand what he was saying. Mikey Mumbles told me, as best he could, "Don't worry, Kyd. It's not so bad. At least you'll have a roof over your head, and get to eat three times a day, and shower, and go to the doctor or dentist, and get medicine if you need it. It sure beats the streets." He laughed as he said it, but I knew he was serious and was taken aback with the obvious relief he found incarceration to offer. It was a bizarre concept for me to grasp, but for the first time I realized that there were people out there who actually preferred jail or prison to their daily struggle of attempting to survive in the untamed, ruthless, relentless jungles of outside life. The sad truth is, most prisoners probably are better cared for than a majority of our poverty-stricken, legitimate members of society.

The best advice I got about being locked up was from Wally.

It scared the shit out of me, and I didn't like hearing it, because I knew it was true. All the same, I'll never forget it. Wally was a huge mountain of a man. At fifty-five years old, he had been in and out of prison most of his life and was about to go back again. One day he told me, "Kyd, three things you need to know about prison and you'll be okay: Hang with your own race, go to church, and don't be the one to change the TV channel. You remember those three things, and you'll be all right."

I spent three months in jail. Because of the severity of my case, I wasn't allowed many visitors. The visitations I did get had to be monitored and were no contact. Melissa came to see me a few weeks after I'd been in. What was left of my heart tore the second I saw her. I knew I looked like hell. I guess I had some kind of panic attack the night all the shit went down, and all the blood vessels in my eyes, on my face, and in my chest burst. The whites of my eyes were filled with blood, completely red, and had gotten infected. I had broken capillaries all over my face, neck, and chest and felt that I looked a little like Frankenstein, with the deep red scar on my forehead from forty-five stitches they used to sew me up where I'd been pistol whipped.

I went to the infirmary in jail for my eyes. They gave me some medicated drops that burned like hell but were supposed to help with the infection. The blood in my eyes and the broken blood vessels had started to clear up, but I still looked pretty fucked, and she was so beautiful. I couldn't help thinking that we should be having a baby in a few months, and I should be at home, studying for a test so I could keep up my grades for Wharton. It was a disturbing visit, and I could tell the whole situation had, rightfully so, completely traumatized her emotionally. The bright light in her eyes had dimmed, and the gleaming Cheshire-cat grin I so adored had turned into a dark and depressive scowl. I could feel the resentment emanating from her as she looked at me with a mix of sadness and disgust. She didn't tell me, but I heard from my attorney that she technically had a miscarriage the night we got robbed but had to have some kind of surgery to remove the rest of the fetus. I'm sure it was terrible. She broke down in tears as she told me about Jefe's memorial service and how she almost couldn't bring herself to go. She was in the car with Becca, balling hysterically, and went back into the house three times before she finally found enough strength and composure to go. She continued to cry, distant and disturbed, sobbing as she asked me, "Why? Why did this have to happen? I really loved you. I just don't understand. Why?"

I cried as I listened, knowing what she meant by "I just don't understand." She just didn't understand why I couldn't be normal. Why we couldn't be normal, with a normal life, normal jobs, normal family. Why I didn't change and make room for all that to happen. All I could do was cry and listen and take my well-deserved emotional lashing, because I couldn't answer.

I knew that Melissa did but didn't want to see me, and the visit was devastating, ultimately leaving me feeling even more worthless and terrible than before. I felt like I had destroyed so many lives, which is the truth, and I know I'll never get over that.

I never believed in suicide. My belief was that we were all here for some reason and part of our job was to stick it out— whatever that means. But I was beginning to second-guess that theory, at least for me, anyway. I truly felt like I didn't deserve to live. The only thing was, there were a couple of things that really bothered me about killing myself, a couple of things I couldn't quite get past, which is probably the reason I am sitting here today. First of all, I have already been the source of enough pain and suffering for the ones I truly loved. If I were to have a bullet for breakfast, for instance, what would it do to my mom or my sister? I had already put them through enough with all this shit. If I took the easy way out, I'd leave them here to pick up all the pieces, to wonder incessantly, for the rest of their lives, how they failed and what they could have done to make things different. They would eternally blame themselves, especially my mom, for having done something wrong, for not having been good enough, for not being "there" enough. I knew it was not right to punish them like that.

The second thing that got me about suicide was I heard somewhere that if you kill yourself in this life, your only gonna come back with a worse set of problems in the next life. And then, if you kill yourself again, you just come back again with an even worse set—again and again until you finally stick it out. There is a part of me that believes in some kind of reincarnation, where we learn lessons, enjoy the good times, live through the shit, and ever so fucking slowly, move up the universal ladder to Nirvana or something like that. I like this whole idea of some kind of ultimate Utopian, God-like, divine existence. It's an ideology that makes all this stupid shit somehow worthwhile, so fuck that killing yourself shit! I'm not going to puss out, and I'm certainly not coming back here to another life with even more problems. This shit is fucked up enough.

So I spent three months in jail. The only reason I got out when I did was because my attorney told me it would help my case if I went to rehab for eight weeks and then to a halfway house for six months. He was working with the DA and supposedly two of the things I had going for me was a possible illegal search, because they never actually got a warrant for the house, and another possible Miranda rights issue. But they wanted at least a part of me, and they weren't gonna let me off scot-free. I didn't want to go to prison. I knew some fucked-up shit happened, and I deserved to suffer and will never stop suffering over it, but I believe I'm a good person. I don't belong in prison, and I am willing to do whatever it takes to stay out and to try like hell to have some kind of a good life. The truth of the matter was, in my heart of hearts, I knew I did need some kind of rehab. I need something—some kind of help.

21

I'm in Portland now, at Mom's, working and taking nine hours at Portland Community College. I had my social psychology class today and it really got me thinking. We talked about Evolutionary Theory and sexual selection and the intrinsic need of the human species to reproduce and propagate their genetic material. All this is something I've always kind of known. I mean, I'm familiar with the idea of 'Survival of the Fittest' and I realize we must have some kind of internal wiring that tells us to survive, procreate and continue our genetic line, but I've never really participated in a direct discussion about it. We talked about human mate selection and how research shows that mate selection today isn't so different than it was with our ancestors long ago. Essentially, women are programmed to want a mate who can provide the necessary resources to keep her and her children alive and well: food, clothing, shelter, and protection. Men, on the other hand, desire a mate who is young and physically attractive. In today's environment the characteristics a woman looks for in a mate translate to: income, social status, age, athleticism, intelligence, and material possessions. Whereas, the characteristics a man desires are: age, health, full lips, clear skin, clear eyes, lustrous hair and good muscle tone.

I was thinking about all this on the way home from class when it dawned on me—The Machine knows this; it's what they play on. Commercialism is geared to exploit our most primal driving force, our basic need for survival. On a subconscious level, this is why we want BMW's, Botox, big houses, personal trainers, treatments at the spa, and on, and on, and on, and on, and on... We've become conditioned to believe we need all this crap to survive—physically and psychologically. And, on some fucked-up level, it's kind of true. As our society has advanced, so has the plethora of shit offered within. The means of survival have increased with more variety, ferocity, and lushness and we are constantly reminded, bombarded with pieces of evidence leading to a survival that exists out there so much more secure, validating, comfortable, and plush than the one we know.

I stopped by the store on the way home from class to buy a pack of smokes. I was standing in the checkout line, waiting for the cashier, Val, her nametag told me, to receive a price check on a box of Western Family Hamburger Helper. Val was not ashamed to advertise her apathetic attitude toward life with the "whatever" tattoo daintily inked in neat, legible, cursive writing on the inside of her right wrist. She stood there awkwardly and impatiently, subtly shifting her weight from one side to another, sighing, checking her nails and pulling little bits of skin or something from her cuticles and then flicking it onto the ground. She sighed again, opened the drawer below the cash register, shuffled some things around, and then closed it, doing everything she could to avoid making eye contact with the customer standing opposite her. Her customer didn't look much older than me and seemed physically and mentally drained from the constant efforts to keep her two young children somewhat under control. She grabbed the youngest one, a boy, probably five or so, by the upper arm, yanked him toward her and smacked him on the ass. "You just wait till we get home!" she threatened. He began to pout, and then cry, and she glared at him as she pulled the Oregon Trail card out of her purse.

I tried not to stare, like everyone else was trying not to

do, so I attempted a little nonchalance and began to browse over the 'little random shit' displays on each side of me that guided my way through the checkout line, like a cattle chute, tempting, enticing, and reminding me with small samples and suggestions of things I *need* that I forgot to get. I picked up a miniature red Sharpie marker that had a clasp attached to the end of it, so one could attach it to the zipper of their jacket or belt loop or nipple ring or whatever and wondered if I should get this, because certainly there was something I needed to permanently mark that all of the other markers I had at home simply could not do. I remembered I only had forty bucks to last me the rest of the week and reluctantly put the marker back. The girl standing in line in front of me picked up the US Weekly magazine with Diddy on the cover in a stark-white suit, white tie, white shirt, white shoes, and dazzling diamonds that dribbled from him like prismed vanilla frosting oozing off the bottom of a chocolate fudge cake. "Diddy's White Party" the cover read in large letters. She turned the page and there was Diddy standing in the center of a round white stage, his shiny white teeth gleaming through a "Yes, I have it all!" smile, one arm extended to the crowd gathered around his feet, praising him as if he were some kind of living god, while his other hand casually held a smoldering cigar.

I watched over her shoulder as she flipped through the magazine pages and saw pictures of Donald Trump, Oprah, Justin Timberlake, Jessica Simpson, Kim Kardashian and her twenty-whatever carat engagement ring. All in expensive cars and designer clothes, walking tall, shoulders back, head up, smiling, dazzling like the stars they are, striding through LAX to hop a private jet and fly off to paradise with their personal trainers, makeup artists, personal chefs, bodyguards, and assistants, and plenty of time to enjoy it all. They have money falling out of their assholes and can afford the freedom and the time for plenty of relaxation, pampering, and self-care. They are solid and secure, relaxed and carefree—or so it seems to the general public.

Sure, this is great for the people who appear to be in this "I have plenty of cash and don't really have to worry about shit but enjoying myself" category, but what about the rest of us out here who are just average, normal, everyday Joes, most of us working our asses off at different rungs on the ladder just to stay afloat? There is an echelon of wealth in this society and the ones closer and closer to the bottom resent the ones closer and closer to the top. This separation, once fully realized, typically through the hardships of those who cannot afford these carrots dangling at various levels beyond their reach, can pit people against one another and lead to a person's or society's feeling angry, mistreated, left out, resentful, oppressed, overworked, undercompensated, underappreciated, and apathetic, ultimately causing their chances of survival to feel threatened.

When people's resentment and apathy grows enough and their needs for survival are threatened, there is a good possibility they will resort to different means of nonconformist, more aggressive ways of taking care of themselves. They start to say, "You know what? Fuck you! I don't want to play your stupid little game anymore. I'm never going to get on top this way. I'm done being a trivial, petty, expendable piece of shit to this laborious machine. It's not worth it. Fuck the group. I'm the only one who is going to take care of me. I don't like your rules, the way you do things. It's not for me; it's not going to get me what I want, deserve, and need." Everything that The Machine thrusts in our eager little faces we want and feel we *need* to survive, to fill some kind of void, the black hole that looms in the pit of our chest.

It happened to me, and the more I look around and listen, I see this attitude, these feelings of anger and resentment building a wall between 'Us and Them'. Even though I realize all of this on some level, I still catch myself feeling as though I need this or that random unnecessary thing for my 'survival'.

I need this shirt, these shoes, this car, this place to live, this shit inside my house and this person on my arm. When I was a kid and my mom couldn't or wouldn't buy me something I wanted, I got mad or upset or bummed out and acted like a brat for a while. When I got a little older and the same thing would happen, I simply became a member of the "black market survival club." I needed and wanted money, and I saw how much could be made selling drugs, and it seemed, at the time, relatively easy in comparison to what a lot of other people were doing for a living, and there was a stigma surrounding it that I liked and was attracted to.

You see where that got me. I swear, sometimes I feel like you can't win for losing.

Well, that's pretty much it so far. I'm here at Mom's, trying to have a positive attitude about my newfound mundane life, attempting to deal with my serious mind-fuck and waiting, with increasing anxiety, for my case to be settled, praying like hell I stay out of prison. I don't belong there, especially for the amount of time I heard them talk about. That's fucked up! I'm no threat. I'm just some pissed-off kid from Suburbia.

Keep your fingers crossed.

About the Author

RYDER STONE lives in the State of Jefferson and spends as much time as possible in the fresh air with good friends.